PRAISE FOR
DEADLY GRATITUDE

"I loved it! It's a real page-turner!"
  Vicky Doehring

"Compelling characters, fast paced, a book you won't want to put down. Perfect for a flight or a cozy read by the fire."
  Josephine Watt, world traveler, librarian of 40 years, and poet

"I had a hard time putting this book down!"
  Karen Milne

"Started Lori Donnester's Deadly Gratitude while waiting for my flight and simply could not stop reading. Finished it in one day!"
  Steve Holzrichter, frequent traveler

"Enjoyable and unpredictable! It kept me in anticipation of what happens next!"
  Sueah Chung

"A novel that reaches many emotions. While feeling the thrills that accompany a crime novel, you'll experience hope, tenderness, and faith. By the end, you will feel inspired. Open this book and see where it takes you."
  Jen Carroll

DEADLY
GRATITUDE

DEADLY GRATITUDE

LORI DONNESTER

Surrogate Press

Published in the United States by
Surrogate Press™
SurrogatePress.com

ISBN: 978-1-947459-10-6

Library of Congress Control Number: 2018932353

Book cover design by: Michelle Rayner, Cosmic Design

Interior design by: Katie Mullaly, Surrogate Press®

For my kids,
"The Homework Mom" is still my favorite nickname.
Love you.

For my husband AKA my best friend,
Love you, dear. You inject fun in my life!
(But I still don't want to ski from 8:30 in the morning
until 4:30 in the afternoon.)

And
For Mom and Dad,
Thanks for helping me find my hallelujah.

PREFACE

Detective Don Layden pulled up to the cemetery as he had many times before, although tonight the crunching sound of the gravel beneath the tires was slightly muffled due to the inch or two of snow on the ground. He turned off the car, leaned his head back against the headrest and closed his eyes. His breathing slowed.

Before long, the cold seeped into the car. Shaking himself, he grabbed the fresh bouquet of flowers and trudged to her headstone in the dark. He removed the dead bouquet that was already there and replaced it with new daisies. Uelle loved daises.

He straightened up and folded his hands. "How are you, honey?" he sighed. "I'm tired. It was another long week, but Luke and I wrapped up the Brown case. The evidence is solid. I think he'll go to jail for a long, long time."

He shrugged. "I don't have too much planned for the weekend. The ski resorts are open. Maybe I'll go up. But the snow levels are still low since it's so early in the season. So maybe not. I'll see how I feel in the morning."

He closed his eyes and dropped his head. His voice came out very close to a whisper. "What I'd really like to do tomorrow is lay in bed with you. Then get up and have coffee together and read the paper." He took in a long breath and opened his eyes.

Instead of the rose-colored headstone he'd chosen for her, scenes of the accident flashed before him. His blonde wife laughing next to him in the front seat. The driver running the red light. The screeching sound of metal as it twisted. Uelle's final screams.

Then nothing.

He regained consciousness in the hospital, and it was then he found out she was gone.

"I wish cell phones had never been invented, honey," he whispered. Putting a hand over his eyes his voice shook as he added, "And you would still be here with me."

Don stood there for a long time, rubbing the headstone. The memories of his life before Uelle's death ensnared him.

ONE

Before the morning light peeked above the mountains, Alicia Kendrick opened her eyes, pulled the blankets up to her chin, and snuggled under them for one more minute as she relished the warmth they provided on this last day of November in Colorado. Never needing much sleep, she rose early every day. Since today was Saturday and her husband was home from work, she wanted to make sure she got her last swim in before he put his foot down and insisted that her beloved heated outdoor pool, a gift from her parents, be closed down for the winter.

Alicia slipped out of bed, taking care not to wake Adam. Last night was the surprise party for Adam's fortieth birthday, and she smiled as her mind replayed the scenes of all their friends eating, drinking, laughing, and even dancing. Her scheme to get Adam out of the house before the party had worked. Her good friend Vicki asked him to come over to her place and assist her with some legal questions, and he had been away just long enough for everything to be ready. All the guests even found places to hide.

Adam was genuinely shocked when he walked into the living room and thirty people sprang up yelling "Surprise!" He even jumped a few inches off the ground himself!

Chuckling at the thought, she stepped toward her sleeping husband and stroked the blanket over him ever so lightly.

He would be in bed until about seven, so she had some nice time alone right now.

Leaning forward and frowning into the bathroom mirror, she touched the bags under her eyes. Then she shrugged and quickly gathered her blonde hair into a ponytail, pulled on her swimsuit, threw on her robe, and padded towards the stairs.

Due to the party, her children, Jessica and James, spent the night with friends. Before moving past Jessica's room, she stepped into it for a moment and fingered the shoes she'd bought as a surprise for her daughter.

Jessica, a sophomore in high school, was going to the winter formal and was excited about it. She looked so beautiful in her new wine-colored dress, and these shoes would complete the outfit. With her long brown hair and her spicy cinnamon eyes, Alicia could hardly believe this perfection was her daughter. Jessica would be so surprised when she got home later today and saw the shoes lying on her bed. Alicia couldn't wait to see her daughter's face. A thrill of excitement ran down her spine and she hugged herself.

Alicia then passed by James's room and stepped in to straighten out a poster of the Denver Nuggets basketball team she'd bought and left on his bed. The fourth grader was a big fan, and if Jessica had new shoes then he needed to at least have a new poster, didn't he?

Finally, Alicia ran downstairs, making no noise on the thick beige carpet. As she approached the first floor, Alicia's brows furrowed in puzzlement. Where was Sunshine? The family's golden retriever was usually at the bottom of the stairs wagging her tail in a happy hello. As Alicia turned the corner, she noticed Sunshine standing guard at the sliding glass door that opened to the back yard, murmuring a low growl.

"Sunshine, what's the matter, girl? Did someone feed you something last night that hurt your tummy? Do you want to go outside?"

At the sound of Alicia's voice, Sunshine looked up and wagged her tail in greeting before returning to her scrutiny of the backyard.

"Hmmm," Alicia rubbed the dog's soft, golden fur and bent down to look into those big, brown eyes. "You're a sweet girl, aren't you?" She patted her pet's head and opened the door. Sunshine dashed outside, disappearing into a small grove of aspens in the northwest corner of the fenced yard.

After flipping the switch to flood the back yard in light, Alicia was about to step outside herself when she glanced over at the Christmas tree in the great room. The ornaments sparkled, reflecting the lights from the kitchen. Alicia smiled and darted over to plug in the tree's lights. She stepped back and sighed with contentment as she folded her arms and looked at the tree. "So glad I put you up for the party," she murmured to herself. For a few moments, the familiar feeling of that special Christmas happiness blanketed her. Then she slid on her clogs, stepped outside, pushed the button to move the pool's cover, and was greeted with the familiar scent of chlorine as the shield rolled back with a quiet whirring noise.

Colorado's Indian summer was only recently over and a couple of inches of snow remained from the first snowfall of the season. But more of that fluffy white stuff was in the forecast. Soon all of Denver would be covered in it, and the ski season would be in full swing.

The water lapped quietly against the sides of the pool as ghostly white steam rose up from the heated water, creating a surreal scene. Alicia rubbed her hands together, threw off her robe and dove into the pool. She was immediately oblivious to her surroundings as she concentrated on her strokes and the feeling of ecstasy that always accompanied her as she pulled her slim body gracefully through the water.

A few feet away in the aspen grove, an intruder petted Sunshine as she ate the meat he brought for her. She looked up and wagged her tail at him, but then she dropped her head and staggered. A violent seizure threw her to the ground. Her lips pulled back exposing her teeth and her eyes rolled back into her head. She choked. Foam came out of her mouth as she writhed on the snow-covered grass. Then, she lay still. The intruder smiled. *It was working just as planned.*

His footsteps crunched on the snow as he approached the edge of the trees, his eyes fixed intently on the early winter swimmer. The time invested in learning Alicia's habits had paid off. The most opportune moment was now here. His heart beat against his chest and his breath came out in little white puffs as it hit the cold morning air. When he observed the party from a distance last night, he was concerned that it might change her morning routine. Luckily, it had not. He watched her for a brief period and listened to the small splashing noises the water made as she repeatedly swam across the pool, expertly flip-turned, and then made her way back again.

Slowly, he ran a finger along the blade of the axe. An outdoor light flickered on the gleaming metal. The intruder gazed at it, mesmerized as he turned the axe this way and that to catch the light. *Quit wasting time. Get on with it.* His lips pressed into a thin line and his gloved hands tightened around the axe handle. His breath created small clouds of steam, like miniature mirrors of the fog coming off the pool. His heart pounded harder with anticipation. It was time. He stepped away from the grove of aspens and inched closer to the swimmer.

As Alicia completed yet another flip-turn, he glanced up at the bedroom windows. There was no sign of any movement. As usual, Alicia was the only member of the Kendrick family up this early. The intruder crept out of the aspens. He stepped to the edge of the pool, raised the axe over his head, and spread his feet apart positioning himself so that it would only take one swing.

She approached. The axe sliced through the air and hit its mark, destroying Alicia's skull.

At first it felt like cutting a melon. But then the blood gushed out of her head. Definitely human. He groped for her in the water and raised her up enough to wrap a beaded chain around her neck and pull it tightly, sneering as he left his trademark. He put the chain back into his pocket as he dropped her lifeless form into the water. Alicia's body floated woodenly in the pool. *Ha! See what happens when you ignore me!* He watched her blood flow into the pool...and smiled.

TWO

The lights beyond the large plate glass windows of Don's workout room were still sparkling like a sea of jewels against the dark of the early morning, but he was oblivious to the beauty. He watched himself jump rope in the mirror, not noticing his sleek muscular build or his chocolate-colored hair now wet with perspiration. Instead he focused on his movements, probing for faults the way an exterminator searches for rats. As his sweat puddled onto the floor, the rope moved faster. The whirling sound of the jump rope as it sailed past his ears and slapped the mat on the floor almost made him miss the sound of his cell phone's ring.

He dropped the jump rope, picked up a towel, and wiped off his face before he answered. "Layden here."

He listened for a minute and let out a breath when he heard the details the caller recited. "Be right there."

He wasted no time in putting his workout equipment away. His six foot two inch frame was silhouetted against the windows of his downtown Denver penthouse as he strode to his bathroom. He quickly showered and shaved. Trouble clouded his granite eyes while his mind replayed the disturbing details from the call.

Before exiting the bathroom, his gaze fell upon a framed photo of Uelle. Picking it up, he ran his fingers along her lips and closed his eyes. Then he kissed the photo and placed it back in its spot.

After putting on a pressed charcoal gray suit and a navy blue tie, he walked out into his contemporary great room. Pausing in front of a birdcage, he greeted a small yellow cockatiel. The corners of his mouth turned up as he placed his hand inside the cage. The bird chirped and stepped onto his extended index finger. Don's face relaxed as he stroked her with his other index finger. "Sorry Belle, gotta go. You have food and water to last all day so you're good. I'll clean your cage tonight. Sound okay? I may be a while, so stay comfortable, pretty lady." Sighing, he placed Belle back in her cage.

Don strapped on his gun, threw a winter jacket on over his suit coat, and left.

Twenty minutes later he stood inside the Kendricks' home. The homeowner, Adam, was wrapped in a towel that covered his wet, bloodied pajamas. He kept running his hands through his auburn hair, his periwinkle blue eyes not blinking. He appeared to be in a trance.

Don walked up to Adam and introduced himself as they shook hands. "I'm sorry for your loss," Don said. "Finding her like that must have been horrible."

"Yes." Adam's shoulders slumped and he sank down into a chair, the towel falling to the floor. He held his head in his hands. "Who would do this to Alicia? What am I going to do without her? How am I going to raise my children?" He rocked back and forth as he spoke.

Near the chair, Don noticed some family pictures with what looked like a teenaged daughter and an elementary-aged son. "Are your children out of the house?" he asked.

Adam nodded. "They're sleeping over at their friends. Alicia threw a surprise birthday party for me last night. Just like always, she had everything planned to the ninth degree, including where the children would be safe." Adam's hands covered his face again. Don touched the grieving man's shoulder, then walked around to take stock of the house, stopping to look out a window. The Kendrick home was in the downtown Denver neighborhood of Capitol Hill, situated near the top with a fantastic view of the city.

Arms folded, Don turned back to survey the great room. The luxurious leather furniture was accented with exotic accoutrements that had been collected from various cultures all over the world. There were also many family pictures, some of which were taken in tropical locations.

Using a handkerchief, Don picked up a photo that was taken at sunset with an ocean background. A smiling, blue-eyed Alicia stood next to a grinning Adam. Also in the photo were two beaming children who looked like a perfect combination of their parents. A polished older couple was with them as well. The grandparents? Don stepped out of the way of a uniformed officer as he dusted for prints.

He went upstairs to inspect the rest of the rooms. Spotting nothing unusual, he made his way out back to examine the scene. Before going over to the body, Don scanned the yard. His lips curled back from his teeth as he looked at the gore. Pool water should be clear, not clouded with blood. As Don studied it he felt his own blood run cold. He forced himself to glance away for a few seconds. Based on the violence, he assumed the killer was male.

The yellow crime tape was already set up, offering a garish barrier in contrast to the surrounding fence. The forensic team used their tools to scrutinize a set of shoe-prints in the wet ground. Alicia's body had been laid along the side of the pool on a large white towel. Don walked over to Alicia and squatted next to her. She was in her early thirties, probably five feet nine and 120 pounds. She had the broad shoulders of someone who had grown up swimming. And now her lifeless eyes stared up out of her ruined head. Don shook himself and then noticed something else. "What are the markings on her neck, any idea?"

"I haven't figured that out yet," the medical examiner, Meg Oliver, replied. Meg knelt down right next to Alicia. "But I do know that she was hit in the head first. The chain, beads, or whatever it was that was wrapped around her neck, happened after the blow. Maybe she was wearing some sort of a necklace and the killer took it by force."

Don scowled. "I doubt that. I don't know any committed swimmers who wear necklaces while they swim. And anyone who swims this time of year is clearly a committed swimmer."

"That's for sure," Meg replied.

Don felt a slap on his back and looked up to see that his six foot seven partner had arrived. There were many times in tense situations when it was a tremendous comfort to have the giant, 240 pound muscular African American on his side.

"Morning, Cheeto." Luke's greeting came out like the rumble of a percolating volcano.

"Cheeto?" Meg blinked in confusion.

Luke grinned. "My partner just loves those orange snacks. We were on a stakeout and had to bolt after the bad guys who just happened to be wearing very expensive suits. Don got that tasty orange grime all over their beautiful clothing. They were pissed as hell." Luke smirked. "A great memory in our illustrious crime fighting history."

Luke turned to view Alicia. "Oh! Oh, man!" His coffee brown eyes turned black as he glanced at Don. In a voice just as dark he said, "This is ugly. Fill me in."

Don brought his partner up to speed as they walked through the trees to examine the dog. A forensic specialist greeted them. "There's a hunk of meat here and I'd bet money it's laced with poison. And the footprints look like garden variety running shoes. They appear to be around a size ten and a half, which is the most common men's size in America. Unfortunately." He raised his eyebrows as if he could read the detectives' minds. "The husband's size is nine and a half."

Don spoke up. "The killer either knew the family well enough to know they had a dog, or he spent enough time watching them to figure it out." He snorted. "That narrows it down, doesn't it?" Sighing, he added, "All right, run all of the tests that you can on that poison. Check the tread on those shoes. If they're new, we might be able to tie them with a recent credit card purchase or something. Since Adam Kendrick is a prosecuting attorney for Denver we're under even more pressure than usual to find his wife's killer."

"That's exactly right!" A female voice from behind them caused Don and Luke to startle. The captain of homicide, Belinda Mann, was on the scene. She stepped forward and stretched her five foot two inch frame to put her pudgy index finger directly in Don's face. Anger smoldered in her mud-colored eyes. "I want this case solved quickly. I want the killer brought to justice. And I want any involvement by those clowns from the media kept to a minimum." She looked at both of them. "Gather all of the information as fast as you can and get working, is that clear?"

Don spoke up before Luke had a chance. "Understood."

"Good." Belinda walked over to Alicia's body and squatted down to take a closer look. The permanent frown lines in her face deepened. "Whoa. What a mess." At 175 pounds, she wasn't agile enough to get up by herself, so she held up her hand for Don's assistance. He hauled her up. She ran a hand through her graying hair, mumbled something representing a thank you, then left.

Luke growled, "What does that woman think we're going to do? Go to a football game and drink beer all afternoon?"

"That's just Belinda. If we want to catch the bad guys, we have to put up with her." His mouth twitched. "But I agree. Gets old."

At that moment, Adam appeared at the back door. Don gestured towards Luke. "Adam, this is my partner, Luke Malone."

Adam shook hands with the detective and Luke placed a hand on the grieving man's shoulder. "I'm sorry for your loss. Let's talk so my partner and I can get to work."

Adam led them into the great room. When he noticed the lights twinkling on the Christmas tree, he stopped. "She must have turned the lights on before she went outside for a swim," he whispered. "Alicia loved Christmas." Tears welled up in his eyes.

Don spotted a box of tissues on a coffee table that was nearly hidden behind a pile of teen magazines. He handed one to Adam and waited for the widower to recover.

Coughing, Adam looked up. "Thanks. Um, do you want some water or anything?" He gestured towards the kitchen.

"I keep expecting Alicia to bring a tray in with coffee and cream and muffins." His face cracked again. He shuffled his feet and gazed at the floor while taking some staggered breaths.

"We're fine." Don cleared his throat. "Adam, I'm going to record this. Okay with you? Many times a detail that doesn't seem significant at first, turns out to be important later."

Adam nodded.

"All right," Don continued. "Take us through what happened this morning."

Adam described coming downstairs expecting to see his wife reading the paper and drinking coffee after her work-out. "Alicia always gets up early," he confirmed. "She usually has her workout in and shower done before anyone else is even out of bed." Adam paused. "Anyway, when she wasn't in the kitchen, the first place I looked was outside. I told her yesterday that I was going to close the pool today. I knew she'd want to get one last swim in." Adam's voice started to shake. "I opened the door and saw her body floating in the pool... and all of the blood. I ran over and pulled her out. But she was gone." The last sentence was whispered. The grieving husband sank into the couch running his hands through his hair. He fell silent, having relived the devastation of his morning.

"Then what happened?" Luke prompted.

"I called 911. Luckily, Alicia told me where each of the kids stayed last night. I called their friends' parents and asked them to keep my kids until I..." Adam struggled to end his thought. "Until I figure out... how I'm going to go on." He put his hand over his eyes. "How am I going to tell them their mother was murdered?"

The room went still. "How old are your children?" Don asked.

"Jessica is fifteen and James just turned nine".

Don placed a hand on Adam's arm. "I want you to know that Luke and I will find this guy."

Adam fixed his eyes on one detective and then the other. "You have to," he whispered. "You just have to."

Don thought for a moment. "I have another question for you. A heated outdoor pool in Denver costs a heck of a lot of money to operate this time of year…" Don cleared his throat.

Adam broke in, "How can a city's prosecuting attorney with two children afford that expense, right?"

"Right."

"Alicia's parents are very wealthy. Alicia's dad started his company from the ground up. He sold it when he retired, making millions. Alicia is their only child. She was a state champion swimmer in high school, then went on to swim in college at the University of Wisconsin. We met there." Adam drifted away lost in thought for a minute. He blinked. "Anyway, when we bought this house her parents wanted her to have a pool, so they paid for it." Adam gestured in a circular motion referring to the house. "They helped us with the down payment for this place too."

That explained the photos with the elderly couple. "I see." Don scratched the back of his neck. "What organizations did Alicia belong to? How did she spend her time?"

"She mainly took care of us. She was on the PTA at Moore Elementary and at the high school. She was in a Bible study group at church, and she was involved in our children's sports activities with the other mothers." Adam shrugged. "That's about all I can think of right now."

"What about your neighbors? Any troubles with them? Or relatives, have you had any disagreements with anyone?"

Adam shook his head. "No, nothing. We are just a normal, quiet family."

Don looked at Luke. "Let's take a look at Adam's enemies. Maybe someone Adam put behind bars wants payback."

Luke agreed.

Adam put his hand over his eyes again. His head dropped.

"You didn't cause this," Don stated in a low voice. "This isn't your fault." He paused. "We need a list of all of the organizations that Alicia was involved in, along with contact info. I also want to meet with Alicia's parents. Explore if there is an old grudge or something from the past that we should know about. Don't want to overlook anything. Do her parents know yet?"

Adam shook his head.

"Do you want to tell them or should we?"

"I will," Adam said. He took a breath. "To be honest with you, the first thing I thought of after I could actually *form* a thought was that someone I prosecuted wants to get back at me. I could meet you over at my office later today to go through my files." He paused. "I have to take care of my kids first, though." He leaned forward and put his elbows on his knees with his head in his hands. "How am I going to do that?"

Don squatted down next to him. In a voice just above a whisper he murmured, "I noticed the religious pictures and books when I walked through your house. You mentioned

Alicia's Bible study group. Do you belong to a church? Could you call your minister?"

"Yes, we go to St. James Catholic Church nearby."

Don continued, "Talk to your priest. No matter what, it isn't going to be easy. But he can help you better than anyone."

Adam nodded.

Don pressed his card into Adam's hand. "If we could get you to give us the address of Alicia's parents, then you could call them and let them know we are coming over to ask some questions. You have my card. Call me any time day or night." Don paused for a minute. "Is there someone besides yourself who knows about your cases? I want to catch the killer, but I don't want to tear you away from your kids right now."

A look of relief crossed Adam's face. "Yes. Why didn't I think of that? Rebecca Van Dyke would be able to help you, probably better than I can. She's my right arm."

After receiving the requested information, Don and Luke left. As they walked out to the car, Luke looked at his partner. "Cheeto, I have a bad feeling about this one."

"Yeah." Don's forehead creased. "So do I."

THREE

Don's phone rang before he even started the Crown Vic. He put the phone on speaker and put the car in gear. "Yes Belinda?" Don braced himself.

"Are you on your way to Adam's office yet?" she asked without a greeting. "Clearly, it's some loser that he sent to jail who's itching to retaliate."

Don squinted as though he could somehow shield himself from her grating voice. "Adam needs to talk to his children," Don explained. "We're headed to meet with Alicia's parents. We might be able to-"

Belinda cut him off, "Alicia's parents! Yeah, you're really going to learn a lot from them. Like what a wonderful daughter she was. What she did in elementary school. Great idea. And while you're learning all of those oh so very important bits of information, her killer is on the run." Belinda snorted. "Another option is to actually play it smart and get over to Adam's office now. Just a thought. All I know is I want this case resolved ASAP! Got it?" Belinda hung up.

Don stared at the phone. "Love you too, Belinda."

"Even sarcasm is too nice for her, Cheeto. Does she think we actually don't want to solve this case? Does she think we want a murderer loose in the city? I just can't believe what comes out of that woman's mouth! Sometimes I wish we lived in the Roman times so we could feed her to the lions!"

Luke smiled and rubbed his hands together as he envisioned the thought.

"Not an idea that two homicide detectives should entertain," Don snorted. "But I get it." He tapped the steering wheel with his fist as he thought. "Adam said his contact told him it's going to take a little time to get the office. Let's just ignore Belinda and go visit Alicia's parents."

"Ignoring Belinda is my daily dream. I'm in."

The O'Donnell home was located in Cherry Creek, one of the most affluent areas in Denver. Don drove up to an elegant stone house set back behind manicured evergreens and an ornamental wrought iron fence. The snow draped upon the spruces made it look like a Christmas card. A six foot tall, silver-haired, fit, elderly gentleman wearing a black cashmere sweater appeared at the door. "I'm Elliot O'Donnell. Are you detectives Layden and Malone?"

"Yes, sir." Don walked up and shook Elliott's hand. "I'm sorry for your loss."

Elliott's face broke and his grieving green eyes bore into Don's. "It's too horrible for words."

Don agreed as he and Luke stepped into the entry way. The interior of the house was spectacular with beautiful wooden beams accentuating the lofted ceilings. Don's shoes sunk into the big Persian rugs that were placed in the center of Italian wood floors. Some well-chosen pieces of valuable art hung on the walls.

Elliott led them to a den where a small woman with short, stylish hair colored with blonde highlights sat next to a fireplace. She cradled her face in her hands and sobbed so hard she seemed unable to take in a breath. Her husband stood next to her with his hand on her shoulder.

"Elizabeth, these are the detectives Adam called about, Don Layden and Luke Malone."

Elizabeth managed a ragged breath and looked up. "Thank you for coming so quickly," she croaked. Then she put her head in her hands and continued to cry.

"Why don't we go into my office?" Elliott suggested. He gently rubbed his wife's shoulders, then turned and led them into another part of the house.

Don found himself sitting next to Luke in a room with solid oak bookshelves lining two of the walls and a huge oak desk, at which Elliott seated himself. The wall directly behind Elliott shimmered with awards and credentials.

After Don received permission to record the conversation, Luke peppered Elliott with questions while Don listened and eyed the paperwork on the desk. He made a mental note of the return addresses of the investment firms. Most of them were recognizable, but of couple of them were not. "Are there any financial issues that could cause any backlash against you?" Don asked. "Try to think of everything, something that may not seem like a big deal to you but could be to someone else."

Elliott sat back in his chair and rubbed his eyes. After a minute he shook his head. "No," he replied. "There is nothing out of the ordinary that I can think of. Recently, I've invested with a couple of new firms, but there aren't any problems there. I do dabble in penny stocks just for fun, but the majority of my investments are with the old, solid firms."

After a few more questions Don handed Elliott his card, and the detectives left. Don was anxious to get to Adam's office downtown to meet with Adam's assistant, Rebecca Van Dyke.

Once they arrived, Don called and waited at the locked door until a small, stylish, gray-haired woman dressed in wool pants and a navy blue ski sweater met them. "Are you the detectives on the Kendrick murder?"

"Yes," said Don extending his hand, "I'm Don Layden and this is Luke Malone."

She shook hands with both detectives. "Hi, I'm Rebecca Van Dyke. May I see your badges?"

Don smiled to himself as she scrutinized first Don's badge and then Luke's. This woman was by the book.

When she was satisfied, she led them over to the elevators and punched the button for the tenth floor. "How's Adam doing?"

"He's devastated," Don replied. "It was a brutal crime scene. Not only is he mourning losing his wife in such a vicious way, but he's also grieving for his children losing their mother. He's struggling with how to explain it to them."

The doors opened and they stepped out into the office. "No one can explain something like that," Rebecca spat. "It's completely inconceivable!"

Her heels clicked on the marble floor as they walked to a conference room. They stepped in and saw piles of files on the wooden center table. Don blinked.

Luke put his hands on his head. "Holy crap!"

"A good prosecuting attorney can process about fifteen hundred cases per year." Rebecca motioned for them to sit down. "Five years is the average time that an inmate serves." She handed them each a file. "It doesn't take a rocket scientist to figure out that we have a lot of files to go through."

"You've got to be joking." Luke looked overwhelmed.

Rebecca put both hands on her hips. "Fear not, oh great warrior. Rebecca Van Dyke is here! I keep a systematic Excel spreadsheet on all of Adam's cases. I'll have it narrowed down to about two thousand files in no time!"

Luke plopped down into a gleaming chrome chair. He groaned as Rebecca, heels clicking, walked out of the room to get more files.

Over at the police station, Belinda Mann examined some charts on her computer. "Okay, now where is that email the accountant sent me for November?" she muttered to herself. "Ah!" Leaning forward, she focused on the screen and then input some data. "Perfect!" She printed out the chart and held it in both hands, staring at it as though it was a trophy. With a painted blood-red fingernail, she traced the crime statistics line for the past three years, which showed a slight decline in blue. Then she traced the green line, which showed data of expenses for the same time period. That line indicated a significant decline at the beginning of the three-year period with continued downturns throughout the rest of the chart.

She sat back in her seat, smiling. "No one can argue with the numbers. Belinda Mann is doing a fantastic job for the citizens of Denver!" She got up and put the latest chart on a big bulletin board in her office. Next to the bulletin board were several framed articles. She stopped and looked at every article for the thousandth time. Each one mentioned how she cut expenses without crime going up. Beside the articles, there was a picture of her with the mayor as he presented her with an award. A mirror hung on the wall at the end of the display. She stopped in front of it, smoothed her hair, and stayed there for some time, smiling as she admired herself.

FOUR

Kate Fitzgerald grinned to herself as she and her mother waited in line at Elmer's Cafe in Boise, Idaho. Kate was in town from Denver to visit her mother, and last night they had gone to watch Boise State University play the last game of their regular football season. The Broncos' win was in front of a sellout crowd at Bronco Stadium. Everyone in Boise was still talking about the many dazzling plays their team made and speculating about the various college bowl possibilities.

The comfortable restaurant buzzed with conversation, bursts of laughter, and the clatter of dishes. As Kate regarded the sea of Boise State orange and blue sweatshirts, jackets, and sweaters, she reminisced about her college days in Boise. Those were good times.

"I've said it before and I'll say it again, Mom. I'm so glad you made the move from Chicago to Boise."

Isabella Fitzgerald smiled. "Yes, me too, dear. Chicago is a great city and I love going back, but it's nice to be out west near you in Denver, and your brother in Salt Lake City."

Kate twirled a few strands of her long, shiny, black hair around a finger. Watching the Bronco fans discussing the game with all of their grins and shouts was such a kick. On a whim she threw her arms into the air in the touchdown signal and yelled, "Go Broncos!" A roar went up from the crowd as everyone cheered and high-fived each other. Kate looked at her mother and grinned.

Before long Kate and Isabella were seated at a wooden table with eggs and coffee in front of them. "Oh, this visit went by way too fast, Mom. I enjoy your friends. They treat me like I'm one of them."

"Yes, between my nursing job at the hospital and the ladies at St. Paul's, it's been easy to make friends here. Boise really is such a warm city." Isabella folded her hands in front of her and regarded Kate, not saying a word for a few moments. "And when all of my wonderful friends ask me if my daughter has any boyfriends, what should I say?"

Kate crossed her eyes at her mother. "Tell them the same thing that I've been telling you for the past year. After that break up with Thatcher, I am not interested in men." Kate pronounced the last six words as though each one was an individual bullet hitting its mark. She pulled a chain out from under her sweater. It held an engagement ring which she shook in front of her mother's face. "Let me remind you that I caught Thatcher cheating on me two months before we were going to get married. When I had this necklace made, I promised myself that would never happen to me again." Her voice rose to a high pitch as her speech progressed.

Isabella's face fell.

Kate sighed. "Oh Mom, don't be sad. Not everyone has to get married and have children to be happy. I'm perfectly happy. I live in a great city, I have a great job, and I have great friends." Kate leaned forward and her voice rose again. "Just understand that I'm not some stupid Cinderella who needs Prince Charming to come along and rescue her. I can take care of myself."

"What's wrong with Cinderella?"

Kate rolled her eyes. "Do not get me started, Mother. You'll be sorry."

"All right, all right. Sometimes I just think that at thirty-one maybe you aren't taking everything that life has to offer into consideration, but I guess I'll just have to accept this, won't I?" Isabella pursed her lips.

"Case closed, Mother."

A moment later, Kate felt eyes on her. She turned to find a young girl of about five standing near her sporting a big pout. Kate raised an eyebrow. "Hi. Can I help you?"

"Why don't you like Cinderella? I think she's pretty."

Kate blinked. "I think Cinderella let the step-mother and the step-sisters abuse her. I think a better ending shows Cinderella running away, getting an education, and taking charge of her life."

The pout turned into thoughtfulness. "What about Prince Charming?"

Kate shrugged. "If Cinderella meets an interesting man who respects her as an equal, then great." Kate wagged a finger at the little girl. "But the point is that Cinderella doesn't need to rely on him, because she can rely on herself."

"Oh." The blonde-haired head tilted. "I never thought about it that way. Thanks." She whirled around and trotted back over to her seat at a nearby table.

Just then, Kate's phone rang. As she listened to the caller, the color drained from her face. "Thank you," she whispered, her hand shaking as she put the phone down. Her lips trembled and her chocolate brown eyes filled with tears as she stared at her mother.

Isabella leaned forward. "Kate! What's wrong?"

Kate swallowed hard. It took a powerful effort to make her mouth work. "Someone murdered one of my friends from church. She was killed in her back yard this morning." Kate looked down at the tablecloth, struggling to breathe.

Isabella gasped, "Who would do such a thing?" She jumped up and knelt by Kate, hugging her daughter. She saw a server and signaled for the check.

A short time later as they buckled their seatbelts for the ride to get Kate to the airport, Isabella contemplated her daughter. "Are you going to be able to fly home today? You're welcome to stay longer."

Kate shook her head. "No, I have a pile of work and I want to get back to be with my friends. I need to be with them right now."

Isabella looked at the steering wheel. She drew a breath and turned back to Kate. "Why don't you consider moving back? You could have fun...some of your old roommates still live here."

The corners of Kate's mouth turned up for a split second. "Sorry, Mom. I know Boise is safe, but it just doesn't have hotels big enough to pay me as much as I'm making now." Kate was a controller for a 750-room hotel in downtown Denver and was itching to move up the corporate ladder. "If I want to advance I have to be ready to transfer to any city." Kate studied her mom's concerned face. "Don't worry, I'll be extra careful," she reassured her mother.

At the airport, Kate bent down and hugged Isabella goodbye. A willowy five foot seven, Kate always felt as though she towered over her five foot one mother.

Before long, Denver's magnificent skyline came into view as the jet circled before landing at Denver International

Airport. The sun reflected off the city's buildings, and the view of the skyscrapers against the majestic backdrop of the snow-capped Rocky Mountains provided a balm for the anguish she'd been struggling to hide throughout the flight.

She got to her car and then headed for Alicia's home before doing anything else. Standing at the door, she braced herself. What does a person say at a time like this?

Adam answered and Kate gave him a heartfelt hug. "Oh Adam, I am so sorry!"

Adam returned Kate's embrace, then looked down at his son, James. James stood right next to his father, almost as though he was sewn to his father's pants. Kate bent down and hugged him. "Hi, James, I love you," she whispered. Kate pulled back from him and reached into a Boise Airport shopping bag. "I know you are too old for Teddy Bears, but this one looked like he needed a friend. What do you think? Do you like him?" A tear rolled down his small cheek and James nodded and hugged it. It was really soft. Kate knew there would be many nights that James might need something to hug. James buried his blonde head in his father's pant leg, cradling the furry brown bear in his arms.

Kate stood up and put her hand on Adam's shoulder. "How is Jessica doing?" Kate and Jessica always had a close relationship. Kate often brought Jessica knick-knacks from Boise State and was always delighted that Jessica put up the posters and other things in her otherwise very feminine room.

"She's upstairs," Adam responded. "She hasn't budged since she found out." His voice broke at the end of his comment and tears glistened in his eyes.

"That's understandable. Is it all right if I go up to see her?" Kate asked.

"Of course."

Kate ran up the staircase and knocked on Jessica's door. "Jessica it's me, Kate." Kate opened the door and found Jessica lying on the bed, staring at a picture of the Kendrick family taken at Thanksgiving and clutching a pair of wine-colored shoes. Kate walked in and put her hand on Jessica's back. "Jessica, I am so sorry for your loss."

Jessica didn't move. "That's what everyone says," she muttered. "Is that supposed to make me feel better?"

Kate sat on the side of the bed so she could rub Jessica's back. "No, of course not. There isn't anything anyone can say that will make you feel better. We just want you to know that we're grieving with you. We want you to know that we love you and that we care about how you feel."

A sob caught in Jessica's throat and she sat up and threw herself into Kate's arms. "Oh, Kate, I was so mean to Mom. I told her she was old and that she didn't understand me. I made fun of her clothes. I argued with her about helping around the house…" Jessica trailed off as she cried harder.

Kate kept rubbing Jessica's back while she sobbed on Kate's shoulder. "Jessica, your mom knew you loved her. All teenagers act like that. I did, your mom did, and now you do." Kate thought for a second. "Your mom used to come to Bible study class and laugh as she told us how embarrassed you were by what she wore. And guess what? We all laughed with her because we have all said the same thing to our own moms." Kate pulled back and regarded Jessica. "I want you to know that she also shared what a good student you are, how cool your science projects turn out, and what a soccer star you've become. Your mom was very, very proud of you. She thought you were the greatest daughter any mother could have and said so all the time. I promise." Kate crossed her heart then pointed up to the sky. "Your mom is up in heaven right now looking down on you because she wants you to be all right. Your mom will be with you all of the time. You know how? Because you carry her with you in your heart. No one can ever, ever take that away from you."

Jessica stopped crying. Kate gave the grieving child a handkerchief so she could take care of her remaining tears. Pulling a stuffed bronco from her Boise State bag, Kate added, "I bought this for you. I thought he could keep you company."

Jessica hugged it. "Thanks," she whispered. Then she leaned into Kate's arms again. Kate continued to rub Jessica's back for as long as she stayed there.

A little while later, Kate and Jessica walked down the staircase into the kitchen. Adam walked over to his daughter and gave her a hug. Noticing the bronco, Adam smiled and thanked Kate for coming.

"I'm going to go over to St. James for a while," Kate said. If you need anything, be sure to call."

On a nearby street in his car up on a foothill, the killer watched Kate through his binoculars as she left the house and got into her SUV. His location today was a different hill from the one he used the previous night when he watched the party. Today's spot was up on a quiet street, hidden behind some evergreens with the Kendrick home still in view. Perfect.

Putting down the binoculars, he took a puff of his cigarette and then placed it into a pile of butts in the ashtray. Regarding his rearview mirror, his arctic blue eyes gleamed back at him. He brushed some strands of fiery red hair from his forehead and shifted his short, portly frame to keep his left leg from falling asleep. A sigh of contentment escaped his lips. This was much more exciting than being at home. There, he could only pace with exhilaration while reliving his glorious achievement. But here he could observe all the comings and goings of the police, neighbors, and friends. It was better than binge-watching *Scandal.* Hours passed by as he watched all the commotion he caused. *You see? I have the power to change lives!*

He returned the binoculars to his eyes and smiled.

FIVE

Kate drove to St. James, a contemporary Catholic Church that felt like her home away from home. It was silent when she walked in. Sunlight radiated through the beautiful stained-glass windows, causing the brilliant reds, blues, and yellows to glow and scatter their incandescent colors throughout the church. She fixed her eyes on the huge cross behind the altar. Her breathing slowed as she soaked up the familiar surroundings. She gazed in turn at the altar with the white cloth over it, the beautiful pictures of Jesus' life throughout the church, and the candles in the back corners that flickered in the darkness where the light from the windows couldn't reach. A feeling of peace washed over her. Kate sat with her hands folded in her lap and absorbed the spirituality of the church for some time. Then she walked over to the candles, put two quarters in the slot for the "candle fund" and lit one. She knelt down on a cushioned bench and covered her face with her hands as she prayed. Time stood still.

Father Tim, the pastor of the church, walked out near the altar and saw Kate. He didn't want to disturb her, so the squat, gray-haired priest waited in the shadows without speaking until she stood up. Then he went over to greet her, and they walked out into the gathering space at the back of the church together. Concerned, he reached out and touched her arm. "How are you doing?"

Kate sighed. "Oh, Father." She stopped and chose her words with care. "There's nothing in the entire English language to describe how awful this is. A husband loses his wife, two children lose their mother, and we lose a wonderful friend." She paused. "For what? Just for hate? It's so senseless! I'm simply devastated! I feel as though a part of me has been destroyed."

"I feel the same way. We're all hurting right now." Father Tim studied the carpet for a moment. "Adam came over earlier and we talked. I don't know how to explain it other than God gave mankind free will. For some of us, we listen to his word and we do our best to abide by it. Others don't. And now we are invited to somehow learn to forgive those that don't listen."

"Forgive her murderer? Sorry, but I'm a long way from being able to do that," Kate challenged. "I just don't see myself feeling any forgiveness for a really long time."

"That's only natural." The priest surveyed her for a moment. "I have a question for you. What are some of the darkest times in history that you can call to mind?"

Kate gazed at the ceiling as she thought. "One of the first things I can think of is the crucifixion of Jesus." She counted on her fingers as she spoke. "Then there are the repulsive acts of the Ku Klux Klan, then the whole Jewish concentration camps horror, then of course 9/11…" Kate looked at the priest. "Wow. When you think about it, mankind can be really gruesome."

"Yes." Father Tim folded his arms. "And what driving emotion do all of those things you mentioned have in common?"

Kate tilted her head as a thought illuminated her mind. "I see, Father. It was hate. All of those things happened because of hate."

"Yes, it was hate. Hate carries a horrific price tag. Don't ever forget that. Rise above it."

Kate sighed. "I know you're right, but how can I change what I feel in my heart?"

"Start by praying for Alicia's killer." Kate scowled and Father Tim continued, "Even if you begin by praying that he can find it in his heart to turn himself in, that's a good start. Do you think you can do that?"

Kate twirled her hair around a finger for a minute. "Yes, I guess I can at least do that."

As she turned to go, Kate's eyes fell upon some posters that Alicia drew for the annual parish Christmas toy drive. Every year the parishioners participated in a program that donated toys to families who otherwise would not be able to give gifts to their children. Several churches in the Denver area participated. The toys all wound up at Regis University, a Jesuit school in Northwest Denver, where the families picked them up. St. James was often the parish that donated the most. Kate knew how much pride the local members took in that. Alicia was in charge of the toy drive this year. She had been moving ahead with it, full force, with posters all over the gathering space and reminders in the church bulletin every week. Father Tim followed Kate's eyes and looked at the poster. "Yes, now I have to find someone else to head the drive."

"I'll do it," Kate volunteered.

"Are you sure? You're already chairing the parish fundraiser in February. That's a huge job." The priest searched

Kate's face. "Don't feel like you have to do it. I'm sure I can find someone else."

"Actually, I really want to do it," Kate insisted. "To be honest, I think that will make me feel a little bit better. I will do it in honor of Alicia. She talked about it all the time, so I already know the whole scheme."

"All right, if you're sure. I really appreciate that."

Kate left feeling better than she had when she'd arrived. She looked up at the sky and asked Alicia to help her with this new task. Then Kate smiled to herself. She was overthinking this thing already. It would be a piece of cake. As long as she did a little planning, what could possibly go wrong?

SIX

After a couple of hours of work with Rebecca at Adam's office, Don leaned back in his chair. He and Luke now had what Rebecca referred to as the "hottest" files. True to Rebecca's word, her Excel worksheet was a great tool. It was organized with the names of the defendants in the first column, followed by columns that contained a large number of details. She could sort the defendants by crime, by verdict, by length of sentence, by address, by neighborhood, by gang if that applied, and so on. Rebecca put the hard files in the order that they had agreed would yield the best results; by neighborhood and by most recent release dates.

Don was impressed.

Luke was overwhelmed.

The detectives now had "only" a thousand cases to review.

"Most of these are drug busts, but some of these criminals could make the jump to homicide," Rebecca observed. "Adam's worked on a lot of cases. He moves a lot of criminals through our courts, that's for sure."

Luke blinked. "Cheeto, if we work seven days a week, fifteen hours a day, I swear it could take us a month to get through all of these interviews." Luke looked up at the ceiling and groaned. "Number one, that'll give this asshole a chance to get away. Number two, we're going to have to endure the daily verbal abuse from our dearly beloved captain."

"Agreed. Let's hope Belinda will assign more manpower to us since Adam is a prosecuting attorney. We know Belinda will feel extra pressure to solve this. So, the faster this case is solved, the better she looks. Her number one priority."

Luke rolled his eyes as Don dialed his phone and put it on speaker. Belinda picked up after the first ring. "What do you want?" she hissed.

"Belinda, we narrowed it down to about a thousand former inmates. If Luke and I do this on our own, it'll take us a month to get through them all. We're hoping you could assign some additional manpower. We want to get this solved. Get this guy behind bars."

"Of course, Don. Of course. Why don't I assign ten more people to this case? Hmm, let me see. Oh, now I remember. There are other cases in this city too. Plus, we have the mayor and taxpayers to answer to." She sniffed. "Darn. I guess it's just you and Luke. You'll just have to figure it out. Call me when you do."

Don exhaled as he ended the call. Luke's head dropped. Rebecca's eyes flashed. "Exactly who was that?" she demanded.

Don looked at her. "Belinda Mann, our Captain."

Luke gave her his own version. "Actually, I refer to her by the title that I believe suits her better: Queen BM."

Rebecca smiled at Luke's play on Belinda's initials. "Yes, she certainly isn't very professional. I just hate that kind of sarcasm. I think that title suits her very well. How long has she been there?"

"Three very long years," Luke answered. "Rumor has it she got the job because she had a rich father who contributed to the mayor's campaign."

Don interjected, "Problem is, she's gained tons of recognition due to running the department so inexpensively." Don felt the heat rising in his face as he spoke. "The mayor's held press conferences and given her awards to show the citizens of Denver how fastidious he is with their tax dollars. Belinda told us that our mayor promotes how our department runs nationally as a model for others to follow. She said she actually gets a bonus based on the reduced manpower cost of her department."

Rebecca winced. "She told you that?"

"Yes. And because of all of that, the police commissioner gives her a long leash." Don sighed. "It's a real struggle to get through the work. So far, we manage to cover for each other without her knowing. But one of these days, a case will come up that we can't cover, and Denver's citizens will suffer. I hope this is not that case." Don paused. "Belinda shines upward really well. Her superiors think she's great."

Luke added, "But around us, she hops on her broomstick and flies around in circles over our heads."

Rebecca folded her arms and grunted. "Let me tell you, I wouldn't mind casting some kind of a nasty spell on her. It sounds like all she cares about is herself and her own upward mobility."

"You just hit the nail on the head," Luke growled.

Rebecca tapped a pencil on a folder for a minute and stood up to move over to Luke. "I don't mean to be rude, but before you go, you just have to tell me how you got that scar above your left eye. I've been trying to imagine what happened all day. It's been driving me crazy." She put her hand over her heart and became dramatic. "Were you apprehending a psychotic bank robber in the middle of his crime? Were you in a bar fight with some gang?"

Luke considered the older woman for a moment. "No, I was trying to save my little brother's life. I failed."

Rebecca gasped and took a step back. "Oh, I'm so sorry!"

"That's all right." Luke shrugged. "I get asked from time to time. I think of it as a good reminder of why I got into law enforcement: to honor my brother." Luke's voice softened. "It's important to me."

"Luke, I'm sure your brother sees what you are doing and appreciates it." Rebecca smiled at him and patted him on the shoulder. Then she looked at Don and tilted her head. "While we're on the subject, how about you? What brought you into this line of work Don?"

"My father was a detective. He was killed in the line of duty when I was twelve. Hundreds of police officers were at his funeral. Many of them told me that he was a hero." Don stared at the wall for a minute as images of his father's funeral ran through his mind. "I have always been very proud of my dad. I guess I want to be like him."

Rebecca blinked and swallowed. "Denver is certainly lucky to have you two working for us, I can tell you that." She took a deep breath and smiled at them both, "Is there anything else you need?"

Don looked around at the room. Pizza boxes and empty cans from the food and drinks she bought them were scattered everywhere, and there was a huge pile of files that had to be refiled. "No, but let's help you clean this up."

She waved them away and insisted that they go work the case. The files that they needed were placed in a box. Luke picked it up while Don signed for them. As they shook hands, Rebecca said, "You have my number. Call me any time, night or day, if there is anything else that I can do to help. I'll be praying for you."

The detectives thanked her and left. As they rode the elevator down to the street, Don looked at Luke. "That is one organized woman. Huge help."

"Yeah, she's a great lady, although I could have done without having the prayers bestowed upon us, or whatever that was."

Don frowned at his partner. "She's just a religious person offering us help in the best way she knows. My mom was just like that. I can't believe you have a problem with it." He rubbed his chin. "Maybe I should pray for you too."

"I don't need prayers. I got me and my family covered."

"To each his own," Don observed as they trudged to the car. After they got settled, Don turned on the ignition and took a deep breath. "Okay, time to start digging."

SEVEN

Hours of interviews later in a Denver neighborhood, Luke stood by the car and put some files back into the box. He stretched. "Okay, Cheeto, we just got a lot of nothin'. We did a lot of driving and talking for zero results."

Don rubbed his jaw. "You know, I'm thinkin' we're on the wrong track. This murder took place about five thirty in the morning." He waved at the box. "These defendants aren't the type to even be awake that early, let alone stand in somebody's yard with an axe." Don squinted at Luke. "I don't know, might be too soon to tell, but the puzzle pieces just aren't fitting together."

"Yeah, I hear you, but don't forget we barely got started, Cheeto. There's still lots of work to do." Then he tapped his watch. "But now, in spite of what Queen BM says, we have to get to that game that was rescheduled for tonight. We have a football team that needs our sage guidance."

Don blinked. "I don't know. Maybe you should go. I can keep working the case."

Luke looked at his partner. "It's just a couple of hours. Don't forget, we keep young boys out of trouble by doing this. I want to catch this guy as much as you do, but these kids need us. Their dads walked out on them." Luke pointed to his heart. "I know what that feels like." He grabbed his partner's shoulders. "We both have to be there."

"You're right." Don's eyes crinkled. "I stand corrected."

Don drove back to the Kendrick's home to drop Luke off at his car. Then he followed Luke to the center where the game was to be played.

Don got out of his car and the corners of his mouth turned up as he gazed at the old, empty warehouse that had been converted into an inexpensive indoor recreation center. There were no bleachers, but the turf worked just fine and the league kept the boys busy. As they walked into the building, Don commented, "No doubt this rec center reduces crime. Big bang for the buck."

"Agreed."

It was ten by the time Don got home after the game. Looking at the huge box of files he'd taken from Adam's office sapped his energy. But he had to find out as much information as he could on these former inmates while working on his computer tonight. That way, he and Luke had a better chance of getting some useful information as they worked though the cases Adam had prosecuted. He sighed as he lifted the heavy box out of the car.

A cheerful little chirp greeted him when he opened the door. In spite of how tired he was, the sound made him smile. He whistled, and Belle chirped again. It felt good to be missed.

Don put down the box and took the bird out of her cage with care. "Hello there, pretty girl. How was your day? Hopefully better than mine."

He held her on his index finger as he walked into his bedroom. "I have to find a very bad man. And Belinda isn't giving Luke and me any help." He chatted on as he changed clothes and then cleaned her cage.

With Belle perched on his shoulder, he picked up the box of files and walked into his office putting them down with a thud next to the desk. Stretching his arms behind his back, he looked around the room, lined on three sides with rich mahogany bookshelves filled with books from floor to ceiling. Don walked over to a window that displayed a glittering blanket of lights outside stretching almost as far as the eye could see. "All right, I'll turn on a little jazz music for us while we work, eh?" He took a seat at the desk, which was situated in a corner so he could look out at the city as he worked.

"Belle, I don't know why, but I'm thinkin' Luke and I are on the wrong track. The first thing I have to do tonight is start the murder book. Got to make sure all the interviews and crime shots are in one spot. Then it's the files. 'Cuz right now these files are about all we have. I'm thinking that if I do as much digging as I can now, maybe I'll find something that will help Luke and me get lucky. I have to do whatever I can think of to speed up this investigation. There is a killer loose in Denver, and I want him behind bars." Don searched into the early hours of the morning.

On the outskirts of Denver, the killer watched a war movie in his living room. His eyes kept drifting to the medieval weapons that were displayed above the fireplace. He got up and fondled the weapons, then walked into his garage. He turned on a heater, took an axe out of a closet, went to his workbench, and polished the axe blade, rubbing it so hard that his head moved in the same rhythm as his hands. He rubbed until the glint of steel shone beneath the cloth.

After a time he examined the axe, turning it this way and that. He brought it up over his head and swept it down, repeating the motion several times. He held it up and peered at his reflection in the blade. "You and I make a good team. Let's do it again sometime, shall we?"

He continued to stare at the shiny axe for a long time.

EIGHT

"Daddy, Daddy it snowed last night! Get up and look at the snow, Daddy! Let's build a snowman today, can we Daddy?" Luke's four-year-old daughter jumped on him as he lay in bed, now wide awake.

He held her in his arms and shushed her, hoping his wife had been able to sleep through all of that. She was seven months pregnant, and Luke knew she was having trouble getting enough sleep. Her job as a physical therapist could be tiring at times and Luke worried about her.

"Lucy, I have to work today. I don't know if we have time to make a snowman before I go to work," he whispered as he hugged his daughter tightly. He glanced at the clock and stifled a groan. It was four thirty in the morning. There was plenty of time to build a snowman. His head sank back into the pillow longingly, but his daughter's big pleading fudge-colored brown eyes burrowed into his heart like they always did, and he suddenly decided it was a perfect time of day to make a snowman. Besides, he knew this case was going to take him away from his family, so he wanted to grab moments with them when he could.

Luke smiled as he got up and tossed his daughter into the air, catching her with ease and giving her a big kiss. He put his mouth near her ear and whispered, "Okay Lucy, you go find a hat and a scarf for our snowman and I'll find some things to make his face." He gently put his daughter down and she scampered off with a delighted giggle.

"Luke Malone, you are spoiling that girl." Luke looked over at his wife and saw that her eyes were still closed but there was a smile on her pretty face.

Luke went over and kissed her on her forehead. "Honey, now you just go on back to sleep and let me complete this important mission." He lowered his voice playfully when he said the words 'important mission'.

"Okay, superhero, I expect to see a perfect snowman when I get up." Sabrina rolled over and snuggled deeper into the covers.

Luke threw on a sweat suit, walked into the kitchen, and started rummaging around for stuff to make the snowman's face. Lucy scurried in, holding up the bright orange wool hat and red scarf that she found. Luke inspected them, scrutinizing each one by turning it over several times and holding it up to the light before giving her a thumbs up. Lucy's eyes sparkled. Then he showed her what he found. "Okay, young lady, we have here a perfect carrot nose…" He put the carrot up to his own nose and Lucy grinned. "And we have here a mouth of red grapes…" He placed the grapes over his own lips and Lucy giggled. "And we have here two cherry tomato eyes!" He put the cherry tomatoes over his own eyes and Lucy chortled with laughter and clapped her hands.

"That's perfect, Daddy! We're going to make the best snowman in the whole wide world!" While Lucy ran to the closet to get her boots, Luke rummaged around for something in a bottom drawer. He found what he was looking for and then helped Lucy with her snow gear. After they were both bundled up, he held out his trophies from the drawer.

"These are head lamps. They are flashlights that you wear on your head. This will help us see since the sun isn't up yet."

Lucy's eyes gleamed as he put the contraption over her blue wool hat. Before long, they were rolling big snowballs and stacking them on top of each other.

An hour later, Luke held Lucy up and helped her put the hat and scarf on their masterpiece. Their snowman was four balls high, not the usual three. He was probably about six feet tall, and his big grape smile showed that he approved of their work. Then with Lucy still in his arms, Luke took a couple steps back so they could both absorb the full effect of their achievement. "Lucy, I do believe that's the best snowman that I ever saw," Luke declared.

"Me too, Daddy, I think that he is the best snowman ever made ever!" Lucy's grin stretched from ear to ear and she hugged her father as hard as she could.

Luke hugged her back and gave her a big kiss. "All right, young lady, your daddy has to get some exercise in before Uncle Don comes over to pick him up for work." Luke carried her into the house and took off her snowy clothes, hanging them up to dry.

Sabrina walked out in her fuzzy robe and slippers and peered outside. Her huge caramel eyes and full lips were even more accentuated due to her close-cropped hair that crowned her head in soft, shiny jet-black curls. Tall and thin, she hid her pregnancy well.

"My heavens! Luke and Lucy Malone, I do believe that is the biggest snowman that I ever saw. He is a prizewinning snowman, and that's a fact!" She bent over and hugged her daughter who was jumping up and down. Luke kissed his wife, picked up Lucy, and encircled them both with his big arms. He sighed with contentment. The three of them stayed like that for a few minutes as they admired the morning's work.

An hour later, Luke came upstairs from his workout, wearing a towel around his neck and dripping sweat. He spotted Sabrina making pancakes and he puckered up his lips as though he was going to kiss her. She held up a spatula in warning. "Don't you even think about kissing me, you sweaty man. Don't even come near me until you take a shower." She punctuated each of the last three words with three matching shakes of her spatula.

Luke grinned and swatted her bottom softly with his towel before heading to the bathroom.

As he looked in the mirror, Don eyed the black circles under his eyes while he shaved. Last night had been long. He kept going back and forth about the investigation. It made sense that a recently released inmate had it out for Adam and killed Alicia. That intent was the only logical motive they'd been able to come up with, at least so far.

But the majority of Adam's cases were drug cases so most of the files had to do with gangs and drugs. Those kids just weren't the type to get up at five in the morning and go out and kill someone with an axe. His night spent searching for more information hadn't yielded much more than what Rebecca had already given them. He wished he would have just gone to bed and gotten a little shut-eye.

Don put on a navy blue suit along with a maize yellow tie and went out to visit with Belle before getting something to eat. He reached into her cage and held her on his index finger, looking into her eyes. Belle tilted her head back and forth. "Happy anniversary, Belle. You've been here for two years."

Don's thoughts made his heart sink. He put Belle on his shoulder and walked over to the fireplace mantel and picked up a photo. He gazed at it, seeing his wife Uelle on her thirtieth birthday, the day he brought Belle home for her.

His memory drifted as he recalled that Luke and Sabrina were over that night, and the photo was taken before they'd all gone out to dinner. Luke, Sabrina, and a very happy and beautiful Uelle with Belle on her finger were all smiling at the camera without a care in the world.

Uelle's long, blonde hair was nearly the same color as the bird's light yellow feathers and the camera caught the sparkle in his wife's cornflower blue eyes. Don recalled telling her the bird's name had to be Belle because he bought a pretty bird for his very pretty wife.

Uelle beamed at him when he said it. Don brought the photo closer to his face. "Today would've been your thirty-second birthday," he whispered. Don closed his eyes and his head dropped.

After a few moments, he wiped his eyes and took some deep breaths. "We miss you, Uelle," Don whispered to the photograph. "We hope you are happy up there in heaven." He kissed her picture, put it back down, and lingered over it for a little while longer. Then he looked at his watch. It was time to get moving. He grabbed some breakfast and hastened out the door.

As Don approached Luke's house, his forlorn mood faded when he spotted the snowman. Luke's house was a modest, but nice bungalow in a modest, but nice part of Denver. The snowman in the front yard, however, was anything but modest. It was a huge, beaming monument that demanded attention. Don knocked on the door and Luke answered. "Good work, my man." Don slapped Luke on the back. "What time did you get up to -?"

Before he could finish his question, Lucy scurried over to him squealing, "Uncle Don! Uncle Don! Did you see my snowman? Daddy and I made it this morning!"

"Yes, Lucy, I couldn't miss your snowman. He is the biggest snowman I've ever seen." Lucy jumped in Don's arms and he gave her a heartfelt hug and a kiss.

"Lucy and I were up at four thirty this morning making that masterpiece, and I decided he is the official snow statue of this entire street," Luke announced.

"That he is," Don declared. "Heck, I think he should be the official snow sculpture of the entire city. And I am honored to be inside of the home of that spectacular super snowman!" Don grinned at Lucy and put her down as Sabrina walked over.

She gave Don a kiss on the cheek and squeezed his arm. "How is Don doing today?" She searched his face as though she was trying to peer into his heart.

"I guess about where you'd expect me to be. Better than last year, that's for sure. Belle and I wished Uelle a happy birthday. But let me tell you that when I woke up this morning, I was very glad that I was going to get to see you and Lucy today before going to work."

Sabrina patted his arm. "We're always here for you."

Don smiled at her. "It helps more than you know, believe me."

Luke took his gun out of a locked safe, strapped it on, and put a jacket on over his gray suit coat.

"Okay, Cheeto, let's go." Luke turned to kiss Lucy and Sabrina goodbye, and handed Lucy a stuffed animal that he picked up off the floor. "Lucy, please go put that back in your room." Lucy turned and scampered off to do his bidding.

"You be careful, Luke Malone," Sabrina commanded. "You have a family to come home to, you hear?"

Luke grinned and posed in a muscleman stance. "I'll be back," he said in his best Arnold Schwarzenegger imitation.

Sabrina smacked him and laughed. Then she looked over at Don. "You be careful too, Don Layden. I don't like the neighborhood that you'll be working in today. I've read about some drug deals going around over there. Those types would just as soon shoot you as look at you."

Don chuckled, "Oh, Luke and I have our share of woman-beaters and robbers too. We don't discriminate."

Sabrina folded her arms and smirked. "Thank you. That makes me feel so much better."

"We'll be careful," Don reassured her. "But we have to catch this guy. The more I replay the murder scene in my head, the more I think that we have a real maniac on our hands."

Luke cuffed his partner on the shoulder. "What are we waiting for? We're the two best maniac catchers I know. Let's go get him."

NINE

In a middle class suburb west of Denver, the killer sat at his kitchen table, watching the street outside. He reached for the cigarette stub that smoldered in an ashtray near his coffee cup. The current stump was just about ready to join the three butts that were already there. Smashing the smoke, he started pacing. Where was the paper? His stomach performed flips. He tightened the belt of his charcoal-gray kimono around his thick waist and kicked a stray Fruit Loop across the cherry wood floor with one of his slate-colored Australian Ascot slippers. A spider crawled up a wall, and he turned and crept towards it. It sped up towards the ceiling and he moved to smash it but missed. It climbed out of range for his five foot nine frame. His icy blue eyes narrowed, and he wiped his forehead with his sleeve, misplacing some strands of red hair. "Grrr!"

Just then the paperboy ran up the sidewalk and tossed the newspaper on the front deck. "Finally!" The killer opened the front door, scooped it up, and spread it out over the kitchen table. After ruffling through the pages, the first section went flying across the room. The second page of the metro section rewarded his efforts: "Axe Murderer Butchers Prosecutor's Wife in a Monstrous Attack." *What a beautiful headline.*

The killer leaned forward to read, then re-read every word. Finally, he smoothed the paper, sat back in his chair, and lit another cigarette. Enjoying a long, satisfying drag he leaned his head back and, with a smile on his face, watched the smoke curling around the kitchen and then float towards the dark, cave-like living room, toward the display of medieval axes, polearms, swords, shields, and halberds that was on the main wall, and then around the thick, tightly drawn curtains. Finally, the smoke thinned and dissipated.

The phone rang. The killer turned toward it and watched as it rang again. He sighed and picked it up, disappointed by the interruption.

"Hello dear, I'm calling you from sunny Costa Rica, isn't that fabulous?" His mother's familiar nasal voice filled the other end of the line and, as usual, she didn't bother to wait for an answer. "We absolutely love every minute of this place. We might just stay here for a while. The condo is enormously expensive, but you only live once, right?"

"Yes, Mother." He sat down and rubbed his eyes, placing his elbow on the table and his chin in his hand. He stared at the table as the call continued.

"We are here with the Pikes. We enjoy being with them, too…" His mother blathered on for several minutes. "Henry Pike told us about his company, so I told him about *your* little company. How is your little company doing, dear?"

The killer eyed one stack of personal unpaid bills and another stack of requests for funds from investors on the kitchen table. "It's never been better."

"That's nice, dear. The Pikes told us all about their son, Charles. Charles started up a company a while ago and he has a Mercedes similar to yours. How is your lovely Mercedes doing?"

The killer closed his eyes. "It's sitting in the garage all nice and clean, Mother."

"That's good. You absolutely must keep it clean. You wouldn't want to be seen driving around in a dirty Mercedes, would you?" She laughed one of her weird, phony laughs. "Charles is shopping around for a jet. Do you think you might buy a jet anytime soon? I'd love to ride around in your jet! I could tell my friends all about it."

The killer dropped his head. *Sure, right after I figure out how to pay my electric bill, I'll go look for a jet.* "A jet is fine for national travel, but most of my travel is international. I've been investing in international funds whose headquarters are located in various places around the world. If I spend my money on a jet, it would just sit unused the majority of the time, whereas if I invest those funds instead, my money grows into even more money. A jet wouldn't be a wise expenditure for me at this juncture. However, if I decide to do more business nationally, of course that is something I would consider."

"Oh." She sighed. "Well, I'm glad it's something that you'll keep in mind." She cleared her throat. "Your father, the Pikes, and I are going to pop a bottle of Dom Perignon and go sit around the pool. But Mary wanted to call her son before we did that, so I thought that I'd call you out of the blue, too. Aren't you surprised?" She said this as though she assumed he would be happy to hear from her.

He didn't answer, but that was all right because she didn't bother giving him a chance to speak. "It was great talking with you. Goodbye, dear." The line went dead.

The killer held the phone away from his face and looked at it. "Don't you mean it was great talking *at* me, Mother?"

He killer hung up the phone, got up, refilled his cup of coffee, and walked back over to the newspaper.

The financial section was out, reminding him of his hard times. There was a story about a number of businesses that had closed their doors in the city in the past month.

Further down, the headline shouted about a Ponzi scheme thief that had been caught but only after millions of dollars were scammed. The killer sighed and ran his fingers through his hair. The economy had not been good to him. He grabbed the stack of unpaid bills and threw them on the floor. They lay there, next to the section of the newspaper thrown earlier and the Fruit Loop.

Heading to his office, he spotted the message light blinking on his answering machine. He pressed the button and listened. "Mr. Witt, we tried stopping by your office, but it's empty. We didn't know you moved. We still haven't received the check from those funds you were going to sell for us. Our son's tuition is due at the end of the month and we were wondering where it is. Please give us a call back." The caller left his name and telephone number and then hung up.

"Yeah sure, I'll call you back. Right after hell freezes over."

The next message however, was much more promising. "Hi, it's David. I have great news. I've been working the membership roster from church and I already have a list of twenty couples interested in investing in the Brazilian fund you told me about. Give me a call and let's discuss the details."

A big smile came over the killer's face. Once again, he spoke to the answering machine, "That's great news, David.

All of a sudden, things are looking up. You and your church were a good find."

He stepped by a table piled with unruly stacks of papers and sat down at his black wooden desk. He usually ignored the cork board behind his computer monitor, but today he paused and looked at the photos: a picture with his parents when they gave him the big check so he could start his own business; a ribbon cutting ceremony when he opened the doors of his real estate financial company; other photos of real estate he secured through investments; and a photo with his associates raising glasses in a toast surrounded by several colorful bunches of balloons as they celebrated his third year in business.

"And then the market crashed and popped my balloons. Haven't recovered yet." He squinted as he regarded his answering machine. "But you, David, are going to help me with that, aren't you? You're going to help me get some new clients so I can pay my bills and pay back some of my old clients." He ripped the photos down, tore them to shreds, and threw them in the trash. Taking scissors out of his desk drawer, he strode back into the kitchen and took his time to cut out the story about Alicia's murder. Bringing it back into his office, he hung it in the top left corner of the freshly cleared corkboard. Then he folded his arms and sat back in his chair and stared at it, smiling.

The phone rang again, jarring his fantasies, but when he saw the caller ID he reached for it. "Hello there Mr. David Johnson, what can I do for you?" He paused. "Why don't I meet you at church for the noon service and you can give me the list of names? I'll invest for them as soon as I have their money. We want the funds to grow as quickly as possible, don't we?" He listened to David, nodding his head. "Sounds good. I'll see you in a little while." He turned off his phone and headed for the shower.

Soon he was in one of his best navy blue suits sitting next to David, a skinny recent college graduate who was still having some trouble with acne. The preacher stood at his lectern and spouted off while the killer thought about the murder. *I planned that very well, didn't I? The police have absolutely no clue. Killing someone without getting caught isn't that hard; it was all a question of planning. Most murderers just aren't as intelligent as I am. They don't think through the details. It's very important to have the mind to build a solid, insightful plan.* Lost in thought, he was surprised to hear the final song indicating the service was over. He and David stood up and exited the main room. As the church members milled in the gathering space chatting, he felt David tugging on his arm.

"I'd like to introduce Mr. Sutherland. I met him at a Christmas food drive last year. I told him about that Brazilian fund you showed me."

The killer broke into a dazzling smile and shook hands. "Yes, it's an exciting opportunity. Let me tell you about the incredibly profitable emerging economy of Brazil."

Mr. Sutherland folded his arms. "Tell you what, I'll listen to your pitch as long as you agree to help with my food drive."

"Deal."

About one hour and five families later, the killer had some nice sized checks in his pocket and drove to his bank's ATM machine. After depositing them, he headed home, pulled on his Nike sweat suit, grabbed the stack of unpaid bills and the stack of requests for funds, and started making phone calls. "Hi, I'm returning your call about the funds. I'll be dropping a check in the mail and you will have it in plenty of time to get that college tuition paid. Also, I have a new fund that's showing a lot of promise, so give me a call. I'd like to fill you in on the details." He sat and smoked and worked. One by one the stacks became shorter.

After a few hours there was less paperwork and zero cigarettes. A grimace appeared on his face. Time to go get some more smokes. He grabbed his car keys and headed out the door.

He drove to a nearby gas station and pulled in. He came here often. It had a big, well-stocked convenience store with lots of knick-knacks. Christmas items had been put out since the last time he stopped by. Silver tinsel on a Christmas tree shimmered in the sunlight and *It's Beginning to Look A Lot Like Christmas* played as he browsed through the displays, looking at the toys that were out for the season.

He stopped and touched a train. Attached to the engine were three cars colored in bright red, orange, and green with a stuffed animal in each car. He pulled out a soft golden puppy with huge brown eyes and long floppy ears and stared at it.

"May I help you sir?" A friendly female clerk gave him a smile. "Isn't that the most darling toy? Any little boy would love it!"

"Yes, I had one of these when I was little. A friend of the family gave it to me. I played with it for hours. I used to imagine traveling away to the best places with these little friends."

"We also have those same stuffed animals in a bigger size right over here." She pointed to a nearby shelf and picked up a larger version of the puppy her shopper was holding. "These have little music boxes in them too. This one plays *We Wish You a Merry Christmas.*" She wound it up and made the dog dance to the music.

"You're a good salesperson," he said with a wink at the clerk. "Sold." He took the dog with him to the cash register to pay for it along with the cigarettes.

When he got into his car he pulled out his phone and searched his contacts for an old friend, Rosalyn Walker. After listening to her voicemail recording he left a message. "Good morning, Rosalyn. I'm just calling to wish you a good Christmas season, if I don't see you. Hey, do you remember that train you bought for me when I was little? The one with the little puppy and the bear and the tiger? They still make those. I just saw one and I wanted you to know that toy helped me to create some of the happiest memories of my childhood." He coughed. "Anyway, I just wanted to give you a call."

He put the phone down and turned his attention to the dog. He held it, staring at it for some time. "Hi Buddy, long time no see. I've had quite a few adventures since the last time we hung out." He stroked the dog's soft, golden fur. "Let me show you something." He pulled a knife out of his pocket, opened it, and polished the blade until the silver shone in the sun.

"Pretty, isn't it? And this is just a little one. I have some bigger blades than this one." He smiled at the stuffed dog. "I can't wait to show you how I use them." He paused. "Maybe you can come with me next time."

TEN

"Okay, Cheeto, so far we're striking out." Luke frowned at Don. "We've interviewed ten more men and they all have legit alibis. At five in the morning on a Saturday, they were in bed and they all have someone who can vouch for them." Luke groaned. "Okay, who is the next lucky man to be visited by Denver's finest?" Luke stared into the open trunk at the box of files.

Don pulled a manila folder from the box. "The winner is Jerome Whiting. Jerome is five feet nine inches, size ten and a half shoe, and he weighs about 160 pounds. He dealt drugs to minors in a school zone and got caught. He attacked the arresting officer but was overpowered. Served five years and was just released two weeks ago." Don looked at Luke. "That fits. Plus, he attacked the arresting officer so he's aggressive. Could be our man." Don examined the file again. "He lives close by. Let's just walk."

"Can do, Cheeto."

As Don trudged through the snow, he observed his surroundings. The homes on the street were run down. For most of the cars on the street, you could see rust on the doors and quarter panels. Traffic was just starting to pick up. Many of the residents they were visiting stayed up late and got up late. So far, the detectives had been the alarm clock for all the men they interviewed, but Don guessed that was going to change.

They got to the ground-floor apartment number 109, and Don knocked. No answer. Don knocked again, this time much harder. "Jerome Whiting, this is the police. We would like to ask you a few questions," Don stated in a loud voice.

Suddenly, they heard some cursing, then some bumping and running inside. Don banged on the door. "I said this is the police. Open up!" Don peered inside through a crack in the drapes and saw what looked like heroin lying out. Drawing his gun, Don threw his body against the door and it burst open. The back window was gaping wide. Don bolted through the apartment and jumped out the back window.

With his gun drawn, Luke checked the rooms in the rest of the apartment. No one was there. Luke radioed Don. "Where are you?"

Sprinting as fast as he could, Don managed to talk into the radio on his collar. "Running south on Steele Street towards 40th Avenue," he shouted. "I have the suspect in sight."

Luke burst out of the front door and leapt down stairs out toward 40th Avenue. His legs churned and his feet pounded the pavement like a jackhammer. Hopefully, he could intercept Jerome from another angle for Don.

Jerome was wiry and fast, but Don was hot on his trail. The suspect dodged in and out behind cars and threw trashcans and anything else he could find in Don's way.

Don hurdled over the obstacles and kept running, pumping hard. The gap narrowed. Jerome ran into the street. Tires screeched as he was almost hit by a car, but he managed to squeak by and kept running. Don slammed the hood of the car with the palm of his hand as he ran by so the driver wouldn't start the car moving again.

Jerome ran by some old furniture that was out to be dumped. He grabbed a chair and threw it at Don. Don dodged it and kept going. Suddenly, Jerome slipped on some ice and fell on his stomach. Don caught up with him and put a knee on his back. Both men created clouds of steam as they caught their breath.

"You have the right to remain silent..." Don handcuffed Jerome and completed the Miranda rights as Luke sprinted up. Luke bent over with his hands on his thighs, sucking air.

"Good job, Cheeto, good job," he said between gasps. He looked at Jerome. "Hey Pal, why were you running? Don't you know you aren't supposed to run from your friendly neighborhood police officers?"

Don hauled Jerome up. Jerome had a dark look on his face. "What's the charge?" he snarled.

"Evading a police officer," Don said. He wanted to keep it simple for now. He called in the address of Jerome's apartment so the drug team could get it processed. Meanwhile, it was time to take Jerome in for questioning.

Two hours later, Jerome faced charges for drugs and evading a police officer, but they could not tie him to Alicia's murder. Don and Luke came out from the interrogation room and wandered over to their respective desks, which faced each other. Luke slammed his hand on his desk and swore. "I hate that. I got my hopes up. I thought we found our man."

"Yeah, I know." Don chewed his lip. "Still feels like we're following the wrong leads." He rubbed the back of his neck. "It's the axe. We aren't focusing on the murder weapon. In all of the files last night I saw no history of an axe or any type weapon of that type. Period. That's not to say that the killer wouldn't have one now. I keep thinking that if we follow the axe it'll lead us to the killer."

Luke booted up his computer. "Let's research the places that sell axes and see if we can cross reference what we find out with an address in the files that Rebecca gave us. Who knows? Maybe we'll get really lucky and find a credit card purchase that matches one of the folks in our fine box of files."

Don felt a burst of energy as he turned on his computer. For the first time in this investigation he really felt as though he was following the right trail. "I'll take the west side of the city, you take the east."

"Sounds good, Cheeto." Luke continued typing. A door opened behind him, but he didn't bother looking up at the noise.

"What are you two doing? You bring one man in for questioning and you think you are done? In case you didn't know, it's pretty difficult to catch bad guys when you're sitting at your desk." Belinda stood next to their chairs with a red leather portfolio in one hand and the other hand positioned on the side of her hip. Her face wore a familiar scowl. "Yeah, I'll bet you didn't think I'd be in today did ya'? I just passed Keith in the hall and he gave me the scoop about your arrest."

Don spoke up, "Belinda, we've been ignoring one of the most important clues in this case: the murder weapon. If we find a connection between an axe and these files that would narrow the field down considerably. Give us a much better chance of finding this guy in a lot less time."

"Oh please, spare me your sob story of not having enough time," Belinda scoffed. "Hmmm...let's see if we can figure this out." She held up an index finger. "Here's an idea for you. Get up off your behinds and go out there and work your leads." She pointed to the door then spun around and stormed back to her office. As she slammed the door, the blinds on her windows rattled as an exclamation point.

A few of the other detectives in the office looked in Don and Luke's direction with sympathy. Don knew each one of them had suffered through a similar speech more than once.

Luke studied the ceiling, clenching and unclenching his fists, too angry to say anything.

Don rubbed his face several times and then looked over at his partner. Luke seemed like he was about to blow. "Let's get out of here." Don kept his voice low. "We'll get Rebecca to follow the axe lead for us while we do what Belinda wants. Who knows, maybe we'll get lucky with the files."

Luke's eyes were still black with fury.

Don stood up and put his hand on his partner's shoulder. "Come on, Luke. If Rebecca helps us, we can really make some progress."

Luke's face was a tight mask.

Don patted his partner on the back. "Come on, big guy. You have a new baby on the way. You have a beautiful family to take care of. You don't want to create a problem for yourself at work. Belinda's not worth it. Forget about her. There's a killer running free in Denver and we have to find him. And we will find him in spite of Belinda Mann."

Luke closed his eyes. He inhaled and exhaled a couple of times with determined deliberation. Then he finally stood up and straightened his yellow tie.

As Don prepared to leave, the Mayor walked in carrying a thick report. Belinda rushed out of her office and greeted him.

"Mayor, welcome to my department!"

"Thanks for coming in so late on the weekend, Belinda." He tapped the report. "As I mentioned when I called you earlier, I just went over the city's budget and I want to thank you for how much you've streamlined your unit. The efficiencies make a big impact in my fiscal policy. I have a budget meeting tomorrow and I wanted to go over a couple of things."

Belinda led him into her office. "No problem, Mr. Mayor. I am happy to be here to answer any and all questions you may have."

Luke stared after the two of them with his mouth open and eyes blazing. Don grabbed him by the arm and they exited the building.

ELEVEN

The sleeves of his Nike sweat suit were rolled up. *Lots to do.* The killer examined the computer screen in his office while he talked on the phone. "Yes, Steven, I know you won't regret this. This investment is a good one. You'll be delighted with the results." He hung up the phone and sat back in his chair.

David's efforts were starting to pay off. He leaned forward and stared at his computer. *This was really going to work, wasn't it? I haven't lost my touch!*

He went back online to look at the Brazilian investment fund. The investor in Brazil was knowledgeable, had answered his questions easily, and sent some forms via overnight mail. The killer had already opened an account, so it would be easy to invest more. *I have money in the bank for myself, I have my old clients quiet for now, so why not? I'm on a roll. Besides, dealing with the investor directly was much more profitable than going through an investment house.* He invested thousands of dollars right on the spot.

Stretching his neck and back, his eyes wandered to Alicia's picture posted on the corkboard behind his computer. A smile came to his lips. He searched through some papers on his desk and pulled out a list of about fifty names and addresses. Eight of them were circled including Alicia Kendrick's name. The killer drew a line through it. *One down.* He put the list near his right hand as he got on Facebook to do some research. *This was going to be fun.*

A couple of hours later, he made a decision. He picked up the list and highlighted a name. Gail Gonzales was the winner. After hours of stalking her on Facebook, he settled on Gail. She taught at an elementary school, played in a co-ed soccer league in the summer, and was single. That would make it easier.

He held some photos that he'd printed from the pictures on Facebook of all the remaining women on his list. Wasn't Facebook a wonderful invention? He came to Gail's picture. It showed a tall, athletic woman with short hair that was an interesting mixture of copper and gold. Her eyes were a couple of shades lighter than a dollar bill, more like a pistachio. She was grinning at the camera while holding up a ribbon that she won in a marathon in Denver last May. There were a lot of exercise psychos in Colorado. Apparently, she was one of them.

He put her picture up next to the one of Alicia and stared at it for a while. Then he checked the time on the Rolex his mother sent him from Switzerland for Christmas last year, which was just another one of many Christmas holidays throughout his life during which his parents had been out of the country.

Hmmm... he wondered where Gail was right now. It might be a good idea to go out and get the lay of the land. He looked up her name online and found her address. Picking up Buddy, he got into his car.

He wound up driving around a while but finally found Gail's place. She lived in a brick duplex and he didn't see any residential security. Turning off the ignition, he studied her residence for a few minutes. "Buddy, it looks like no one is home. Let's go check, shall we?" Stuffing the dog into his pocket, he went up to her door, examined the lock, and knocked. No one answered. He looked around and didn't see anyone walking along the street, so he stepped off the front porch and trudged around in the snow to look at the locks on any other doors. The back door looked promising. There was no deadbolt there. As he walked back to his car, he smiled.

Kate sat back in the chair in her office and rubbed her eyes. One downside of being a controller for the downtown Denver Marriott was budgets. She referred to budgets as an occupational hazard due to the seven-day work weeks and the numerous hours she spent creating and scrutinizing worksheets with lots of numbers. Budget season was almost over, and her eyes stung due to the time spent staring at her computer screen. Her cell phone buzzed.

"Hi, Father Tim. What's up?"

"Hi Kate. Father Bill asked me to give you a call to see if you could swing by Regis at some point to give him an opinion on the toy drive. The building he was planning on using for it is being painted and they aren't going to be done on time."

"Are they ever?"

She heard a chuckle on the other end. "No, I guess not. Anyway, would it be a problem? It shouldn't take long."

Kate looked at her watch. "I'm still at work so how about if I swing by there on my way home?"

"That'd be great. I'll call him back and let him know you'll be there tonight."

Kate closed down her computer and headed over to Regis University. As she got into her car, thunder roiled.

After a short drive, Kate stood on the front porch of the priest's residence and rapped on the door. it opened before she even had a chance to put her hand down.

"Hi, Father Bill. Wow. Were you standing by the door waiting for me?"

The clergyman was just a couple of inches taller than Kate and she found herself looking right into his twinkling blue eyes. He pointed to the ceiling. "Maybe the Holy Spirit told me you were here."

Kate tilted her head. "I think that might be a stretch, Father."

"Okay, okay." He bent over and picked up a couple of lanterns. "I was bringing these to the door to be ready when you got here. The place where I was thinking we could use for the toy drop off doesn't have any electricity."

Kate wrinkled her nose. "Why not?"

"We're going to store the toys in an entrance to an old chapel that was first built here back in 1887. The electrical system that was installed later is old and would cost thousands to bring up to code. We have a beautiful modern church and I just can't justify spending that kind of money." He handed her a lantern.

"Makes sense."

Lightning flashed as they made their way to the old chapel. "Looks like we got ourselves a storm coming in," Father Bill observed.

Kate made her way through the grove of trees that nearly surrounded the old chapel. As they approached the gray limestone structure, she looked up and saw some old gargoyles adorning the building. A shiver ran down her spine.

Father Bill noticed her apprehension and let out a belly laugh. "Don't you love those? Those are the rain gutters of the days of old. Kept the rain from damaging the masonry. The style just sort of stuck for a while."

Kate continued to gaze up at the gargoyles. A muscle in her jaw twitched as she pondered their creepy faces.

Father Bill fiddled with the lock and the chapel's door creaked as it swung open. A pungent musty odor rushed to Kate's face and she drew back. Father Bill held out his lantern and motioned her inside.

She stepped forward and looked around. As she swung the lantern, shadows moved and jumped. Tree branches tapped against high ceiling windows. They sounded like a creature knocking to get in. "Wow. This is crazy." She looked at the priest. "I don't think I would want to be in here by myself."

"Yeah, I guess I can see why someone might find it a little scary. I should air it out before we put the toys in here. Let me walk the perimeter of the room so you can see it better. This is the entrance of the chapel. I think it will be big enough to store the toys until the Alumni House is ready."

"I don't think you want to put them on the floor." Kate bent over and touched it with a finger. "It's filthy. Can you bring some tables in here so we can stack them when people drop them off?"

"Sure can. I'll make sure it's cleaned too. So, do you think this is okay if we store the toys here?"

Kate straightened up and walked around holding her lantern out. Some cobwebs adorned the walls. "You'll want to get rid of the resident spiders. I don't think the kids want them crawling out of their toys."

"Good idea. Come to think of it, I'd better get an exterminator out here in case of rats."

"I could have gone all night without hearing that." Kate moved toward some oak doors. "Is this the entrance to the chapel itself?"

"Yes. Want to go inside?"

Kate clapped her hands together. "Absolutely!"

Following Father Bill, Kate held her lantern in front of her and explored the room. Small stained-glass windows with artistic etchings lined the walls and old, cracked wooden pews sat in rows leading up to a stone altar. Paintings, dimmed with age, showing various scenes from the Bible were on the walls behind the altar. The stone ceilings were vaulted, making the room feel bigger than it really was.

"This is gorgeous," Kate whispered. "I love the paintings! I'll have to come back here sometime when it's light outside." Her stomach sank. "It's too bad the cost to get it up to speed is so high."

"I agree. But my fiscal responsibility is to my students." The priest turned to Kate. "Do you want to see the basement? It's pretty cool too."

"I'd love that."

Father Bill found a skinny door in a corner and led them downstairs. "There are so many little rooms down here." He led Kate around opening doors. "And some of them even have smaller rooms inside." He showed her the tiny spaces. "I think these were used to pray."

Kate brushed the cobwebs out of the way as she examined her surroundings. "I love it down here. I can imagine someone kneeling in this room, praying her heart out." She turned to the priest. "Thank you for showing me this. It's just what I needed after a hard day of budgets."

Kate followed Father Bill outside. A fresh dusting of snow was on the ground and more floated down from the sky. Thunder crashed. She hugged herself. "Thudersnow! I love it!"

The priest smiled. "Life is always full of surprises, isn't it?"

TWELVE

"Forty files." Luke heaved a big sigh and looked at Don. "We busted our butts and went through forty files and the most productive things that we have done is nab a drug dealer and start Rebecca working on the axe angle."

"Yeah. A long day and night. Let's call it. We can start early again tomorrow. We made faster progress in the morning when the people we were trying to connect with were all in bed and we didn't have to drive all over the city catching up with them. I'll drop you off at home. Should I come by about the same time tomorrow?"

"Yup, that'll work."

Don pulled up in Luke's driveway, and Luke exited the car and waved a hand as Don drove off. Luke unlocked the front door and walked into the house. "Sabrina?"

"I'm in here." Sabrina lay in bed watching TV, waiting for him. "Lucy is in bed for the night." Luke sat down on the side of the bed next to her and kissed her. "How'd it go?" Sabrina asked. "Did you find your maniac?" She listened as Luke told her about his day and his frustrations. She patted his arm as he spoke.

"I'm gonna turn out the lights. Be right back."

As he walked toward the kitchen, he glanced into the living room and stopped. The furniture had been moved around. He shut off the lights and hurried back into the bedroom. "What happened to the furniture in the living room?" Luke asked frowning.

"I moved it while I was vacuuming today, and I thought I would let you put it back. Is that okay with you Mr. Fussy-man?" Sabrina pursed her lips at him.

"No, that is definitely not okay with me, Sabrina. Especially while you're pregnant. I told you I would vacuum." Luke waved his finger in her face. "There's no way you should be moving heavy furniture." He put her hands in his. "I want you to promise me that you won't do that again."

"Okay Mr. Fussy-man, I won't do that again." Sabrina's eyes crinkled. She rubbed his shoulder and smiled at him. "Now come to bed and keep me warm."

Luke's frown changed into a smile and he kissed his wife's hand. "Okay, Mrs. Malone, your wish is my command."

A few miles away, Don stood in front of Uelle's headstone. He tied a couple of birthday balloons with bright purple ribbons to the vase he kept there. "Happy Birthday, Uelle." He looked up at the sky and shook his finger at it. "You remembered her birthday, right?" He smiled at the tombstone. "I'm sure they remembered. After all, how could they forget the birthday of the most wonderful person they've ever met?" He stood and rubbed the tombstone for a while, head bowed.

About an hour later, he sat at his computer with the files next to his desk and Belle on his shoulder. As he talked on his cell phone, he studied a list on his screen. It was from an email that Rebecca sent.

"Thanks, Rebecca. You worked hard on this. This will help." He listened for a minute. "Yes, we had background checks done on the members of the PTA and the Bible study group but came up with nothing. No surprise there." There was another pause. "Yes, I'll call you if I need anything else. You're definitely helping us narrow it down. Thanks again. Bye."

He sat back and folded his arms, still looking at the list. "Belle, I think I've got tomorrow mapped out. It's better than it was before. Rebecca came through with those cross-checks. We really don't have anything that connects with axes, but we do have some knife references."

He took Belle off his shoulder and looked at her. "The jump from knife to axe could happen, don't you think? I don't know, maybe some sort of an attraction to a steel blade?" Belle cocked her head and a small smile formed on his lips as he put her back on his shoulder. When he looked at the box of files, he ran a hand through his hair and a small groan escaped his lips. "It's the best we have right now, anyway."

He printed the email and rearranged the files according to the list. Then he got up and stretched and brought the box into his entrance placing it near his front door. He carried Belle over to her cage.

"Good night, pretty lady. It's time to dream about eating bugs or some other wonderful fantasy." He stroked her feathers for a few minutes as Belle looked at him. Then he placed her in her cage and put the cover over it so she could sleep well.

He hoped he would too.

THIRTEEN

The alarm sounded and Don reached over to turn it off with his eyes still closed. Man! That was a short night! How could it be five already? He kept pushing the snooze button but the ringing continued. He finally opened his eyes. "Oh." With his head still on the pillow, he picked up his phone and held it to his ear. "Layden here."

Luke was on the other end of the phone and Don could hear the strain in his voice. "Don, Sabrina has some bleeding going on. I'm taking her to the hospital."

"Oh, no." Don sat up. "Does she have any cramps or anything?"

"A little bit. She vacuumed yesterday while I was gone and moved our living room furniture around!" Luke's voice grew louder as he spoke.

Don grimaced. "Not good. Just get her to the doctor. Let me know how she is doing, all right? Do you have someone to watch Lucy? How will she get to pre-school?"

"Yeah, I already got that all set up," Luke replied. "Hey sorry to leave you like this with the case being so tough and all…"

"Don't worry about it. Take care of your wife and your baby. Besides, Rebecca came through with some cross-checks. I have the day all mapped out."

"Do you have someone that can go with you?"

"Luke, you worry about your wife. I'll worry about the case. Now get off this phone. Go take care of your family. Let me know how things go, okay? Talk to you later."

Don placed the phone back on the night table, looked at the clock, and groaned. It was four in the morning. He blinked a few times, and then rubbed his face with both hands hard so that he could wake up enough to get up and exercise. He might as well get going.

Since it was so early, Don stopped by the station's shooting range in the basement of the downtown station. He greeted the shift manager as he signed in. "Hey Simon, how's it going?"

The pear-shaped man grinned at Don. "You're here early! This time of day it's usually the guys that are getting off the graveyard shift who come in."

"Yeah, I woke up early so I decided now was as good a time as any to get my practice time in for the month. Have to go out and interview people all day. I'm guessing pounding on the doors of Denver's citizens this early might get me in hot water."

"Roger that. See you when you're done."

About forty-five minutes later, another detective, Zach Daskalis, came in to work on his practice shooting in the stall next to Don. "Hey Don, how's it going?"

Don shook his head and gave the short, husky man a weak smile. "Been better." He told Zach about the case, and about Belinda's insistence that the files were the only key to the answer. "I just hope she's right and that I can make some inroads today." Don explained Luke's challenges and then asked, "How goes the task of solving crimes for you?" Don remembered that Zach and his partner Jim had been working on a series of murders that were occurring amongst the homeless community.

"It's tough, too." Zach's forehead creased. "They either won't talk to us because they're scared or sometimes they just don't have the mental skills to communicate very well. Many of them believe we are going to hurt them when that is the furthest thing from the truth."

Don sighed. "Yeah, the mentally ill are a population at risk. Problem is they are easy for everyone to ignore." He grimaced at Zach. "I guess we're paid to clean up the mess, eh?" The two detectives nodded to each other.

"Good talking to you. Don't go out there by yourself. Wait until you know what's going on with Luke." Zach raised a hand to signal goodbye as Don turned to leave.

Don went upstairs to check his email before getting out for the interviews. He hoped he could get that done before Belinda arrived. She rarely came in this early.

He just turned off his computer when Belinda walked up behind him. "Well?"

Startled, Don jumped and then closed his eyes before turning around to face her.

"Good morning, Belinda. What brings you in so bright and early?" Don made his voice as pleasant as possible as he turned to face her.

"Following up on my detectives." Belinda glared at Don. "Oh come to think of it, you have a case going, don't you?" Her eyes narrowed. "Any progress?"

Don kept his voice calm. "We're moving forward. We worked late last night. Then I did more research after I got home. I think I can make good headway today."

"Cool. It'd be amazing to see some sort of progress on a murder that occurred two days ago." Her eyes widened. "Don't you agree?" With that she turned on her heel and stomped to her office.

Don clenched his teeth, got up, and exited the station.

Belinda turned on her computer and responded to an email from the mayor. When he read it, she hoped he would notice the early time of day it was sent. Then she got up to go grab breakfast at her favorite spot near the station.

Outside, Don stood by the Crown Vic for a couple of minutes. Doing the interviews alone was definitely not the smartest thing to do, but he didn't see any way out of it today. He opened the trunk and pulled the first file. Then he climbed into his car and headed out.

FOURTEEN

The first file Don pulled was for a man named Chris Koster who was jailed due to a domestic violence crime. Reading about someone beating his wife made Don's blood boil. He stalked up to the door and pounded.

No answer.

Don pounded again. After a few more moments, the door swung open. Standing there was an overweight man of about five feet ten inches. The few hairs left on his head were gray and dirty. His clothes were wrinkled and his face was grizzled in gray scruff.

Don showed his badge. "I'm investigating a crime. I'd like to ask you a couple of questions. Are you Chris Koster?"

"Huh?" Chris appeared to be confused.

As Don asked his questions, he stepped into Chris's house and looked around. It was a mess. Empty bottles of beer and alcohol were mixed in with old, barren boxes of pizza. There were no signs that a female either lived there or visited. Chris's former girlfriend was obviously long gone. An ancient bloodhound looked at Don without even raising his head, his soulful brown eyes needing no words.

Don finished the interview and escaped. He got back into the Crown Vic and grimaced. "That was ugly," Don muttered to himself as he put the file back. "That guy couldn't make it out to the curb let alone to Alicia's house."

Don drove to the next address, parked, and looked at the file. Armando Rahmin got out of jail about five months ago. Adam prosecuted him for dealing drugs on the grounds of an elementary school, attacking a police officer with a deadly weapon, and running from the police. Armando studied the martial arts and was also good with knives. He was six feet tall and 190 pounds. "Luke, I miss you already," Don said to the empty passenger seat next to him. Don braced himself, got out of the car, and bounded up the stairs to Armando's apartment.

Hearing noises coming out of the apartment, Don slowed his approach. Men's voices were mixed with music. Don wanted to see how many men he might have to be dealing with. He put his back against the outer wall of the apartment so he could look into the room through the window. Three men were doing a drug deal. There was about two ounces of what was most likely cocaine out on the table. He could see them testing it to see how pure it was. Don retreated a few steps and called for backup when a neighbor opened his door, spotted Don, and yelled, "Hey! It's the cops! What are you doing here?"

Chairs scraped against the floor in Armando's apartment. Don pounded on the door. "Open up, this is the police!"

Don burst through the door and rolled as guns fired at him. He took cover behind a couch and returned fire. Just then a bullet zinged by him from behind. Don looked over his shoulder and saw a young boy turn and run away.

Chairs fell over as the dealers headed for the fire escape. Don jumped up and chased them. Don was faster than all of them, and he was able to take one down and cuff him while watching where the others headed. The culprits split up and Don followed in Armando's wake, legs pumping.

A gray-haired woman inclined her head in the direction of a grimy alley and Don slowed down. Holding his gun low, he eased into the alley. The hairs on the back of his neck prickled. Step by step, he moved forward. He saw a fence at the end of the alley. Approaching a trash bin, Don sprang out and found nothing.

Before Don knew what was happening, Armando pounced on Don from behind. Don's gun fell out on the ground and spun out of reach as he and Armando wrestled on the ground. Armando had a knife, but Don was quick and stopped the knife several times. The scuffle continued. Armando was able to slice into Don's arm, but Don got on top of him and cuffed him just as he heard sirens in the distance.

Don retrieved his gun and put it away then hauled up Armando. "You have the right to remain silent…" Don dragged Armando towards his car as the police backup came running.

Two hours later, Don sat in a room in ER getting stitches from a young, black haired doctor when Luke strode in. A nurse chased after him. "Sir, sir you can't go in there! Only family can go in there!"

Luke turned and looked down at the tiny nurse. "I am family." Luke walked over to Don and put his dark face right next to his partner's face. "Can't you tell we're brothers?"

The nurse looked from Luke to the doctor. Luke flashed his badge and the doctor spoke up. "It's okay. Thanks, Cindy."

"He's my partner." Don rolled his eyes. "See what I have to put up with?"

The doctor's eyes crinkled and he continued stitching while Luke stood in front of Don, shifting his weight from one foot to the other. "What happened?"

"First tell me about Sabrina. How is she?"

Luke exhaled in relief as he responded. "She's okay. She just has to lie down and rest for a couple of days, but she'll be fine. I talked her sister into staying with us for a little while." Luke folded his arms. "Your turn. What happened?"

Don filled him in and watched Luke's eyes flash as he listened.

"Cheeto, I told you not to go anywhere without someone to help you! What were you thinking?"

"I was thinking Belinda would kill us if we didn't make headway on the files. Armando and his buddies are being processed right now. As soon as I'm done here, let's get down to the station and see where we are."

"You really should lie down for the rest of the day," interjected the doctor. "You lost a fair amount of blood."

"Don't worry Doc, I think I can take a couple of stitches and still do police work."

"Against your physician's advice."

About thirty minutes later, Armando was in an interview room with his hands cuffed behind his back and his feet cuffed as well. Don and Luke stood outside of the room for a minute, observing, before they went in. Luke grabbed a chair and tossed it so that it landed backwards. He straddled it and stuck his face close to Armando's.

"Very impressive," Armando sneered.

Luke's eyes narrowed. "I'm not here to impress you, sucker, I'm here to get answers." He moved his head closer to Armando. "And you had better think about the consequences of withholding information. Not a good idea."

Don walked over and stood at the end of the table. "So tell me, Armando, how was your life in the penitentiary? Canon City is such a beautiful town, don't you think?"

Armando's lips drew back across his teeth and his hickory eyes darkened a shade. "Hey man, it was like staying at the Hilton. Turn down bed service, maids to clean, fresh linen every day…"

"And I'll bet you can't wait to go back." Luke raised his eyebrows. "That must be why you were dealing drugs this morning. So you could get back to an upgraded suite right away."

Armando scowled and folded his arms. His eyes shifted from one detective to another.

Don leaned forward. "Then again, maybe the idea of going back isn't really so appealing after all. Maybe you hated it. Maybe you thought about how you got there and decided to get even."

Armando frowned. "What are you talking about?"

"What were you doing at five thirty in the morning this past Saturday?" Luke's face was so close to Armando's face that he could feel Armando's breath.

"Five thirty in the morning?" Armando laughed. "Hell, I was sleeping! What else would I be doing at that time of day?"

"You sure?" Luke squinted at Armando. "I better not find out that you're lying to me. I assure you, you will be very sorry if I find out that you are."

Armando looked down his nose at Luke. "Go talk to my ol' lady. She'll tell you."

Luke sat back and looked at Don, frowning. Another dead end.

Don and Luke hustled out to verify Armando's alibi. Sure enough, it was true. They got back in the car and sat there for a few minutes, staring at nothing.

Cursing, Luke slammed his fist on the dashboard.

"I know." Don leaned his head back and looked at the Crown Vic's ceiling. "The axe has to lead us somewhere. It's the axe. We keep focusing on these files, but we can't ignore the axe."

Just then, Don's phone rang. He looked at the caller ID and put it on speaker. Then he took a deep breath. "Layden here."

"Have you and Luke transferred to the drug unit?" Belinda's sarcasm dripped through the airwaves like a toxic chemical. "You've made a couple of nice drug busts, but no murder busts. You're looking for a murderer, remember? You're supposed to be homicide detectives. Have you finished checking out the rest of those files?"

Don closed his eyes. "No Belinda, we have not."

"Then get to it! And by the way, you managed to cost the department money again. Armando's landlord called and wants payment for the damages to the apartment."

Don tried not to snarl. "They shot at me first." The call ended.

"I'll get in touch with Rebecca again to see if she's come up with any other possible connections on the axe." He gritted his teeth. "I know we've already done that. Maybe she found something new." He stared at the floorboards. "This might be the case that is too big to solve under Belinda's way of doing things."

"Yeah, no kidding." Luke's tone smoldered. "To be honest, Cheeto, I'm really troubled about this." His voice dropped. "Let's just hope our killer didn't develop a taste for what he did. I'm gonna say it again. I have a bad feeling about this one."

FIFTEEN

The bell rang and Gail Gonzales looked at the twenty-nine fourth graders sitting in their seats. "Okay students, class dismissed. Don't forget about the book reports that are due tomorrow." Immediately the scraping of chairs against the floor combined with the sound of young voices excited about the end of the school day. Soon, only one student remained in the classroom, standing next to Gail's desk. Gail smiled at Hillary. "Yes, Miss Hillary, what can I do for you?"

The young girl bit her lip. "Miss Gonzales, I really didn't get that about fractions today. I couldn't do any of the problems that you told us to practice." She looked down at the floor. "I was too scared to tell you in class," she said in a voice that was almost a whisper.

Gail put her finger under Hillary's chin and raised the young girl's head. "That's okay. Fractions are kind of tricky," she smiled. "All you have to do is practice them a little bit and then you will get it. Do you want to practice with me right now?"

Hillary's brown curls bounced as she nodded, relief evident in her big, blue eyes.

Gail pulled up a chair next to her desk and worked on some problems with Hillary. After about thirty minutes, a smile broke out on Hillary's face. "I think I get it now." She wiggled in her chair as she looked up at her teacher.

"Okay, Hillary. Just remember, the best way to get math is to practice it. And good job asking me for help. That shows that you are a very serious student."

Hillary's smile widened, and she scampered out of the classroom.

Gail sat back down at her desk and looked up her grade book on her computer. She got out a file of her students' work and updated their grades one by one. Then she gathered her things and headed out.

At home, she stretched her arms to the ceiling ready for a break after a long day with her energetic ten-year-olds. It was starting to snow. She sighed. Today she just couldn't summon the energy for a jog. First, a snack was in order, and then maybe a little Facebook. After getting comfortable on her couch with her laptop and her cat, Dewdrop, she chatted online. In no time, she sat up a little straighter. Wow. A great-looking guy who competed in ironman competitions wanted to be her friend. That sounded interesting – and so was his post: "Hi. I'm a guy who loves to compete and I saw your picture with your medal. Maybe we should meet and go for a run together."

Gail stared at the screen for a minute and then accepted his request to be her friend. "Hi. Funny you should contact me now," she replied. "I just blew off running tonight. I could use a little motivation. Running with an ironman could help, no doubt!" She held her breath.

"Me, too!" he wrote back. "Always harder to run when it gets cold. Where do you like to go?"

"I'm not too picky. Maybe we should meet at a coffee shop sometime, then head out for a few miles."

"Sounds good. Name the time and the place and I'm there!"

Gail picked her favorite coffee shop and made plans. She signed off as her stomach started to growl.

She opened her refrigerator and rummaged around, which didn't take very long since there wasn't much to inspect. "Dang it, Dewdrop, I have to go to the grocery store!" With a groan, she put on her coat and grabbed her keys.

The killer saw Gail back out of her driveway. He shut the laptop he had been using to chat with her and followed her to the grocery store. He grabbed a small cart and trailed her, staying several feet away while keeping an eye on her.

A short time later, Gail picked through some apples in the produce aisle, putting those with any blotches or bruises aside.

"It's worth the trouble to choose a good apple, don't you agree?"

Hearing a man's voice, Gail looked up and saw a thick red-haired man speaking to her. He grabbed an apple and moved very close to her with the fruit almost touching her mouth. His eyes seared into hers.

"Yes," Gail replied as she turned away, dismissing his advances. Something about him gave her the creeps, so she didn't want to encourage any further conversation. She shivered as she felt his stare burning a hole through her back. The store's canned version of John Denver's *Colorado Rocky Mountain High* suddenly sounded eerie. It was time to end this little outing and get home as soon as possible.

In the store's parking lot, she loaded her groceries into her trunk, unlocked the driver's door, and then heard "It looks like you made some good food choices. I'll bet you are going to make a nice dinner." Startled, she swung around and saw the red-haired man again. This time, he was standing right next to her.

"Yes, thanks." Just then a couple rolled two carts out of the store and loaded their contents into an adjacent Suburban. When the man looked up to see who was making the noise, Gail jumped in her car and locked the door. The man just stood there staring at her as she backed out of her parking space and took off. She gripped the steering wheel as hard as she could to keep her hands from shaking.

SIXTEEN

Don felt the early morning air on his face as he got into his car with a bouquet of daisies in his hand. Thirty minutes later, he stood at Uelle's marker. "Hi honey." He placed the flowers in their spot and tossed the old ones. He shoved his hands in his pockets. "Boy, Luke and I have a bad case. The crime was so violent and personal. He planted an axe in the back of a woman's skull." Don shuddered. "I want to find this guy ASAP. Problem is, we have a ton of interviews and Belinda won't give us any help with them. We're operating on the hunch that the motive is retaliation for jail time. It makes sense following up on these files is the right way to go. But what if we're wrong? What if we're wasting our time? I don't want this guy to get away!"

Don sighed. "Enough of that. The Eagles are doing pretty well..." Don chatted a little longer and then drove over to Luke's.

"How's the arm?" Luke asked as he got in the car.

Don shrugged. "No big deal." Don and Luke got to work on the files. Hours passed, but the only progress they made was to put a large number of files in the "dead end" box.

At Moore Elementary, Gail sat at her desk in her classroom while supporting her chin in her hand. She could not stop yawning. Her class was busy reading an assignment and she decided to slip out to the teachers' lounge and grab a cup of coffee.

A pot of coffee was still on from lunch. Hooray! Another teacher walked in the small room as Gail poured a cup. "Hey Gail, what's up?"

Gail smiled at Teresa. "I am so tired today. I couldn't sleep last night." Gail gave the Wikipedia version of the grocery store scene to her colleague.

"Ew, creepy." Teresa wrinkled her nose. "Maybe you should change grocery stores."

Gail sighed. "Yeah, I guess so. It stinks though, because the Safeway I go to is only a few blocks from my house, so most of the time I just jog over there." She tilted her head. "It's so weird. I keep thinking that I've seen him before." She shrugged. "Oh well, hopefully I won't ever see him again." She glanced at her watch. "Time to get back to work." Gail gulped the last of her coffee and hurried back to her class.

Out in the suburbs, the killer hung up the phone after working another lead from David. He cracked his knuckles as he studied an entry on his computer. The phone interrupted him. As he listened a smile crept over his face. "David, you're doing a great job. Your church connections are working out splendidly. Keep the money coming. I believe this investment vehicle is going to turn out well for all of us. Email me those names, drop off the money tomorrow, and I'll take it from there."

The killer got up and wandered into his kitchen. Some dirty dishes sat in the sink. He reached for a knife and polished it until it gleamed. Turning it this way and that, the light's reflection on the blade was mesmerizing. He pulled Buddy out of his pocket and showed him the knife. "Buddy, that blade is fascinating, don't you think? A little blade like this can cut into a thick piece of meat. You do that enough times, you destroy it. It's powerful. And just wait until I show you what a bigger blade can do." He whistled as he went to retrieve his axe.

Finally! The last bell of the day sounded throughout the school building. Gail breathed a silent sigh of relief as she smiled at her students while they departed. Hillary hung back for a few minutes. "Guess what, Ms. Gonzalez."

"What, Hillary?" Gail's fatigue vanished for a moment.

"I get fractions now. I got all of the homework problems right, every single one."

Gail clapped her hands together in delight. "Way to go! I just knew you could do it!"

"Thanks. I really wanted you to know." Hillary grinned up at her teacher. Gail held up her hand for a high five and Hillary giggled as she complied.

Gail cleaned up her desk and checked the time. She wanted to get home early so she could relax and get a good night's sleep.

The killer parked his car and pulled the axe out of the trunk, stuffing it under his coat. Closing the trunk, he bent down to study his handiwork on the license plates. *That will work.*

The paint on the plates disguised the real numbers quite well.

He smiled and straightened, adjusting his dark leather gloves and pulling the wool cap down over his hair. Acting nonchalant, he strolled along in front of Gail's residence. When he reached her place, he glanced over both shoulders and snuck around back to work on the lock. *Let's see if the video I watched on how to do this was worthwhile.* After a couple of tries, it clicked.

He held his breath as he pushed open the door and looked around. His heart pounded as he stepped in, crept down a hallway, and entered her cozy kitchen. The oxygen felt thin suddenly, and he had to breathe through his mouth so that he could get more air. A cat peered at him as it crouched under the kitchen table. Turning around, he got his bearings. Some sunlight streamed in through the windows, providing a natural glow on the wicker baskets and other knick-knacks scattered throughout the room. It took him a while to decide what to do. *Find her bedroom.* Glancing through the house, he located the bedroom and tried to listen over the pounding of his heart. He closed his eyes. *Man, this felt good! What a feeling!* He was Superman with super powers.

Thirty minutes later, Gail pulled into her driveway with the music blaring. She turned off the car and continued singing. Tommy DeLuce from Angels and Airways always got her rockin'. After she unlocked her door, she dropped her papers on the front hall table. Maybe she would grade them, or maybe she wouldn't. "Hey Dewdrop, where are you? Did you have a good day?" Gail took off her coat and hung it in her front closet. Dewdrop strolled into the entrance and rubbed up against Gail's legs, ready for some attention. Gail picked up her cat and stroked her as she walked into the kitchen, filled a glass with water, and ate a couple of crackers.

Walking back to the front door, she sorted through the mail and tossed it on the table next to her papers from school. She chatted with Dewdrop as she made her way to the kitchen once again. "I wish I could have been lounging around here napping with you today, Dewdrop. I'm beat. I'm ready to change into some sweat pants, pop some popcorn, and watch a movie."

The killer waited in her bedroom behind a tall wooden dresser, hearing every step as though it was magnified ten times. He heard her stop at the sink and fill a glass with water. He heard her open a cabinet and rustle around. He heard her walk back to the entrance. Then, a door closed. *What was she doing?* A toilet flushed, and the door opened. He wiped his palms on his pants as he looked around the room. It was painted a sunny yellow and the drapes were white with yellow flowers. Running shoes and slippers were near the bed and her closet door was partially open. *Maybe I should be hiding in there.* He swept the back of his hand against his forehead.

Gail walked over to the kitchen table and stood over the newspaper. "Huh. What are the legislators going to do to the education system now?" She sat down and browsed the paper, reading occasional articles.

The killer rolled his eyes. *How long am I going to have to wait? Alicia was so much easier than this.* He stared at a shelf bristling with shiny trophies and medals with colorful ribbons. The glow from the trophies seemed to mock him. He rubbed the stuffed dog in his pocket. The sounds the pages of the newspaper made as she turned them was like fingernails on a chalkboard. *Why don't you read it in the morning like everyone else?*

Gail's doorbell chimed, and she disengaged herself from the kitchen table and her cat. "Why do you like to sit on my feet? One of these days I'm going to trip and fall right on top of you. Then you'll be sorry!" Gail laughed as she walked to the front entrance.

Blood drained from the killer's face. *Is someone coming over? Didn't she say she was going to watch a movie?* Once again, his heart hammered in his ears so hard that he could hardly hear.

Gail opened the door and spotted the familiar brown of a UPS truck driving away. She grinned as she picked up the package on her front step. "Christmas is arriving early!" She trotted back into the kitchen and ripped open the box.

The killer dropped his head as relief flooded his body. *No visitor.*

Gail pulled some gleaming red and gold Christmas tree ornaments out of the bubble wrap. "Oh, these are going to look so much better than my old stuff. Maybe I should go out and buy a tree tonight and decorate it while I watch that movie." Gail hugged herself as she looked down at her cat. "That actually sounds like a lot of fun. That will cure me of the creeps from that guy at the grocery store." She picked the cat up off of her feet and rushed to her room to change clothes.

Okay, this is it! Remember what a rush it was last time? As Gail stepped into her bedroom and walked by the spot where he was hiding, he raised his arm over his head and buried the axe into the back of her head. It tore the bone in two and the soft brain tissue was destroyed as it sprayed everywhere. Gail dropped, and Dewdrop went flying out of her arms, yowling. The killer stood and watched in satisfaction as Gail's blood pooled out onto the floor from her lifeless body. Then he wrapped the beaded chain around her neck and squeezed it tight, just as he had done with Alicia. He put the chain back in his pocket, wiped the axe off on her sweater, and left.

SEVENTEEN

Don and Luke walked out to the Crown Vic and Don opened the trunk and looked at the next file. "Let's check out the address on our next interview and grab a burger on the way there."

"Okay, Cheeto." Luke sighed as another long night of pounding on doors loomed ahead.

The next morning, Don pulled into Luke's driveway and greeted his partner as he got into the car. "I have an idea. I think you'll like it 'cause it's sure to piss off Belinda."

Luke raised his eyebrows. "Sounds like a step in the right direction."

Don continued, "We both want to explore other paths but can't because Belinda doesn't support spending any time looking for one." Don paused. "I get it that it takes a lot of legwork to solve a crime. I don't have a problem with that. It's just that the killer is still out there and if we just had a couple of guys to help us get through these files we could cover other angles as well."

"Agreed."

"I think we should talk to Adam again and dig deeper into Alicia's relationships and activities. Adam was in shock when we talked to him the first time. Let's turn over different rocks and see what crawls out."

"Sounds good, Cheeto, I'm in."

"I knew you'd say that. I already called Adam. Alicia's funeral is in a couple days and he has to make some runs out to the airport to pick up Alicia's relatives. He said we could come over at three. So, let's put as big of a dent as we can in that box of files until then."

At the stroke of three, the detectives sat around the kitchen table at Adam's house with Don's tape recorder in the center of the table.

Don began, "Adam, our first guess on motive was the revenge of one of the criminals that you prosecuted. But that just isn't playing out. We're still working that slant, but we also wanted to take a deeper dive into Alicia's activities. Maybe there's something out there that could provide some kind of a connection. Maybe you were in such a state of shock that you forgot something. Or perhaps you just didn't recognize something as a problem." He paused and inclined his head in empathy. "That would be normal. It happens all the time."

Adam's shoulders slumped. He stared at the table without seeing it. "She was such a good person. She never did anything to hurt anyone. There's just no way…"

"Adam, there's no doubt your wife was a good person," Don reassured him. "This isn't going to wind up being about Alicia. It's going to be about a madman who's out there and can't function in society. We're trying to figure out what triggered him. Somehow, somewhere, some way, something happened that drove this guy over the edge. Please help us answer that question. We have to find him and get him off the streets."

Adam blinked. "Okay." Adam started counting on his fingers. "She was the PTA president at Moore Elementary.

She was involved with our kids' soccer clubs and science clubs. She was a member of the Bible study group at church and they did a lot of community service." He looked up. "That's about it. Her big thing was taking care of us."

"What about her last day? What do you know about that?"

Adam studied his hands for a minute. "She threw me a surprise party for my birthday. She wanted the tree up. We fought about that a little, but I gave in. She loved Christmas, and now I know she just wanted it up for my party." His eyes glistened and he dropped his gaze. "I guess I noticed the fridge was a little full, but I didn't think too much about it because that was her department. Then she got me out of the house so she could get ready. I don't think she left home that day."

"Did you suspect anything?"

"No, her good friend had some legitimate legal questions and I went over to her house to give her advice. Took a couple of hours or so. When I came back, everyone jumped out at me. You know, the surprise part." At the memory, his lips turned up a fraction.

Luke leaned forward. "Any jealousy going on in the soccer club or anything like that?"

Adam shook his head. "None that I know of. I could ask…"

Don's phone interrupted. "Layden here."

"Detective Layden, you've been too slow," Belinda reprimanded. "Get over to 2603 Aspen Avenue. The killer struck again." Then the line went dead.

EIGHTEEN

The crime scene was in a state of organized mayhem when Don and Luke pulled up. The street was packed with the various official cars and the forensics team was scrutinizing every square inch of the duplex and the yard. The detectives walked around back and saw that there was no deadbolt on the back door. No real obstacle for the killer.

Don spotted a member of the forensic team. Even though the man's back was turned and he was of average height and build, Don knew that head of curly black hair. "Hey Greg, give us the scoop."

"Twenty-seven-year-old female." Greg turned and led them into the bedroom. The victim was on the floor and the back of her head was split in half. Blood was everywhere. A cat had been walking back and forth from the body to other rooms in the house leaving bloody paw prints all over the duplex. Meg was kneeling next to the victim.

"I hate this guy." Luke's voice was quiet, but intense. He stood near the doorframe, shoulders drooping.

Don squatted down next to Meg. "Tell us what you know so far."

"I'd say she's been dead about twenty hours. There is no sign of a struggle."

Greg picked it up. "It looks like her attacker broke in the back door and was waiting for her when she came home."

He looked at the detectives. "I'll bet we'll be able to prove that the shoeprints leading up to the back door match those that we found at Alicia Kendrick's house." He led Don and Luke to the front door. "She came in here and put her work on this table. These papers have yesterday's date on them."

Don pulled out a pencil to sort through them without touching them. "It looks like she was a school teacher."

"Yes," Greg affirmed. "The school called the police this afternoon to report that Gail Gonzales wasn't in yet and they couldn't get in touch with her at home. They said she hadn't done that in the four years that she worked there."

"What school?"

"Moore Elementary." Don sucked in a breath. Same school where Alicia was PTA president. He walked back into the bedroom while Luke inspected some other rooms. Meg was still next to Gail. Gail was now lying face up, green eyes wide open and vacant. He walked near the body and knelt down. "She has the same markings on her neck that Alicia had."

As he leaned closer, Meg tapped him on the arm and handed him a magnifying glass. "Strange markings, aren't they? It's some kind of a beaded necklace but it's not quite a normal spacing pattern. It's really odd."

"Yes, it is." Don scrutinized the markings through the glass. "This reminds me of something, but I just can't think of it." He put the glass down and chewed the inside of his cheek. "Have you found any stray hairs that might be from the killer? Something that will give us more to go on?"

"Yeah, you need someone to make your job easier for you, don't you Detective Layden?" Belinda's voice of gravel was right behind Don. "You have the records that will give you the answer, but you just haven't had the time to get through them, isn't that right? Now you can see that your inefficiency has led to: another murder!" Belinda glanced briefly at the body, then moved away to look around the rest of the duplex.

Don didn't move. His eyes were closed. Meg put a hand on his back and spoke in a low voice. "Don don't listen to her. This guy is smart. And it hasn't been that long since the last murder. No one could have prevented this."

Don took a deep breath. He got up and walked out the front door to get some fresh air. Just then, a television truck pulled up. Don hung his head. It kept getting worse.

When he looked up, he saw Sarah Snow getting out of the truck. At least he knew her. She'd interviewed him in the past.

He watched as the cute, petite news reporter marched up the sidewalk, her blonde curls bouncing, and her cobalt blue coat bright against the drabness of the snow. She recognized him and waved. "Why, it's my superhero, Detective Don Layden! How are you?" When she got near him he put out a hand, but she laughed and gave him a hug. "You think I'm going to settle for a handshake from one of the most handsome men in the city of Denver? You must be crazy, Don Layden."

"Oh." Don blinked and scratched his neck. "Hi, Sarah."

"I was hoping you would give me a call after we went out on our date that night." She smiled up sweetly at him. "Didn't you enjoy yourself?"

Don shuffled his feet remembering the last time he saw her. She'd practically broken his arm to have one drink at a bar after she interviewed him about a case. She thought that was a date? "Uh, yeah, sure Sarah. I've just been busy keeping the citizens of Denver safe."

"Except for what's been going on lately it seems." By this time the camera crew was set up. Someone handed Sarah a microphone and she turned to face the camera giving an update as to their location and what she knew, which was not much. She introduced Don and then turned towards him.

Don took a breath. Man, she worked fast.

"Detective Layden, what did you find when you arrived?"

"We found a female homicide victim in her late twenties. We aren't releasing her name until we notify her relatives."

"This is the second female homicide victim in four days. Were there any similarities with the Alicia Kendrick case?"

Don paused. There was a serial killer on the loose and the people in Denver deserved to know. "Yes."

Sarah leaned forward. "Do you have any leads? Where are you on this investigation?"

"Actually, we have a plethora of leads. Turns out that's the difficulty. We're working as fast as we can. Problem is, it takes a lot of time to pursue that many. But I want to assure you that we are very committed to solving these crimes."

Just then Belinda burst outside. She gave Don a stony look as Sarah turned to her.

"Captain Mann, what are your thoughts on these horrible crimes?"

Belinda straightened her back. "The Denver Police Department is a lean, mean fighting machine. As you know I was recently given an award by the Mayor for the efficiency of this department. I am certain we will get this case closed in a matter of days."

Sarah pursed her lips. "We certainly hope so. Based on the timing between Alicia Kendrick's murder and this one, a few days are all you have before someone else gets murdered."

NINETEEN

As they finished up at the crime scene, Don's jaw twitched. Only a psycho would do this.

"We've got to find this monster," Luke hissed. "Let's hustle on over to the principal's house."

"My thoughts exactly."

Don listened as Luke called the department to tell them to get clearance to give the news to the principal and let her know they were on their way over. As he drove, Don glanced over at Luke. His partner had his forehead pressed against the glass of the passenger side window, staring at the passing scenery. Don guessed he was seeing nothing.

Within thirty minutes, Don pulled into the principal's driveway. He knocked on the door and a somber blonde man of about fifty answered. He was somewhat short and had the thick build of a man who enjoyed eating. Don presented his badge. "I'm Detective Layden and this is Detective Malone. We're here to see Mrs. Gladdick. It's about…"

The blonde man interrupted, "I know what it's about. I'm Dean Gladdick, her husband."

Don and Luke followed him into a comfortable living room and found a small woman of about fifty with short red hair sitting on a floral sofa, crying. Don squatted down near her. "Good evening, Mrs. Gladdick. I'm Detective Layden and this is Detective Malone."

She nodded to them and gestured towards some chairs. Her husband came in with a handkerchief for her, sat next to her, and reached for her hand. The grief in her face relaxed by a degree as she clutched his hand, and she composed herself.

Don leaned forward and looked into the principal's eyes. "I'm sorry for your loss. Thank you for getting in touch with the police when Gail didn't respond to your calls." Don pulled out a notebook and his tape recorder. "Okay if I record this conversation? There might be some information that won't seem like anything today but might mean something later on when I listen to it again."

"That's fine."

"When did you realize that something was wrong?"

"Classes start at a quarter to nine," whispered the distraught principal. Fighting back tears, she struggled to speak. "When Gail wasn't in by a quarter after eight, I called her, but she didn't respond. All of a sudden it was noon and I still hadn't heard from her. That's when I called the police."

"Okay, do you have a list of the teachers and other staff in the school?" Don asked.

"Yes, I'll get that for you right away." She opened a desk drawer, rummaged through it for a minute, and then produced a roster.

Don took the list. After thanking her, he and Luke went back to the car. "I think we need to take care of this list tonight."

"Exactly. Hand it to me and I'll tell you where we're headed, Cheeto."

Hours later, Luke made another check mark and drew a circle around one name on the list. "So far we just heard a whole lot of nothing. The only person we haven't talked to yet is Teresa Whitham. She hasn't answered her calls and didn't come to her door."

Don's heart pounded. "I hope she's okay," he whispered. He called Mrs. Gladdick. "Hi, this is Detective Layden. Sorry to call you so late but we were not able to get in touch with Teresa Whitham. Would you know if she had plans tonight?" Don exhaled and leaned his head back as he listened to the response. "Thanks for your help. And be sure to let me know if you think of anything else." He turned to Luke. "She's in New York right now. If she doesn't return our calls, we'll just have to interview her as soon as she gets back."

"Okay, that's the best we can do. Let's get back to our desks and run through everything we know."

At the police station, Don and Luke stood in front of a white board. Luke placed Alicia's photo in the left corner of the board and Gail's photo in the right corner. Don had his tape recorder out along with the murder book, which included his notes from Alicia's murder, and was updated with the notes from their interviews with Gail's parents and her colleagues. Some notes caught Don's eye and he looked up. "Gail was in the Bible study group Alicia was in too."

Luke's eyebrows shot up. "Interesting."

Don hunted for a marker for the white board. "Okay, we have the Bible study group at St. James Catholic Church and Moore Elementary in common." Don reached for his cup of coffee.

"I say we take a harder look at Moore Elementary. Maybe there are some crazy politics going on there. Plus, I asked Sabrina to do a little research on whacked out parents and that scene can get nutty. Maybe we could find something there." Luke looked at Don. "This predator is definitely whacked." Luke's brows furrowed. "What about James, Alicia's son? What sports is he into?"

Don moved to his tape recorder as Zach passed by and stopped. "Hey Don, hey Luke. How's the case going?"

Don shook his head. "Lots of leads, but nothing's panned out yet." He pointed to the pictures of the victims on the white board. "We're looking at what these ladies had in common. We're hoping that will help us break it." He rolled his shoulders to loosen them up. "How 'bout you? Any progress on the homeless murders?"

"We're in the same boat you are in terms of following up on leads," sighed Zack. "I wish I was rich and could do more to help all these homeless people. It's driving me crazy that we can't solve this case."

Just then Belinda stormed into the office. When she saw Don and Luke she stopped short. "This looks like a really efficient way to get those files done." She walked over to Don and stood right under his nose. "And now you're a movie star."

"Huh?"

"I just saw you on the news. And you told that reporter that the two murders were similar. We agreed that this killer has a revenge motive on Adam Kendrick. But I guess you didn't think that would play as well on TV. So, you made something up to create a big splash like they do in the movies."

Don chewed on the inside of his cheek. "The revenge motive was plausible until Gail's murder. Gail's murder and Alicia's murder have the same MO. We really believe there is someone out there that both of these women knew who is a lunatic. It's even possible that he could be executing some sort of a plan against a group of women."

"Oh, please! Spare me." Belinda almost spat. "I really hate to burst your bubble, but this is Denver gentlemen, not Hollywood. You two are watching too many police shows. I'll bet both murders have connections to Adam Kendrick. Period. Figure that out, get to work on those files, and get both of these cases solved. Now!" Belinda spun around and stomped out of the office.

Don, Luke, and Zach looked first after her and then at each other.

Zach spoke first. "That's tough. Sorry guys."

Don looked at Luke. Luke's face appeared to be made of stone. "Let's get out of here. I'll go through the files at home. Who knows? Maybe I'll find some connection to Gail. I'll call Rebecca and ask her to work on that as well. That way if Belinda asks us about the files, we're still working them." Don paused. "But we're going to Moore Elementary tomorrow." Don locked eyes with Luke. "Belinda or no Belinda, you and I are going to get this guy."

TWENTY

Kate poured another cup of coffee from the thermos at her desk. She straightened her shoulders and closed her eyes as she rolled her head from side to side. Then she took a stack of papers from her printer and started reviewing each line one more time. About sixty minutes later, she reached her arm behind herself and patted herself on the back. "Kate, you did it girl. Budgets for the upcoming fiscal year are done. And now you are officially on vacation. Wahoo!"

As she clicked her mouse and emailed the files off to corporate headquarters, she felt the relief surge through her body. Every year she wondered how she got through the long hours of the budgeting process. As she was closing her office door, her phone rang. "Who the heck is that?" she muttered to herself before she answered.

"Kate?"

"Hey, Vicki! It's good to hear from you. What's up?"

The voice on the other end of the line shook. "It's Gail. Gail's dead. She was murdered just like Alicia."

Kate braced herself against the wall. "Oh my God, no!"

"Why don't you come over to my house? I know it's late but a few of the ladies are already over here."

"I'll be right there." Kate turned to face the wall and leaned her forehead on it. Then she beat it with her fists and sank to the floor in tears.

A few blocks away, Don pulled into his garage. He opened his front door and threw the car keys across the room. He pounded the door until his fist bled. Belle's musical, welcoming chirps sounded in contrast.

Head hanging, Don trudged over to her cage and peered at his pet. She kept chirping and stretching her wings as she looked at him, letting him know she wanted to get out and be with him. Don's frown faded a bit as he pulled her out of her cage. He stroked her feathers and felt some of the stress slip away. "Belle, I've had a really horrible day." As he put her on his shoulder, his eyes strayed to a photo near her cage. It was a picture of his family when he was growing up in Michigan. It was taken at a ski resort there. He touched the picture of his father. Then he opened a carved wooden box next to it, which contained some letters. On top of the letters was his father's badge. He took the badge out and stroked it, then sank down into a couch and held it against his forehead with his eyes closed.

"Dad, I had a bad day. We've got a killer out there murdering women and my boss won't let me follow my gut. I've got to stop him before he kills someone else." Don pondered the badge. "I wish you were here so I could give you a call. I miss you, Dad."

Don reached for the box to put the badge away, then thought better of it and carried it into his office. As he put the badge down, he tilted his head for a second and then rushed back into the entrance and grabbed his tape recorder. He sat down in a reading chair, picked up the badge and rubbed it as he closed his eyes and listened.

The words from Adam's interview on the morning of Alicia's murder washed over him. He heard the words 'church' and 'Bible study' and 'man of the cloth'. He stiffened. His eyes flew open and he jumped to his feet so quickly that Belle fluttered off his shoulder. He picked her up and looked at her. "It was a rosary! The markings on the necks of both of the victims were from a rosary!"

Don grabbed his notes from his conversation with Adam. "What was the name of that church?" He called St. James and left a message. Then he called the medical examiner's office, but no one answered. He looked at his watch. "It's already tomorrow." In spite of his excitement, he yawned. "All right Belle, I've gotta get a few hours of sleep. But not too much because that killer has a taste for murder now and I don't want him to hurt anyone else."

TWENTY-ONE

The killer stood next to his coffee maker, watching it drip. He glanced out the window to check on the sky's progression as a lighter shade of gray unfolded from the deep black blanket of night. *Ah, yes. Any moment now.* He poured his coffee and looked outside again. His lips curled. It was there.

He opened the newspaper, and this time he was on the front page. He looked down at the headlines screaming out about the destruction and pain wrought by the "Serial Killer Stalking Denver Women". His heart swelled with pride. He put his feet up on a stool and started reading, savoring each word. The smoke from his cigarette swirled around his head.

Paper in hand, he moved to his office and examined the corkboard. He cut out the article and pinned it up next to Alicia's.

The phone rang and he picked it up. "Hi David, how are you? Yesterday's meeting with the church finance committee was very successful. I just wrote your first commission check and will get it in the mail today."

"Thanks. How about just giving it to me at the food drive?"

"Oh yes, the food drive. Sorry, I'm just waking up. I have that circled. Wouldn't miss it for the world. Today is my birthday and I can't think of a better way to spend it."

"I didn't know that! You don't have to do this. I can tell Mr. Sutherland you had other plans."

"David, I assure you I cleared my calendar for this. No other plans. This is important to me."

He ended the call and looked at his calendar. There were no other appointments besides the food drive. *So what else was new?* He ignored the sinking feeling in the pit of his gut. He was used to it by now.

Just then his phone rang again. The caller ID showed his mother. *Did she actually remember?*

"Hi, Mother."

"Hello, Dear. I'm just back from vacation, and I have something to show you today. Want to meet me for breakfast?"

"Yes, I can do that. Tell me when and where and I'll be there."

He even smiled when he ended the call. *Could what she wanted to show him be a birthday gift?*

He stepped into the shower with a sense of happiness. It felt good for a change.

As he drove to Luke's house, Don was lost in thought. He pulled up in Luke's driveway and found Luke standing out in the cold, ready to go. "Hey Cheeto, you call the priest?"

"Yes, he's waiting for us."

A few minutes later the detectives arrived in front of St. James Catholic Church. A small building to the side was the rectory, the priest's residence. Father Tim answered the door after the first knock and showed them in, poured them coffee, and offered muffins. "I'll help you in any way that I can," he declared.

Don sat down and got straight to the point. "Father, Adam Kendrick told us about Alicia's Bible Study group. He gave us a list of the members. Gail's name was on that list. Our medical examiner just confirmed that the markings on both Alicia's neck and Gail's neck were from a rosary and thought both victims were already dead when it was wrapped around their necks." He paused. "Can you think of anyone that would have a vendetta against Alicia, Gail, or anyone else the Bible group?"

The priest shook his head. "No. Both women were wonderful ladies. I can't think of anyone who would do this to them. It makes no sense."

"What kinds of activities does the group do?"

"Over the years they have gathered food supplies for the homeless, toys for underprivileged children, supplies for poverty level newborns and their mothers, and they have assisted with the mentally ill."

"What about social activities? Do they go out regularly or anything like that?"

"Yes, sometimes they meet for lunch or cocktails." The priest smiled. "I've heard that margaritas have become a favorite of the group recently. Just a couple of weeks ago they went to a Mexican restaurant east of town and Alicia told me about all of the different flavors that they had. She said they were like smoothies for adults."

In addition to the recorder, Don took notes. "Okay, I have a recent list of the group. I'd like some older lists as well. I'm countin' on finding a former member out there who knows something." He tapped his pencil on the paper. "Have they done any community service projects lately?"

"They organized a Thanksgiving dinner and gifts for the mentally ill at the hospital out east."

"Okay, get us the information for the contacts there too. Thanksgiving wasn't that long ago. Maybe we can find some sort of a connection."

Armed with the information, Don and Luke split the list and went out to interview each member of the group. They met up in a coffee shop late in the morning to compare notes.

Don took a sip of coffee. "These are some of the kindest people I've ever met. They all live very normal lives. I haven't found even a shred of a motive so far."

Luke agreed. "Yeah, I guess one thing that you can say about the holy rollers is they do seem to be nice."

Don raised an eyebrow at Luke but then thought better of his retort and glanced down at his list instead. "There is still one person I haven't interviewed yet. Let's go pay Kate Fitzgerald a visit."

Forty minutes later, Don sat next to Luke in Kate's living room. As Kate put together a tray of cheese and crackers she insisted on making, Don took note of the framed diploma from Boise State University and a picture of Bronco Stadium. Kate brought out the tray and moved Don's recorder and some travel brochures to an end table near Luke, so she could place the tray on the glass coffee table in front of them. The detectives sat on a tan leather couch, and she seated herself on a matching loveseat facing them.

Luke picked up one of the brochures. "Going somewhere?"

"No, not this year," Kate looked at the brochure and shook her head. "I just finished budgets for my company and I usually go out of town right after I'm done, but for some reason nothing appealed to me this year. So, I decided to organize my house instead. You know, do a little spring cleaning in December." She frowned. "Speaking of being organized, why the heck haven't I thrown those in the recycling?" She glared at the brochures as though they had committed a crime.

"Where do you work?"

"The downtown Marriott. I'm the controller there."

Don cleared his throat. "Kate, we are very sorry for your losses."

Her lips tightened. "Thank you."

"Tell us about Alicia and Gail. When did you meet them? How? Give us your history together."

"We were acquaintances for years at St. James, but one exceptionally beautiful spring morning we all decided that we wanted to show God our gratitude for this beautiful world and the beautiful people in it. So, we organized our Bible study group. Since then we've become really good friends." She leaned back in the loveseat and looked at Don. "That's it. That's the big story about how I got to be such good friends with Alicia and Gail."

"Seems like someone out there has a deadly objection to your club. Can you think of any reason why anyone would have a grievance against you, Alicia, Gail, or St. James?"

Kate shook her head. "No, I really can't." She raised her eyebrows. "Unless you have something against margaritas."

"Father Tim told us about the adult smoothies."

Kate's eyes crinkled as she thought about going out with her friends. "Yes." Then she frowned. "Come to think of it, we did deal with a less-than-courteous waiter at Jose's a week or so ago."

"What happened?"

"It was the Wednesday before Thanksgiving. We just finished putting on a dinner with gifts for the patients at the mental health hospital east of town. We decided to stop in at a Mexican place Gail knew about for cocktails. The waiter overheard us talking about church and Bible study and got irritated." She paused. "We had designated drivers and a few of the non-designated drivers got a little loud, I guess." She looked at Don and Luke. "But it wasn't bad or anything. There weren't that many people there. You'd think that he would have been glad for the opportunity to make a good tip, wouldn't you?"

"What kinds of things did he say?"

"Oh, derogatory remarks about Christians and their beliefs and stuff like that." She shrugged. "Not that big of a deal. People have their own opinions." She paused. "Then he made a derogatory comment about Jesus Christ and that one didn't go over well at all. Some shouting started. A couple of us jumped up and managed to get everything calmed down." She raised a brow. "Then we just continued with our drinks and snacks. As a matter of fact, Vicki Zurn asked him to make some copies of the membership list so that we could organize a calling tree about our Christmas party."

Don looked up from his notes. "What information was on that list?"

She stared at Don. "Names, addresses, phone numbers... oh my God." She put her head in her hands.

Don leaned forward. "Which women were giving the waiter the hardest time?"

"I would say it was Alicia, Gail, and Wanda Benaducci. Vicki was a little noisy too." She folded her arms. "I guess he could have listened to us talking to each other and figured out who was who."

Don leaned back for a minute. "I hear what you're saying. But it's a pretty far stretch from complaining about Christians to murder, Kate. On the other hand, it might be a good idea to make sure everyone in your group takes some extra precautions. Tell them to lock their doors. Plus, they all need to be aware of their surroundings. Can you call them? Get the word out?"

"Absolutely."

"Also, while we're here, I'd like to take a look at your locks. Just see your setup, okay?"

"I guess so." Kate blinked. "But I'm sure that I'm fine."

Don walked into the kitchen and over to the sliding glass door that led out to a deck overlooking a pool. Kate had a nice corner unit and the deck stretched all the way back to another sliding glass door. "That your bedroom?"

"Yes."

Don observed the fire escape near the deck and fiddled with the lock on the glass door. He turned around and walked into her bedroom with the others trailing behind.

Luke smiled when he saw more of the Boise State paraphernalia. "BSU, eh? Good school, good football team."

"Awesome school. Awesome football team!"

Don examined the sliding door in her bedroom. He spun around. "This lock is pretty worthless. So is the lock on your other door. Plus, it's easy to get from the fire escape into your place."

"But the doors downstairs to the courtyard are locked, and there is a security guard in the lobby." Kate put her hands on her hips. "I'm safe here."

Don's forehead creased. "If I were you, I wouldn't want my life depending upon someone who is paid what those guards are paid with the kind of training they get." He motioned outdoors. "Maintenance is done out there and doors can get left open." He paused for a second. "You said that you work at the Marriott. Any chance you could stay there until we get this case solved?"

"I suppose." Kate straightened her shoulders. "But I don't think that I really need to. I even have a gun-with a permit of course."

"Gun or no gun I think if you saw the two murder scenes that we've seen, you would change your mind." Don felt his eyes burning as he glared at Kate.

Kate drew in a breath. "Yeah, sure. Okay."

As they walked into the living room, Don continued talking. "Luke and I are going to run out to Jose's. You remember your waiter's name?"

Kate pursed her lips, then held up a finger. "I'll bet that I still have my receipt. Maybe his name is on that." She left the room.

Luke watched her disappear and looked at Don. "What kind of a person has a receipt for a few margaritas from a couple of weeks ago?"

"She's an accountant. It fits."

Kate hastened back into the room and handed a piece of paper to Don with a flourish. "His name is Treavor."

"Treavor, the Christian-hater, eh?" Don looked at Luke. "Let's go pay this guy a visit."

TWENTY-TWO

The killer stepped into the elegant restaurant and scanned the room for his mother. When he didn't see her, he asked for a table for two. Ten minutes later, she strutted through the door. She was wearing boots with heels giving her thin, five foot two inch frame an extra four inches in height. Her short, platinum blonde hair bounced along with her stride. Her granite gray eyes, which the killer always thought matched the color of her heart, searched for him. Her painted face displayed the usual dark red lipstick, but her eyes were shadowed in a soft plum color now. New fashion, he guessed.

The smell of her perfume wafted around the table as she walked up and gave him the required hug. He started to help her with her coat, but she raised her hand.

"Hold on for a minute. Let's go out to the valet parking."

They walked out and there it was: a brand Mercedes Maybach S550.

"It's the new model. Isn't it gorgeous?"

Bile rose up into the killer's throat. *She had no idea it was his birthday. She just wanted to show off her new car. Of course.*

They sat back down in the restaurant, and his eyes fell to the blade of the knife placed near the sparkling white china plate. As his mother's voice droned in the background, he stared at it. It seemed to be speaking to him.

Jose's was a small, dark restaurant on the east side of the city. Don ducked the low hanging red lamps that hung down from the ceiling and noticed Luke doing the same. They stood next to each other at what appeared to be a hostess stand for a couple of minutes, then Don motioned to the bar. They walked past some plastic-lined booths to a small bar where a brown-haired burly bartender stood chewing on an unlit cigar. His green vest did little to hide his girth.

He pushed the cigar over to one side of his mouth with his tongue. "What can I get ya'?"

Don paused. "How about a couple of drafts?" As the bartender turned his back, Don and Luke exchanged glances and Luke gave a slight nod.

Don made a show of tasting his beer and smacking his lips. "Ah, that hits the spot." He looked at the bartender. "Worked here long?"

"'Bout five years." He responded as he wiped down some glasses. He didn't stop cleaning or even look up.

Just then, a short, beefy waiter with dyed ink blue hair hustled across the room to the bar service station next to Don. "Hey Max, I need a couple of blackberry margaritas." He handed Max a chit and drummed his fingers on the bar while he waited.

Don sipped on his beer and glanced sideways at the waiter's nametag, which displayed "Treavor" in green lettering.

Treavor left and Don cleared out the tab with Max so that he and Luke could go sit in Treavor's section. Soon Treavor came over and handed out a couple of menus.

"What's good?" Don asked.

"Smothered burritos are a popular choice," Treavor muttered.

"Sounds good to me," Don said. "Put me down for that." Luke asked for the same and Treavor darted away.

Soon he came back carrying a big tray with huge plates of cheesy burritos. After placing each plate, he stood back. "You good? Need anything else to drink?"

Don waved a drink menu at him. "You're the Baskin Robbins of margaritas."

"Yeah. Brings in a lot of ladies. Sometimes they even buy the glasses the drinks are served in to bring home. Go figure."

Don grinned. "Can't argue with lots of ladies being around, right?"

Treavor shrugged. "Depends."

Don nodded. "Yeah, I hear ya'. Sometimes they can really be annoying. That pisses me off. I mean, who do they think they are, ya' know?"

"Yeah."

Don waved his hand to include the restaurant. "How do you handle it when that happens in here? That must be tough."

"Most of the time I just ignore them."

"Yeah, but I'll bet once in a while you get a group of ladies, they have some margaritas, then they have some more, then they start gettin' all bossy or whatever. That would just drive me nuts, you know what I mean?"

"Sure bugs me," Luke chimed in.

Don continued, "I couldn't handle that. How do you do it?"

Treavor's sooty gray eyes darkened and his voice became sharp. "I work for tips, I'm not stupid." He paused for a split second. "Do you want anything else?"

Don shook his head and Treavor left. Luke dug into his burrito. Moving the food around in his mouth he mumbled, "How do you want to play this?"

Don moved his head from side to side, stretching his neck as he contemplated his answer. "I think we need to follow him after he gets off work. Let's check out what he does. He definitely didn't like it when I pressed a little."

"Good call."

Thirty minutes later, Don and Luke headed to the Crown Vic. Don opened the trunk and looked at the files, studying a cover sheet Rebecca gave them. "There are a number of files with an address nearby. Let's go check them out while we're in the neighborhood. I overheard Treavor tell one of the other waiters that he's working the dinner shift, 'til about ten. That means we have a couple of hours until we have to get over to our Eagles' game. Let's knock some of these out."

"Sounds like a plan."

Soon the two men found themselves sitting in front of a row of low cost apartments. "Okay, Cheeto, who is the lucky man that gets to meet us next?"

Don picked a file up off of the console, glanced through it, and snapped it closed. "His name is Falco Ferez." He turned to look at Luke. "Let's go find out how Mr. Ferez is doing since he got out of prison, shall we?"

Five minutes later, a small dark-haired young man opened his door. "What may I do for you?" His accent was hard to place. Northern Africa, maybe?

Don and Luke showed their badges and started to ask him some questions when Luke's nose twitched. "What's that smell?"

Falco's eyes gleamed. "It's worship time. Care to join me?"

Don felt the hairs on the back of his neck rise. "Sure."

Falco led the detectives into a room filled with smoke from incense so potent that Luke coughed. He stopped when he saw Don's face and followed his partner's gaze. The room was red and black and in the center was a huge statue of...what?

Falco enjoyed the reaction. He reached for a cigarette that was burning in a nearby ashtray and inhaled then exhaled slowly as he studied Don's face. He smiled and said, "You do know who that is, don't you?"

"Lucifer," Don breathed. "It's Lucifer." Don stared at the huge, black hideous statue of a man-beast. The face looked more like that of an open-mouthed ape, displaying fangs. With a mountain lion's body, the claws were long and twisted and it held its tail as though petting it. The creepiest part were the eyes, which seemed to glitter in its head. Don stared at Falco. "You worship Lucifer?"

Falco laughed. "Yes, detective. I worship the devil!"

Don took a step forward so that he was right in Falco's face. "Tell me Falco, what do you think about Christians?" His voice had become a deep growl.

"I hate them," Falco sneered. "They repulse me!"

Don gripped Falco's arm. Luke touched Don's shoulder for a second, and Don loosened his grasp but did not let go. "Where were you last Saturday morning Falco?"

Falco bared his teeth at Don. Don looked closer and noticed Falco's canine teeth had been sharpened to look like vampire teeth. He tightened his grip again and shook him. "Where were you Saturday morning?" Don bellowed.

"I was up late Friday night. I slept until noon."

"Care to prove that?" Luke asked.

"I live alone. I do what I please," Falco snapped back.

Luke cracked his knuckles. "Falco, it sounds like we have a problem," Luke said in measured tones. "You see, we are investigating two murders and you have ties to the first victim." Then he gestured to Lucifer. "And because you worship this guy, we could make ties to the second victim as well."

"Who was killed?" Falco's face remained unchanged, but his eyes darted back and forth from Luke to Don.

Luke took a step forward. "The wife of the prosecuting attorney who tried your case and her friend who was in the same Bible study group."

"I certainly didn't have anything to do with that." Falco sniffed. He gestured towards Lucifer. "Perhaps he had something to do with that."

Luke leaned against a wall, folded his arms, and tilted his head. "I dunno, Falco. I like you for it. Let's say you are out one night, and you hear a bunch of nice ladies partyin' after they've done some good deeds in the community." He rubbed his jaw in thought. "Then they start talking about their church, or their priest, or something like that." Luke walked over to Falco and looked down at him. "This ticks you off. After all, isn't a priest one of his greatest enemies?" Luke motioned towards the statue.

"As much as doing something like that might please my master, I did not." He snorted. "I think my master got someone else to do it."

"You don't say." Luke studied Falco for a long moment. Then he leaned down to look at Falco's teeth. "I like what you've done to your teeth, Falco. You remind me of some dogs I know."

Falco growled, "Get out, both of you! You don't have any right to be here. I don't have anything to do with your case."

Don moved towards Falco, but Luke held up his hand still keeping his eyes on Falco. "Okay Buddy, we'll leave. You invited us in, remember? I guess we've worn out our welcome. Not a problem. Bye."

Don locked eyes with Falco as he walked out the door. After they got into the car Don found himself gripping the wheel. His knuckles were white.

"Chill, Cheeto." Luke put a hand on his shoulder. "I grabbed this." Luke held up the cigarette Falco had been smoking. "If Falco had anything to do with Alicia's or Gail's death, we have some DNA to help us out." Luke took out a plastic bag and placed his evidence inside.

Don took a deep breath. "Good work, partner." Then he shook his head. "Man, that guy gave me the creeps."

Luke raised his eyebrows. "Yeah, he was a weird one. Let's get this evidence to Forensics."

The killer pulled into the parking lot where food drive was being held and was greeted by truckloads of food. Before he knew it, David was at his side.

"Hey, thanks for coming. Great you could make it." David pointed to the trucks. "The food has already been gathered. Today we're going to organize it and then bring some down to the homeless shelter. They feed hundreds of homeless there every day, so they go through a lot of food."

The killer blinked a few times. "Wow. I had no idea it was this big." *This looked like a lot of work.*

David's eyes glowed. "Yeah, isn't it great? Mr. Sutherland – you remember the guy at church? He gets this going every year."

"Of course, I remember Mr. Sutherland." *After all, his investment helped me pay my bills.* "There's a ton of people here."

David pointed to one of the trucks. "Yup. Why don't you help that group over there? They'll show you what to do."

TWENTY-THREE

Kate Fitzgerald's kitchen looked as though a cyclone had just gone through it. All of her dishes were out on the counter as she washed the interior of her cabinets. She was dressed in Boise State sweats with her shiny black hair pulled back in a ponytail. After everything was clean to her satisfaction, she placed each piece back where it belonged. As she reached for a glass, she stopped for a moment. It was a margarita glass from Jose's that she bought the night she was there with her friends. Her eyes grew moist, and she stroked it as she held it against her cheek. Then her eyes snapped open. "The tattoo!" she exclaimed out loud. She rushed to pull out a paper and a pen, drew for a few minutes, and then looked for the business card Don gave her.

A few minutes later she called him. "Detective Layden, this is Kate Fitzgerald. You talked to me earlier today, do you remember me?" She listened for a couple of seconds. "Good. I thought of something I forgot to mention when you were here. Treavor had a freaky tattoo on his arm. I just sketched it out and I really want you to see it. Can you stop by my place, or can I bring it to you?" She listened again. "All right, I'll take a picture of it and text it to your phone. Let me know if you don't get it."

Two minutes later her phone rang.

"Hi." She listened. "You know, I bet if I take another picture, it'll just be blurry again. I'm happy to meet you somewhere so I can just give it to you." She paused. "Oh, how about if I meet you at your game? To be honest, I'd love to watch it. I'm a big football fan. I know just where that building is! I'll see you soon."

Hours after he got to the food drive, the killer put his hands over his head to stretch his back. *Whoa. That was a hell of a lot of work.* He looked around. Pallets and pallets of food sat in a warehouse, ready to go.

David walked up. "Isn't this great? It gives you a good feeling, doesn't it?"

The killer considered for a moment. "Come to think of it, it really does."

"Okay, let's head to the shelter. Wait until you help there. You'll feel even better. Follow me."

The killer shrugged. "Will do."

After they arrived at the shelter, they unloaded the food and brought it into the building. The killer sniffed. Good smells abounded. Dinner was cooking.

Once again, David stood by the killer's side. "Okay now we help serve."

The guests were dressed in ragged clothing and shoddy shoes, but they expressed appreciation for each spoonful they received. The killer found himself smiling and joking with many. *This is crazy,* he thought. At the end of the evening, he sat with David as they ate their own meal.

"So, I guess this probably wasn't much of a birthday for you, was it? We really appreciate your help though."

The killer gazed at David. "You know what? I never would have thought it in a million years, but this is the best birthday I've ever had."

Over on Pecos Street, Don and Luke facilitated warm-ups for the football game.

Kate approached and stood in the background. She didn't want to interrupt the preparations.

Once it got going, the game was a tight one, a battle of the running backs. One team drove down the field to score, then the next team did the same.

"Dang. Their coverage on our receivers is good," Don grunted under his breath. "Need to change up the routes."

By this time Kate's coat was off and the sleeves of her blue and orange Boise State sweater were pushed up to her elbows. She found a moment to pull Don aside and handed him a paper. "I think if you just change the routes for your receivers, it could work for you. Here, I sketched something out for you."

Don looked at her sketch and raised his eyebrows. "This is crazy. That's really close to what I just did."

Kate didn't miss a beat. She thumped Don on the shoulder, hard. "Okay, good! Go get 'em!"

The end of the game neared, and the Eagles had the ball with two minutes left and ten yards to go. Their quarterback made a short pass to the tight end and he ran. Kate sprinted down the sidelines to the goal line, screaming encouragement to the player as she went. Right before he reached the goal line he got tackled, but he reached the ball across the goal line before he hit the ground. Kate threw her arms up in the touchdown signal and the entire Eagles team jumped up and down.

But the referee blew his whistle and walked over to where he thought the player was down, two inches from the goal line. As far as the referee was concerned, it wasn't a touchdown. Kate ran over to him. "He reached across the goal before his knees were down. He broke the plane with the ball! It's a touchdown!"

The referee shook his head.

"But I had a better line of vision than you did! I was right on the goal line! You were a few steps behind!"

The ref turned and walked away.

Kate stomped her feet and stared at his back in disbelief.

Don, Luke, and the team were still hollering their objections. The ref stepped up to them and confirmed, "Game over. You keep it up and I'll file a complaint against you." He pivoted and left.

Luke held his head with both hands trying to regain control. "Okay team huddle up." A group of very sad-faced boys encircled the coaches. "That was a tough call," Luke said. "Sometimes that's how it goes. But we made good adjustments and we learned hard lessons tonight. I'm proud of you. We have a good record, and we can rise above this and win our next game." He stopped when he noticed some of his players looking at something near the goal line. Smiles crept across their faces. He turned and saw Kate making faces at some sort of an imaginary person. First she was crossing her eyes, then she was blowing up her cheeks, and then she was scowling.

Don turned and watched Kate for a moment, then called over to her. "Hey Kate, are you okay?"

Kate ran over to the team. "Not really. I'm pretty mad. And sometimes when I'm dealing with someone who I think is really hardheaded then I pretend that he's right in front of me and I make faces at him. It helps." She addressed the players. "Let's try it together." The entire team made faces at each other and soon they were all laughing so hard they could hardly stand up. Before long, everyone had to catch a breath.

Don looked at his team. "Okay guys, it's Eagles' pizza time. Let's go hit our spot. I'm buying." He looked at Kate. "You're welcome to join us."

"Nowhere I'd rather be."

In no time the pizza was gone, and Don and Luke said good-bye to the team. After everyone was gone, Luke, Don, and Kate all sat together, and Kate pulled out her sketch. "I can't believe I didn't think of this while you were at my place earlier. I noticed this tattoo on Treavor's arm when he served us. He had his sleeves rolled up and I saw it."

Don's jaw dropped. Kate's sketch was an exact replica of the statue of Lucifer that they had seen in Falco's apartment.

TWENTY-FOUR

Don recovered first and looked at Luke. "It looks like we may have a stumbled upon a ring."

"Yeah." Luke folded his arms. "I do believe that Mr. Treavor deserves the honor of our company."

Don filled Kate in a little bit on the trip to the restaurant and the subsequent stop at Falco's apartment.

"So, these devil worshippers who hate Christians have a list of the names and addresses of the members of the St. James Bible Study group." Kate clenched her fists and her eyes flashed. "I wouldn't mind having a little conversation with Mr. Treavor myself."

"That's our job."

"But Don, listen to me. I have knowledge that you don't. Treavor might say something that only I can respond to. I think it's really important that I come."

"No. We're trained for this. You're not."

"But I have a huge stake in this!"

Don leaned forward towards Kate. "Another good reason why you aren't coming." Don cleared his throat. "By the way, have you moved into the Marriott yet?"

Kate shook her head.

Don checked his watch. "Today's your lucky day. There's just enough time before Treavor gets off for two of Denver's finest to help you move a couple of things over there. We'll follow you home."

Before she knew what was happening, Kate found herself in a room on the second floor of the Marriott saying goodbye to Don and Luke. She stepped outside of her door and watched them head towards the elevator.

On impulse she ran back into her room, grabbed a coat, her gun, and her key and headed as fast as she could down the stairs and out to the Crown Vic. She was in luck! The back doors to the car were unlocked. She opened one, slid in and huddled unnoticed on the backseat floor, just as the detectives got in. Kate kept quiet.

Luke looked over at his partner. "I'm not religious, but I sure as hell don't understand why anyone would want to worship the devil."

"Yeah, plus between the tattoo on Treavor's arm and the exact same statue at Falco's place, let's hope checking Treavor out leads us somewhere."

Soon Don parked near Treavor's place, opened his door to get out, but then stopped. "What do you know?" He pointed to a man getting into a car across the street. "Treavor got off early and now he appears to be going somewhere."

Luke grunted. "Looks like we'd better find out where, Cheeto."

They followed Treavor for miles out to the eastern outskirts of town near some partially constructed office buildings. After the downturn in the economy, construction in many projects such as this were abandoned. Everyone knew these buildings had been empty for years.

Don cut his lights, staying at a distance behind some trees. He noticed a few other cars parked several yards in front of them with people sitting inside. "What the heck is he doing way out here? And who are all these people?"

"Who knows? This group is full of a bunch of nut cases, if you ask me." Luke reached into the glove compartment for some binoculars. "As far as I can tell, it looks like we have about eighteen nuts right now."

Before long, a big van pulled into the area. Everyone got out of their cars and went to the back of the van. They opened the doors and pulled out two people with gauzy black hoods covering their heads and handcuffs around their wrists.

Luke sat straight up. "Cheeto! They have hostages!"

Don was already on the radio calling it in. "Unit twelve requesting backup." He described what was happening and put the radio down. Without another word Don pulled his revolver out as he exited the car, aware that Luke did the same. He retrieved their bulletproof vests without making a sound and handed one to Luke. The two officers then crept up behind the group unnoticed.

Eyes wide, Kate heard every word. Holding her breath, she eased herself up off the backseat high enough to see outside. She stifled a gasp when she observed the surreal scene. The pitch black of night surrounded a group of men carrying lit torches as they led two hostages over rocks and through the ghostly construction site. Kate's heart pounded against her chest.

Without making a sound she exited the car and crept forward, following the detectives from a distance.

The group of men climbed over a few half-built walls and walked across rickety hand-made bridges. Don waited for a couple of minutes before he followed with Luke nearby. Eventually they came upon a makeshift outdoor room with a deep fire pit. A bright, blazing fire roared increasing the ominous rumblings in Don's gut.

Behind the fire sat a large table that looked as if it was intended to be some sort of an altar. Behind that was a gigantic statue of Lucifer. The flickering light from the fire made the statue's eyes glitter. It almost looked alive. Don felt the hair on his arms stand on end.

Don squatted and took cover behind a pile of abandoned refuse a few yards away from the fire pit. He observed Luke hiding behind a similar pile concentrating on the scene in front of him.

The group of men took out red hoods similar to the white ones worn by the Ku Klux Clan and put them on. After that, a few of the attendees pounded drums to commence a ritual. The black hoods worn by the hostages were then ceremoniously removed. That's when Don noticed that the clothes of the forlorn victims were filthy, their shoes tattered, and their hair dirty and straggly. *They were homeless!*

The hostages were tied with ropes and the group of men chanted in rhythm to the drums as they lifted one of the homeless men up onto the table. One of the kidnappers brandished a tactical knife with a large blade and held it over the homeless man as he chanted.

The homeless man cried out, "Please don't hurt me! Please let me go!"

Don didn't wait to see more. He jumped up and roared, "Freeze! This is the police! Drop your weapons or we'll shoot!"

Pandemonium broke out. Like a hurricane blasting a house apart, the group scattered. Several of the men had guns and before they knew it, Don and Luke found themselves in a gunfight.

The homeless man curled up as much as he could, trying to make himself as small as possible given his restraints.

The men tried to advance on the detectives, but their aim was poor, so their bullets winged from the refuse. Slowly, between bullets whizzing near them, Don took turns with Luke moving forward. Their choreography involved aiming, firing, ducking, and rolling.

In the distance sirens blared, growing closer. Soon their attackers were down and wounded. The detectives confiscated their assaulters' weapons and Don called for several ambulances while he watched Luke provide first aid to the more seriously injured. None of them were dead, at least not yet.

As Don went to help one of the hostages, a bullet zipped by his head. He dropped, rolled, and pointed his gun. Then he heard a shot from a different direction and a groan from the man who fired first. That man was hit in the shoulder. He staggered and went down. Looking towards the sound of the shot that brought him down, Don sucked in his breath when he saw Kate standing there with her gun pointed at the fallen man. Luke rushed forward and grabbed the man's gun, cuffed him, and checked his wound.

Don stared at Kate. "What are you doing? Are you nuts? How did you get here? Get down so you don't get hurt!"

Still holding her gun, Kate crouched down and shouted back. "I'm backing you up, that's what I'm doing! And I think we all still need to take cover because a couple of those guys got away and they might double back like this one did and kill us all!"

Just then, a group of officers ran up to help. Don took charge. "Okay, while some of you help the wounded, we need men to guard against anyone who might come back and attack. A couple of you take the homeless men in for questioning. Zach Daskalis will want to be there. Give him a call. And get a forensic team down here. Call in the K-9 unit so we can round up anyone who escaped." A grimace masquerading as a smile appeared on his lips as he added, "You might want to tell Forensics to bring coffee. This is going to be a long night."

Don observed as officers read the injured detainees their rights, loaded them into ambulances, and took them to hospitals.

When he was satisfied the operations were going in the right direction, he turned toward Kate. Her gun was at her side and he noticed Luke making his way toward her from the other end of the fire pit. Don strode up and glared at her. "How did you get here? Did you follow us from the hotel?" His voice sounded loud and gruff.

"I ran down the stairs and got into the back of your car before you got down the elevator," she confessed.

Don's voice climbed a few more decibels. "What were you thinking? We are professional detectives investigating a murder! This isn't a game, Kate!"

"I know it's not a game! Two of my friends are dead! I have to live in a hotel because I might be the next one to get an axe buried into the back of my skull by devil worshipping jerks! Guess what? If you think that I'm the kind of person to just sit around and let someone devastate my life, then you are wrong!"

"Yeah, you're right, I am wrong. Because until a few minutes ago, I thought you were an intelligent woman!"

Luke put a hand on Don's shoulder. "Take it easy, Cheeto. She's not hurt and this all turned out as well as it could." He turned to Kate. "My partner has a right to be pissed. I understand that you lost your friends but getting into our car without us knowing is against the law. One of the reasons why is because we're trained to deal with dangerous people, but you're not."

Kate put one hand on her hip and looked at the ground.

"Where's your gun?" Luke demanded.

She held it out so that he could see it.

"Is it still loaded?"

Not able to hide her sheepishness, Kate emptied it.

Luke ran a hand over his head. "All right. Let's give Kate a ride back to the hotel and get to the station so we can talk to Mr. Treavor and the rest of these lunatics."

Luke held open the back door of the Crown Vic for Kate, then planted himself in the front. Don turned the ignition switch and gravel flew as he turned the car around. "Hey Cheeto, we're not responding to a call. Chill out. Do I need to drive?"

"No, I'm good." Don took a deep breath but his knuckles were white.

Luke watched him for a few seconds then took out his phone. "I want to text Sabrina to let her know her man's safe."

The window for the cage to the back seat was open and Kate watched Luke's face soften as he texted his wife. She noticed his ring. "Do you have any children?" She was surprised when her voice shook a bit.

Luke looked back and a big grin spread across his face. "Yes, I do. I have the absolute cutest daughter on this planet. Without a doubt. Here, let me show you." He held up his phone so Kate could see a picture of Lucy. Kate leaned forward and studied it.

"She really is cute. I'd say the world better watch out about ten years from now."

Luke looked at the picture and grinned. "Don't you worry about that. Her daddy will be the one watching out, just like always. Lucy Malone is well protected." He kissed his daughter's picture and stared at it again.

Kate watched Luke stare at the photo of his daughter the exact same way all parents look at photos of their children. His expression reminded her of Alicia's face when she looked at her children's photos. And now her friend was gone. She pounded the seat next to her.

Luke exchanged glances with Don then turned around. "Uh, what's wrong?" he asked Kate.

"I...I can't believe what I just saw. Those men...that statue...then when they put that poor, defenseless man up on the table and took out that knife...that just sucks!" She pounded the seat again.

"You're right. It sucks." Luke paused. "And not only that, but now I have to spend all night interviewing these looney tunes, and I'm hungry!"

Don snorted. "All right. I'll grab us some food. You get the party started at the station."

"Fish tacos from Billy's!" Luke looked at his partner and grinned.

"Can't argue with that. Those fish tacos have fueled us through many hours of crime fighting."

Don dropped off Luke and turned to Kate. "Billy's is on the way to your hotel. All right with you if I grab the food first?"

"Sure."

Don drove with Kate to Billy's Tavern. They found a table and ordered the fish tacos for take-out and a couple of Cokes to drink while they waited.

Kate excused herself to go the ladies' room and Don took a big sip of Coke. He sat back, closed his eyes, and relaxed as he felt the cool liquid slide down his throat. Man, what a day.

Kate came back and sat down. She stirred her soft drink and stared at a commercial playing on the TV above the bar. In it, an actress was crying. "You know, I've always wondered how those movie stars still look so pretty while they cry. And their make-up doesn't run down their face. How does that work?"

Don smirked. "Who knows? Maybe they have some special scientific makeup."

Kate studied her glass and giggled. "I can see them selling it in the store." She held up a menu card from the table sideways, pretending it was a case of makeup. In a nasal tone she said, "Hello, Ma'am. We are having a special today on our famous Stone Face makeup. For a mere $500 an ounce, you too can have a face of granite!" Then she leaned back in the booth and laughed so hard her shoulders shook. "You must think I'm nuts," she said through guffaws.

Don smiled. "I take the fifth."

Kate sat up straighter and regarded her Coke again. Her smile faded. "Do you see stuff like what happened tonight very often?"

"We see the underbelly of society more often than most, Kate. There are some bad people out there."

Kate was silent for a minute. "Humans can be so awful. But they can be so beautiful, too." The corners of her mouth turned up. "Luke was so cute when he showed me that picture of his little girl. And that beauty of a parent's love contrasted with the hate of the devil worshippers is just so hard to understand."

"Reminds me of a story I read once. About a boy who'd been in a Jewish concentration camp. He remembered the acts of kindness that occurred every day. In spite of the evil." Don poked the ice in his glass with a straw. "He became fascinated by goodness. He realized goodness and love are the ultimate power inside reality."

"Wow, that's amazing." Kate twirled her hair around a finger. "Actually, I think that's why Jesus came. He showed us the beautiful way to live. Then he suffered a horrific death, but he came back to life so that the story of his triumph over evil would carry on. So that we wouldn't forget." Her eyes glinted. "But we forget all of the time, even to the point of people worshipping the devil."

Don was quiet for a minute. "I suppose people get so wrapped up in their day-to-day lives that it takes over and they forget about the higher level."

Kate's eyes widened and she leaned forward. "I know, that's the problem. So many people think of life as an idle game, a festival for profit." She snorted. "You see where that's getting us."

She sat back and held up an index finger. "Just imagine what the world might be like if there was a deeper awareness of God's word." She tilted her head. "A church service is just one hour per week to help you deliberate on words that are zoomed in on goodness. One hour to get you re-focused in the right direction. In the direction of love." She paused. "Is that really asking too much?"

Don studied Kate for a couple of minutes, considering her words. "I hear what you're saying, but you are aware that there are really good people out there who don't go to church, right?"

"Yes, I know that." She sighed. "I guess I get a little too zealous sometimes." She shrugged. "It just seems like a positive way to combat all of the hate."

Don chewed on the inside of his cheek for a minute. "You can't control the way people live their lives or what they believe. All you can do is just be the best you can be."

"Yeah, you're right. You'd think I'd know that by now." She stared at her Coke and stifled a yawn.

"I should get you back to your hotel room." Don signaled for the waitress. "Are you all right now?"

Kate dropped her head a little bit and looked at Don through her eyelashes. "Yes, Detective Layden."

Don sat back and folded his arms. "I'm sorry that I yelled at you, but don't *ever* pull anything like that again."

"I'm sorry that I yelled at you, too." Kate squirmed. "That really was an awful scene."

"We agree on that one." The waitress brought Don a bag with the takeout food. Don signed the check and stood up. "Next stop is the Marriott." Don dropped Kate off at the hotel, then went down to the station. He watched on the other side of the one-way mirror as Luke interrogated Treavor.

Luke leaned over Treavor. Treavor's head was down. "So, Treavor, how often do you offer sacrifices in your *church*?" Luke growled.

Treavor didn't move.

Luke slammed his fist on the table and raised his voice. "No, let me rephrase that. How often do you kill people in that deserted building?"

Treavor continued to study the table. "They were homeless," he muttered. "Nobody misses them."

Luke held onto the back of a wooden chair and squeezed it so tightly that Don thought it would snap from the pressure. Luke was quiet for a number of moments. Then he took measured steps over to a manila folder perched on the edge of the table. He opened it and placed two crime scene photos in front of Treavor. One was of Alicia's body and the other was of Gail's.

"So, you got a taste of what it was like to kill people who you thought meant nothing and then you progressed to see what it was like to kill someone who obviously meant something." Luke's voice lowered. "These ladies look familiar?"

Treavor's jaw dropped when he saw the photos. For the first time, a flash of alarm dashed through his eyes.

"You know who they are, don't you?" Luke leaned forward. "I suggest you start talking, pal. Because we've already got you for the homeless men and making the leap to these women won't be very hard."

Treavor stared at the photos and gulped. "I didn't have anything to do with them. Yeah, they were in my section at the restaurant a couple of weeks ago, but that doesn't mean anything."

"That doesn't mean anything?" Luke bared his teeth and wagged his finger at Treavor. "You got too cocky, devil worshipper. Those ladies pissed you off with their talk of Jesus Christ. So, when they asked you to make a copy of their names and addresses, you made an extra copy for yourself and decided to start picking them off."

"No, man, you've got that wrong. I didn't have anything to do with that."

"I'm going to let you sit here for a while. Might help your memory."

Luke came out of the interrogation room and Don handed him the taco which his partner wolfed down in short order. Still chewing, Luke sat back. "You want to take Falco and I'll keep after Treavor?"

"Sounds good."

Luke stepped back in and went after him over and over but got no further.

Don's interview with Falco met with the same denials.

Shortly before sunrise, the exhausted detectives reconvened outside the interview rooms.

Don spoke up first. "Have you called the team from the crime scene to see if they were able to catch anyone that escaped?"

"Yup. The K-9 unit was on the way."

Don stretched his arms over his head for a minute. "Maybe some more time in here will break them down. Or maybe we can recover some DNA from the crime scenes." He looked at his watch. "The good news is that we take the rest of the day off while the shooting at the devil worship scene is investigated. They'll have to push the paperwork through fast though."

Luke nodded, then made a lot of noise as a big yawn overcame him. "I gotta get some sleep. Let's call it until that investigation is over." He sighed with relief. "I'm lookin' forward to a nice, relaxing sleep, like you get when you solve a tough case, you know what I mean?"

Don squinted. "Yeah, I know what you mean, but something doesn't feel right. I can't put my finger on it, but something just doesn't feel quite right."

"Don't you even be sayin' that, Cheeto!"

As he deliberated in his office, the killer squinted while his cigarette smoke coiled around the computer screen. He reached for a white coffee mug with brown stains that sat next to an ashtray filled with butts. The worksheet on the screen was entitled "New United Community Church" and contained a multitude of columns and rows filled with names and numbers. Finally, he sat back in his chair, folded his arms, and smirked. It was all coming together.

A strong sneeze caused a newspaper clipping sitting on the corner of his desk to flutter to the floor. *Ah yes.* Alicia Kendrick's funeral was going to be held at St. James Church. *Might be time to make another impact. Where did I put that notebook?* Reaching into a drawer, he retrieved the mahogany-colored portfolio. Then he pulled out the file containing Alicia's name and Gail's name. Time to look on Facebook to see who next would strike his interest.

TWENTY-FIVE

As Don drove to St. James Catholic church at seven o'clock that night, he observed the full parking lot. In addition, no parking was left on the streets nearby. A black hearse sat in front, leaving no doubt to passersby as to the occasion. A media truck was in front too. When Don pulled into the parking lot Luke commented, "You'll never find a spot here."

"Watch me." Don somehow managed to squeeze the Crown Vic into a spot in the parking lot that was on an unusual incline.

Sabrina was in the car too, and Luke helped her out. "Don Layden, only a crazy man would park here," she remarked as she stood up and steadied herself in her heels.

Don waved off her comment and they walked in.

Many, many people were there already, and Don, Luke, and Sabrina found themselves sitting shoulder to shoulder with others mourning the loss of Alicia Kendrick. The soft lighting illuminated prominent focal points not only on the altar, but throughout the church. Candle stands with twenty flickering candles were situated behind the many lovely flower arrangements that were placed in the front. Don kept looking around watching the attendees. The music began and Father Tim started the service.

Don settled back to try to absorb the culture as much as he could in the hopes he might get some sort of an insight into the case to help him figure out how to make those devil worshippers talk. After some prayers, there were three Bible readings. Father Tim stood at the lectern, speaking to the congregation as he read the last reading. He then looked up and spoke about Alicia.

"I knew Alicia for years. She was a wonderful woman. She loved her family, loved her neighbors, and she loved God. I also think she had a special gift with children. I once heard a child ask her why Jesus came down to earth and I want to share her answer with you.

They happened to be near one of those five gallon aquariums filled with colorful fish and rocks. Alicia asked the boy if he could swim. I remember how his eyes lit up when he thought about swimming. 'Yes,' he answered.

'How did you learn?' Alicia asked him.

'My mom taught me how.'

Alicia directed the boy's attention to the fish swimming in the aquarium. 'Do you think you could have learned by watching a fish swim?'

The boy giggled so hard he could hardly talk. 'No, silly! I'm not a fish!'

Alicia smiled at the boy. 'Of course you're not. You had to learn from another human, right? That's one of the reasons Jesus came here. Even though Jesus was God, he understood that we humans didn't really understand what God was trying to tell us through those prophets who were in the Old Testament. He knew we needed to hear it from God himself, but he had to be a human for us to understand. Just like you needed to learn how to swim from another human.'"

The priest paused and smiled. "I'll never forget the boy's face as the lightbulb flipped on. Then the boy asked, 'But he knew people were going to be mean to him, right?'

'Yup. But he recognized that many of the people would love him and learn from him and teach others what God wants us to know. And that they would carry it on after he rose up and went to heaven.'"

Father Tim looked around the church. "That little story gives good insight into Alicia's heart. We'll miss her. But take comfort in knowing that she helped to make her part of this world a better place." The priest walked back to his chair near the altar and sat down for a few minutes. The room was silent as the congregation absorbed his message.

Don leaned over to Luke. "The devil worshippers would definitely have a problem with Alicia."

Soon the service was over and the attendees were invited to dinner in the church's social center. As Don, Luke, and Sabrina stood near the Crown Vic, Kate walked up.

"Hi, it's nice to see you. Thanks so much for coming. Are you going to the social center to grab a bite?"

Don shifted weight from one foot to the other. "Well…"

Luke butted in. "Yeah, I'll eat!"

Sabrina rolled her eyes. "Luke Malone!"

Kate laughed and extended her hand towards Sabrina. "I'm going to take a wild stab and guess that your name is Sabrina Malone. I've heard great things about you. I'm Kate Fitzgerald."

Sabrina took Kate's hand and returned the smile. "Good guess, Kate. I've a lot heard about you, too."

Kate clasped her hands together and looked at Sabrina with pleading eyes. "Please don't judge me on my police car stunt alone! Please give me another chance."

Sabrina waved her hand. "It's nothing. It just sounds to me like you have some spunk, girl. I like that."

Luke watched everyone head over to the social center. "Do you think there's going to be enough food for all of these people?"

Sabrina scowled at her husband.

Kate giggled as she fell into step with Don, while Luke and Sabrina walked behind them. She found a table for them, and she and Sabrina held places for Don and Luke as they went to get the food.

Don looked around and noticed that at one end of the room there were pictures of Alicia throughout her life. A small crowd gathered around them, and Don watched as some of them laughed and some wiped their tears.

Kate spotted a television camera and a reporter making her way through the crowd. She grimaced. "I don't think this is the place for a television crew."

Sabrina turned to look and there was Sarah Snow. Sabrina watched as Sarah spied Don and Luke as they finally started to make a path back toward their table.

Placing Kate's plate in front of her, Don said, "I don't really know what you like to eat so I just got a little of everything. I brought you a glass of white wine, too. One of the ladies there thought you might like one."

Kate laughed. Her plate was piled with food. "Wow. This looks great. Thanks."

Sarah burst upon them, grabbed Don and gave him a hug and a kiss. "How is my favorite detective?" She smiled warmly at him.

Don took a step back. "Good, Sarah. I'm good."

Sarah moved between Don and Kate. "Tell me about the investigation. How is it going?"

"No news for the media right now."

Sarah flipped her curls and batted her eyes. "Oh, Don Layden, we are more than just friends talking here," she said. "You know me. I wouldn't betray a confidence from you."

Don held up a hand. "Sorry, Sarah, no news."

She frowned and turned to Luke. Somehow, she managed to wedge herself in between Luke and Sabrina.

Kate watched as Sabrina's face tensed. Kate got up and talked to someone near Sarah and waved her glass of wine around. Some of the wine spilled on Sarah.

"Oh! Oh! My sweater!" Sarah glowered at Kate.

Kate turned. "Oh, I'm so sorry." She dabbed Sarah's sweater with a napkin. "Here, let's run to the bathroom and get some water on that pretty sweater." As she turned to leave, Kate looked over at Sabrina and winked. Then Kate coaxed Sarah to follow her to the rest room.

Standing next to a sink, Kate dampened a paper cloth and turned towards Sarah. "Let me get that cleaned up for you."

Sarah snorted. "Not only is it a new sweater, but I can't be on camera with a wet spot like this! I wish you would have paid attention to what you were doing!"

Kate kept her eyes on the sweater. "I apologize again. There is no need to worry because it's coming right out, and it will dry in no time in this arid Rocky Mountain air. No one will ever know what happened."

"But I'll certainly know!" She narrowed her eyes at Kate. "So, how do you know Don Layden?"

"He's investigating the murders of my friends."

Sarah's eyes widened. "You knew both of the victims?"

Kate stiffened. "I'm sure there are others in the city who knew both women." Her voice sounded tinny in her own ears as she struggled to keep the annoyed tone at bay.

"How did you know them?" Sarah started digging.

"Oh, I'd see one or the other of them at various places." Kate threw the towel away. "There you go. Give it five minutes and you'll be good as new." She spun around and exited the restroom as fast as she could.

Kate hurried back to the table. "I think I just screwed up." She described what happened in the bathroom. "I don't think Sarah knows the Bible study connection between Gail and Alicia, but thanks to me she's probably going to figure it out pretty quickly."

Luke scrunched up his nose and shook his head. "Don't worry about it. It's only a matter of time before the media figures it out anyway."

Sabrina stretched her arms over her head and looked at Luke. She poked him teasingly. "Hey you, since we have a babysitter, your wife is thinking she might want to go out and listen to some good music." She snapped her fingers and danced in her chair. "Maybe Don and Kate should come too."

Don sat up straight. "Sabrina, Kate is mourning the loss of her friend. She may not feel like going. Besides, I just don't do that sort of thing anymore."

Sabrina wagged a finger at Don. "And that is exactly why you should go." She turned to Kate. "Kate, I hope that you don't think that this is disrespectful. I just thought that it might be nice for you to go out instead of being by yourself tonight."

"Actually, it would be a good way to remember Alicia. She loved to go listen to music and dance." Kate's smile was small. She blinked back tears. "Actually, I think Alicia would approve."

"I want to speak to Adam," Don stated. "He's been swamped with people throughout the evening, but not as much now." Don turned to Luke. "At first I wasn't sure the devil worshippers were the killers. But Father Tim's talk made me rethink that. I can see devil worshippers going after someone like Alicia. She would be an enemy." He squinted. "I guess, anyway. Hard to imagine what they think."

"It's possible some of them might want to get rid of the real holy rollers. Okay Cheeto, let's speak to the people here and see what we find."

Sabrina folded her arms. "Then it's settled. Let's meet at the door in thirty minutes." With that, Sabrina gathered some plates and headed towards the kitchen to help clean up.

Don's jaw dropped and he turned to Luke. "How does she do that? I never even agreed to go."

The corners of Luke's mouth turned up as he watched his wife. "I don't know, but she sure is cute while she's doing it. Come on, let's go talk to these folks."

Kate went over to greet two friends, Wanda and Vicki, who stood near the photos of Alicia. "Hello. You guys hanging in there?"

Both ladies took turns hugging Kate. "As well as can be expected, I guess," Vicki answered for both of them. "It was a beautiful service, don't you think?" Kate agreed and the women spoke together for a few moments.

Before long, Wanda stretched and groaned. "All right, I think I need to go home and take a long bath. Pete's out of town for a couple of days and I've been going to bed early and getting up early while he's been gone."

Vicki looked at her friend. "Be careful with Pete not being home. Maybe you should come and sleep over at our house while he's out of town. Mark won't mind."

Wanda ran a hand through her close-cropped, blonde hair and then adjusted the black jacket she was wearing to cover her short, somewhat plump shape. "Thanks for the invite, but I'll be okay. My neighbors are watching out for me."

Vicki looked hard at her friend. "Okay, but like I said, be careful. Sleep with one eye open. Kate says those people in jail haven't talked yet and she isn't sure they were all caught."

Near the kitchen, Sabrina was still gathering plates. As she took another stack to the sink, she accidentally bumped into a man wearing a black trench coat with a black wool hat pulled down, not quite hiding some unruly straggles of hair the color of fire. A red plaid scarf hung loosely outside of his coat. "Excuse me," Sabrina murmured. The man grunted and walked away from her. She stared after him. There was something about his arctic, icy blue eyes that made her shiver. She shrugged her shoulders to rid herself of the feeling, but she couldn't stop watching him as he made his way close to where Kate had just been standing.

The strange man stopped and looked at a poster that encouraged participation in the Christmas toy drive. Then he peered at some of the ladies Kate had mentioned were good friends.

Just then, someone jostled Sabrina from behind. Sabrina turned and realized that the cameraman had backed into her. She saw Sarah Snow interviewing some parishioners, then scribbling notes. Sabrina put the plates down and approached Sarah. "Excuse me, may I talk with you for a second?"

Sarah backed away from the parishioners. "Yes?"

Sabrina drew herself up to her full height causing Sarah to look up even farther since the top of her head was only about as high as Sabrina's mouth. "How do you know the deceased?" Sabrina demanded.

Sarah flipped back her blonde curls. "I don't. I'm a reporter."

"You're a reporter," Sabrina repeated. "Did it ever occur to you, Miss Reporter, that people are grieving here and maybe they don't want to be interviewed right now?"

Sarah blinked. "This is news. The citizens of Denver deserve to know all of the details."

"Miss Reporter, I do believe that you have your news. You have pictures of the hearse in front of the church, you have pictures of this social hall and you have spoken to friends of the deceased who are in mourning right now. I think you've gotten what you came to get, and I think you should have the decency to leave now."

Sarah's face darkened. "You think I should have the decency to leave." Her voice rose. "And who made you the gatekeeper of this service?"

Father Tim appeared. "Is there something I can help you with?"

"Yes!" Sarah turned towards the priest. "This woman just told me to leave. Exactly who is she to tell me what to do?"

"I am merely a fellow human being who thinks people have a right to grieve without a camera in their face for hours on end." Sabrina wasn't quite successful in withholding the growl in her tone.

Father Tim inclined his head and looked at Sarah. "Jesus Christ would say that we should treat others the way we would like to be treated ourselves. I'm just curious. Have you ever lost a loved one? Not only that, but have you ever lost a loved one in such a grisly way?"

Sarah's mouth opened but no words came out. Hearing the exchange, the cameraman stepped in and touched Sarah's arm. "Come on, Sarah. Let's go."

Father Tim watched the news team gather up their equipment and leave. The priest turned to Sabrina and extended his hand. "Hello, I'm Father Tim. Welcome to St. James Catholic Church. I appreciate your concern for Alicia's relatives and friends. Thank you."

In the parking lot, Kate stood next to Wanda's car chatting and shivering.

Wanda poked Kate. "You go on and get back inside. I'm fine."

Kate hugged her friend goodbye. "Okay. Take care of yourself." She then scurried back into the social hall.

The killer's eyes followed Kate as the door closed behind her. Only then did he move out of the shadows, his red plaid scarf flapping in the winter wind. He looked up and watched Wanda's taillights pull out of the parking lot as he hurried to his own car with a grim expression of anticipation on his face.

TWENTY-SIX

As Wanda drove home, she passed by a toy store. At the last second, she swerved into the parking lot and got out. Hugging herself with excitement, she ran towards the entrance.

The killer pulled in a minute later and parked in a spot about five spaces away from Wanda's car. He sat and watched the front doors of the store.

At St. James, things wound down. Don and Luke walked over to Sabrina after they finished trying to get information and Kate soon joined them.

"I didn't have any luck. How about you?" Don asked Luke.

"Me neither. But it was worth a shot." He turned to Kate. "Now, are you sure you don't want to ride with us?" Luke asked her. "We all know how much you love to ride around in police cars."

Kate blushed and shook her head before she turned to go to her own car holding the address that Sabrina wrote down for her.

Before long Kate, Don, Sabrina, and Luke found a table in a jazz bar and sat down to listen to the music.

"Now, isn't this nice?" Sabrina turned to Kate. "Do you like it, Kate?"

Kate twisted her hair with her finger as she nodded. "Yes, I do. It's definitely a good change to be out listening to music. Normally I'd be at home reading *Sports Illustrated*."

"Oh no," Sabrina groaned. "Don't tell me you like football, too."

Don spoke up, "She actually has some really good knowledge."

"Hmm…that comment is telling. You think just because I am a woman that I couldn't possibly understand football the way you do, don't you?" Kate frowned.

Don held up his hands and sat back. "Sorry, I meant it as a compliment." He looked to Sabrina for help.

Sabrina drained her water glass and motioned to the men's empty beer mugs. "Will you two gentlemen please go get me some more water when you go get another brew?"

Sabrina drummed her fingernails on the table for a minute after the men left. "Don't be too hard on Don. He lost his wife a year and a half ago. He's been in a fog ever since. Sometimes he doesn't know what he's saying."

Kate's face fell. "Oh, that's awful. I'm so sorry for him."

"He really loved that woman." Sabrina's voice softened. "He still does."

"That is really sad. I'm so sorry to hear that."

Motioning towards the necklace around Kate's neck, Sabrina cocked an eyebrow. "Change of subject. What's up with the necklace?"

Kate grabbed the chain around her neck, a little off balance by Sabrina's question. "This is my reminder to myself about how awful men can be. My fiancé cheated on me during our engagement." Kate folded her hands. "And that led to my decision to blow men off for the rest of my life."

"I see." Sabrina pursed her lips. "Stereotyping. Always a good option."

Kate's eyebrows drew together. "I'm really not one to stereotype."

"No, of course not. You're just going to blow off all men due to the actions of one man."

Kate blinked. Her lips parted but no words came out. Just then, drum sticks crashed against some cymbals and the band started playing right as the men returned to the table. Sabrina stood up and put one hand on her hip.

Luke glanced at Don. "I'll be back."

Kate swirled a straw in her margarita and looked at Don. "Do you like this music?"

"Absolutely. I'm a big fan of all music." He took a sip of beer. "Have you heard about the studies they've done listening to the rhythms found in nature?"

Kate shook her head.

"They found that the sounds from birds, frogs, bugs, et cetera have certain rhythms. Interestingly enough, those exact rhythms are found in music. From Mozart to The Who, music has the same basic rhythms as the rhythms found in nature."

Kate's eyes widened and she leaned forward. "That's crazy! Really?" She sat back again and giggled. "After all of these years of hating bugs I can't believe I have something in common with them." Her lips twitched. "I do like frogs though." She got up and started dancing while singing "Ribbitt, ribbitt," making motions she thought a frog would make. She stuck out her tongue as she danced. She looked so ridiculous Don broke into laughter and couldn't stop. Soon Kate was laughing too. When Sabrina and Luke got back to the table they found two hysterical people wiping their eyes.

"What's so funny?" Sabrina demanded.

"Oh, you had to be there," Kate gasped. "Ribbitt." She and Don broke up again. Then the band played another song and this time all four of them went out onto the dance floor.

Just a few miles away, Wanda walked out of the toy store hugging a three foot tall snow-white teddy bear. She took care as she placed it into the passenger seat and almost had to stop herself from putting it in a seat belt. "I wonder what my child will name you. I guess I will have to wait until my baby is born and learns how to talk, won't I?" Giggling, she sang "The Wheels on the Bus" at the top of her lungs the entire ride home.

Looking at the empty space where Pete's car was usually parked brought a frown to her face, so she took out her cell phone, dialed her husband, and told him all about the events of the day, as she walked into the house holding the bear close to her body.

The killer pulled up and stopped his car near her house. *She left the garage door open!* He closed his eyes. *Too good to be true.*

Wanda was on the main floor upstairs hanging her coat in the closet. "Alicia's funeral was beautiful, Pete. The music was gorgeous and the flowers were so nice. And the readings and the speakers were wonderful. Everybody kept saying over and over how uplifting the service was." She listened for a minute. "Yes of course. Every night I lock the doors, I set the alarm, and I'm careful." She moved towards the bathroom and held up a stick. She put the pregnancy test back down and started hopping around.

"Pete, I was going to wait until you got home to tell you this but I just can't. Honey, I'm pregnant!" She held the phone away from her ear as she heard her husband's joyful exclamations on the other end of the line. "Yes, it's true. After all of these tries, after all of these years, it's finally happened. You're going to be a daddy!"

By now she was in the living room and she sank down on a contemporary couch right next to the teddy bear, wiping her eyes. "I'm so happy, too. I have my first doctor's appointment next week. Do you want to come?" She and her husband talked on and on.

Outside, the killer bolted out of his car. He pulled on some gloves, opened the trunk, and reviewed its contents. He found himself holding his breath as he looked over each shoulder. *Coast is clear.* Retrieving the axe, he put it under his coat. Still looking around, he crossed the street and slipped into the garage.

After finishing her conversation with her husband, Wanda moseyed around her house, cradling the bear. Wandering into the guest room, she straightened her arms out and held the bear in front of her. "What color do you think would look good for the baby's room?" She wrinkled her nose. "I don't like the idea of pink or blue." She looked at the bear. "Maybe a creamy color like beach sand." She pursed her lips, then started nodding. "I like that idea. But maybe we should get Pete's input too. We want him to feel included, don't we?" She chuckled and hugged the bear.

The killer flattened himself against the wall and waited, heart pounding. He panted and concentrated on forcing himself to stop. He heard some joggers go by and froze, trying to stop the sweat from dripping off his forehead.

Inside the house, Wanda sat down at her computer, turned it on, and placed the bear next to her. "Let's look at some furniture. You would look so cute sitting in a little chair when we bring the baby home."

The killer pried himself away from the wall and inched his way to the door that lead into the house. He opened it with caution.

On the main floor, Wanda absorbed the choices on her computer screen. She scrolled through a website, clicking on items of interest. She sat back in her chair and folded her arms. "Hmmm. That's pretty cute." She chewed on her lip as she contemplated the image before her.

The killer inhaled and exhaled, trying to calm himself as he stayed quiet. Step by step, he crept around the first floor of the home.

Upstairs, Wanda leaned forward and grabbed the computer mouse. "I'll keep looking, but that's a start." She scrolled through some more images and then she picked up the bear and meandered over to the kitchen table for a quick review of the different drawings of the building she designed for work. She put her hand on her stomach. "Wish your Mommy luck at her presentation tomorrow, little one."

Her phone rang and she answered it. "Oh, thanks Grace. I was on the phone with Pete when I got out of my car, and I guess I was so excited to talk to him that I forgot to close the garage door." She paused. "No, don't be silly. Clyde doesn't need to come over. I'll just run downstairs and close it. And yes, if I need anything I'll be sure to call."

Wanda pattered down the stairs and closed the garage door. It was noisy as it shut and she didn't hear the killer edge next to the stairs.

As she turned to go back upstairs he raised the axe high and buried it into the back of her head. A small scream escaped her lips before the axe destroyed her brain and she fell to the ground dropping the teddy bear next to her. It didn't take long for the white bear to become soaked with Wanda's blood. The killer's eyes were slits as he pulled the rosary out of a pocket and wrapped it around her neck. Her lifeless eyes were wide open as he tightened the chain. Then he put the rosary back into his pocket, picked up the axe, and walked out through the back door.

He wiped his shoes on the snow and inched around to the front of the house. The street was quiet. He hurried over to his car and sped away.

TWENTY-SEVEN

Dressed in sweats, Don stood out on his back deck with Belle on his shoulder while sipping some steaming coffee and watching the early morning sun's ascent into the pink sky over the mountains. "Belle, I really don't want to go in to work today. I want to get away from everything. Just go skiing." He sighed and put his finger near Belle so she would climb onto it. He brought her around so they were face to face. "But I've got to go in. I got the green light to start working again after the shootings with those devil worshippers. We've got to get them to talk. I want this case closed." Belle blinked her eyes in response.

With that, he placed Belle in her cage and got dressed.

He picked up Luke and they both entered the station after picking up their guns. As they walked in, Don stopped to pick up a piece of paper Zach Daskalis dropped from his desk. Zach looked like he was filling out some paperwork.

"Hey Zach, what's the update?" Luke walked over to Zach's desk. "Have they broken their silence on our case yet?"

"Nothing doing." Zach sat back in his chair. "Get this: a couple of them are surprised that they are going to be prosecuted for killing homeless people!" He shook his head in disgust. "At any rate, thanks to you two we've got the homeless murders solved, but they still won't admit to killing Alicia and Gail." He paused. "And now they've got lawyers."

"Crap!" Luke ran a hand over his head. "I'll call and see where they are on DNA and the rest of the evidence. If we get something even somewhat solid, that could start the ball rolling and then they'll talk." He picked up his phone and dialed.

Don wandered over to the whiteboard, his eyes narrowing as he studied it. Something bothered him, but he couldn't figure out what.

Just then, his phone rang. "Layden here." As he listened, his heart fell. He hung up and his head dropped. He just stood there, eyes closed, pinching the bridge of his nose. He exhaled and sank down into his chair, turning towards Luke as though in a trance. "The reason why those bozos haven't confessed is because there's a good chance that they didn't do it. The killer struck again." Don stared at Luke for a long moment and watched as his partner turned and pounded his fist on the desk. Don leaned over and held his head in his hands. After a few long minutes, he raised himself out of his chair, and took a deep breath. Without a word, he and Luke took off to the crime scene.

When Don and Luke arrived, Meg was already there. Don viewed the scene. Wanda lay in a heap at the bottom of the stairs in a drying pool of blood. A teddy bear soaked in her blood was next to her.

Meg spoke up, "It's the same guy. Axe to the back of the head, chain wrapped around after the chop. I'd say she's been dead about thirteen hours."

"Her name is Wanda Benaducci. She's an architect and she missed a very important meeting." A police officer held up the pregnancy test stick. "And we found this in the bathroom. It's positive."

Don closed his eyes, threw back his head, and a groan escaped his lips. Shaking himself, he opened his eyes and clicked on his tape player. "What information do we have on Wanda so far?"

"We know her," said a voice from behind him.

Don looked over his shoulder and saw an African-American couple standing in the background, holding hands. Don stepped towards them and introduced himself. "How do you know the victim?"

The man answered "We are her neighbors. I'm Clyde Floyd and this is my wife, Grace."

"Wanda is an architect," Grace said. "Her husband is in sales. We've been neighbors for years. Before Pete went out of town, he called us and asked us to watch out for her while he was gone. I called her last night because she left her garage door open after she got home." Grace's voice shook. "I offered to have Clyde come over and make sure everything was okay, but she said she was fine." Grace's eyes filled with tears and she covered her face with a handkerchief.

Clyde put his arm around his wife's shoulders. "That was about nine last night."

"Which fits with the time of death."

Clyde continued, "This morning Grace called Wanda to see how she was doing and she didn't answer. I came over and saw the blood in the snow. We got worried and called the police."

Don finished scribbling in his notebook and then regarded Wanda's neighbors. "Anything else you can tell us to shed some light on this? Strange cars in the neighborhood? Someone walking around in the cold who really didn't belong?"

Clyde and Grace looked at each other and shook their heads.

Grace returned her gaze to Don and her brown eyes filled with tears. "We can't think of anything."

"That's all right," Don reassured her as he handed her his card. "Right now, you are in shock. Here's my card. Give me a call any time day or night if you remember something. Even if you think it's insignificant, just call."

Heads bowed, the couple trudged out the back door.

"There is no sign of forced entry," a police officer said. "We checked all of the doors and windows."

Don examined a piece of paper. "She's on the list of the Bible study members at St. James."

"Crap!" Luke pounded a fist against the wall. "We were there with her last night!"

"Maybe he was there, too." Don's face hardened. "Maybe this guy wanted to see his victim alive before he killed her. Plus, I think he gets off on the publicity that surrounds this case." Don narrowed his eyes. "The homeless killers avoided publicity, but I think this guy likes it. That's the part that bothers me about both cases. They just don't line up."

"I'll tell you what's bothering me about this case." Belinda walked up behind Don and Luke. "That it isn't solved yet! What the hell have you two been doing, besides working on everyone else's case but your own?"

Don turned to face Belinda. "We've been working *our case*, Belinda. Following up on leads, exploring every avenue."

"Yeah, I heard what you said to Sarah Snow about the plethora of leads you have." Belinda's eyes burned. "Interesting. I know of a detective or two who are no longer detectives. They talked to the media too much." She raised her eyebrows.

Don flushed bright red and he leaned down so his face was right next to Belinda's. "Do what you gotta do Belinda." His voice came through his teeth in a snarl. "But good luck on solving this case if you're down one more detective." With that, he turned, strode out of the room, jumped into the Crown Vic, and took off.

The room was silent as the team standing near Wanda's body stared after Don. Luke cleared his throat. "Huh. My ride just took off. Looks like I'm going to have to hitch a lift back to the station."

"I can't believe you're being so cavalier about what your partner just did," Belinda spluttered. "We are in the middle of a murder investigation!"

"Yeah, and whether you want to believe it or not, we've been working it, Belinda. We've been spending time on those files as ordered and we've also been following as many other leads as we can. We don't want to see another woman meet her death. We've hardly slept." Luke's eyes narrowed and his voice dropped. "We're not lazy pieces of crap. We're working our butts off."

Belinda shot a penetrating glare at Luke then stormed up the stairs. Her footsteps pounded above them as she stomped around the room. They heard cursing as pieces of the conversation she was having with herself floated down the stairs to them.

Luke turned to face the others. "Let's just get back to work and let her blow off some steam." He snorted. "Ain't no way she'll let Don go. She can't. She needs him." His eyes flickered. "And she's figuring that out right now."

Luke watched the team come back to life and get to work.

TWENTY-EIGHT

Don drove home, parked the Crown Vic and stormed into his condo. Minutes later, he was in his ski clothes. He threw his skis, boots, and poles into his SUV and headed up I-70 to Breckenridge.

A few miles away, the killer held the phone to his ear. "Yes, David I am in the process of sending the funds out for the Cook family. International money isn't quite as liquid as money invested domestically." He listened for a moment. "Yes, Mr. Cook's accident was terrible, and I understand that the family needs cash to keep going. I will get it to them as soon as I can."

He set the phone down and leaned back, his eyes not moving from his computer screen. After repeated attempts to talk with someone, the lack of an answer from his Brazilian investments concerned him. He touched his stomach as an uneasy feeling came over him.

Shaking himself, he sat up and found the website for Delta Airlines. It was time to take a trip to Brazil. *Sometimes a personal visit paid huge dividends. These people need to see that they were dealing with a professional. They better not even try to ignore me!*

Driving up to the ski resort on I-70, Don's hands tremored as he gripped the steering wheel. The good news was that, for once, the traffic wasn't bumper to bumper. He got out of the car and in no time got off the chairlift. Then, he skied several runs at top speed. The cold mountain air invigorated him, and he could feel the stress peeling away in layers, run after run. Sometime later, he found himself sitting next to three young female snowboarders on a quad chairlift.

"Hi, how's your day going?" A young woman with blonde braids sticking out from under a pink helmet grinned at him.

"I've had better." Don paused for a minute. "How about yours?"

"Oh, I'm having a great day! I just finished up all of my exams at Colorado State. Wahoo! It's vacation!" She pumped her fists into the air.

Don had to smile at her animation. "What are you studying?"

"I'm a marketing major. I'm going to convince all of America to buy the brand of whatever company I work for!"

This time Don chuckled. "You're making a believer out of me already. When does America get to see you in action?"

"I'm only a freshman even though I'm twenty-one. I started down the wrong path out of high school. But eventually I figured things out. That's when I enrolled in CSU."

"Impressive. What made you figure out that you were on the wrong path?"

The sun gleamed on the lens of her bright pink goggles as she tilted her head. "I wasn't getting anywhere, and finally it occurred to me that the only one who could change that was me."

The chairlift came to an end and Don watched the girls as they strapped on their boards and took off, pumping their fists amidst hoots and hollers. Don squinted. "So, you were on the wrong path and you figured out the only one who could change that was you."

"You say somethin', bro?" A young boarder standing nearby looked at Don.

Don shook his head. "Just thinking out loud." He tightened his boots and streaked down the hill to his car and his phone.

His phone had been busy while he was gone. There were five missed calls from Luke, four from Sarah Snow, but not even one from Belinda. Interesting. He listened to his voicemail and had to steady himself against the car when he heard the news. Lucy had been hit in the head in a sledding accident and was in the hospital in a coma.

Don drove straight to The Children's Hospital on Franklin. When he arrived at Lucy's stark white room, Luke and Sabrina were sitting next to each other gazing at Lucy. Sabrina was holding Lucy's hand and Luke's big hand was gently wrapped around his daughter's tiny forearm. Lucy's little body was surrounded with tubes and monitors. Her head was wrapped in a bandage. She was propped up slightly and she looked like she was sleeping, but the tension in the room made it clear that wasn't the case.

"What happened?"

"She went sledding with some friends from pre-school," Luke replied. "Someone built a snow jump and they went off of it without looking and ran right into her. She had a seizure on the hill and they brought her here in an ambulance." His voice didn't sound human.

"What have the doctors said?"

Sabrina answered, "She has had what is called a TBI which stands for Traumatic Brain Injury. They did an MRI and they are draining some cavities in her brain to reduce the swelling."

"She's on drugs to try to prevent any more seizures and to help keep down the inflammation," Luke added. "Esther, her main nurse, told us we just have to sit and wait." His spirit lifted just a bit when he said, "Esther said Lucy's age is a positive."

Don looked at Sabrina. "Were you there?"

Sabrina shook her head. "The mother of Lucy's friend called and invited her to go sledding, and I just thought it would be okay." She put her face into her hands and started sobbing. "Why did I let her go?"

Luke put both arms around his wife. "You let her go because kids go sledding. You couldn't have seen this coming, honey. Don't beat yourself up."

Time passed. Don was looking out of the window when his phone rang.

"Don?" Kate's voice was shaking. "Were the devil worshippers in jail last night?"

"Yes, they were."

"How could this happen? How could Wanda have been killed? Were all the men caught that night? Could it be one of the guys that got away?"

"We aren't certain that we caught all of them so that's still a possibility, but it just isn't holding up. And you're right, the killer is still out there and every single member of your

Bible study group is a target for him." Don sighed. "I think we need to review everything. Now that we know what we know, I'd like to go through the details with you again. You might remember something you didn't remember before. I think we got off on the wrong path with this devil worship stuff and we have to get back on the right one."

"Okay, you name the time and the place and I'll be there."

"Actually, I'm at The Children's Hospital on Franklin. Lucy was in a sledding accident. She's in a coma."

"Oh, no!" Don heard Kate suck in her breath. "Is it okay if I come down?" she whispered.

Don put his hand over the mouthpiece and checked with Luke and Sabrina. "Yes, it's okay. Room 403 in the intensive care unit."

"I'll see you in a little while."

Don sat back down by Lucy's bed and rubbed his chin. "So, am I still employed by the city of Denver or am I solving this case *pro bono?*"

Luke brightened up for a fraction of a second. "Queen BM was pissed as hell when you left. She stomped around and cussed for a while, but when it comes right down to it I think she knows you're right; the case won't get solved if you aren't on it." He inclined his head towards Lucy. "Especially now. I'm out for a while. I already talked to HR."

"Don't worry about anything but your family, partner. I've got the case."

About an hour later Kate walked in and Sabrina stood up to greet her. The two women hugged.

Kate held up a bag. "I brought some things." She pulled out a stuffed toy. "Here's a puppy to keep Lucy company."

Next Kate pulled out some books. "I thought you might like to read to Lucy." She handed them to Luke.

The next thing Kate pulled out of her bag was a white ceramic angel. One wing was slightly chipped and there were a couple of scratches on it. "This is a little angel my mom gave me when I was young. She told me it was my guardian angel. I used to rub it when I was scared or upset when I was small. I'd like to give it to Lucy, is that okay?"

"That's very sweet, Kate," Sabrina took it and placed it on a stand next to Lucy's bed.

Luke paced near the window.

"And I brought a medal of St. Jude." Kate pulled a small silver medal out of the bottom of the bag. "He is the patron saint of desperate situations. Would it be okay if I put this near Lucy's bed too?"

Sabrina started to agree, but Luke spun around. "Fat lot of good that'll do!" he spat out.

"Luke Malone, what are you saying?" Sabrina frowned. "If there is anything we need right now, it's prayers!"

Luke's eyes went vacant. "Sorry, baby, I just don't believe in all of that stuff. Where was God when my brother was dying, huh?"

Kate put the medal in a pocket and held up her hands. "I'm sorry, I shouldn't have brought it. I was just trying to help."

Don cleared his throat. "Kate, why don't you and I go down to the coffee shop and go over the case from the beginning. Luke, you are welcome to join us if you want to or stay here, it's up to you."

"You go on." Sabrina stared at her husband. "I'll stay here."

Luke turned to walk out. "I'm going to step outside for a minute," he said in a clipped voice. "I'll meet you in the coffee shop."

The elevator took Kate and Don to the coffee shop. Don retrieved a small notebook and pen from a coat pocket after they found a table and sat down. He and Kate put their heads together as Don reviewed each page step by step.

Before long, Luke rambled over and stood near their table, shifting his weight from one foot to the other.

Kate looked up at him and placed a hand on Luke's arm. "I'm sorry if the medal upset you. I swear, I was just trying to help."

"I know." Luke waved his hand. "I don't want to talk about it right now. I want to talk about the case." He pulled up a chair but positioned it so that he was facing Don, not Kate.

After about thirty minutes, they wound up back at the meal at Jose's. "I keep coming back to the waiter there because he was just so mean." Kate's forehead creased. "It isn't very often that you meet someone who is just plain mean."

Luke readjusted his chair a bit, sat back, folded his arms, and studied Kate. "Let me ask you something. Do you like everyone that you meet? Do you really think that everyone is a good person?"

Kate tilted her head and twisted her hair around a finger for a few seconds as she considered Luke's question. "Well no, even though Jesus told us to love our enemies I have to admit that I honestly don't like everyone I meet. Unfortunately, I still have a long way to go on that one." She held up a finger. "But, I at least think everyone has a light of some sort inside of them and I always challenge myself to find it. I have to tell you, there are very few people I have known whose light can't be found." Kate paused and stared at the table for a minute. "Although there was one guy that I worked for a few years ago when I first came to Denver…" Eyes wide, she stopped and grabbed Don's arm. "Holy crap!" Her lips parted and she stared straight ahead as if in a trance.

Don's eyebrows drew together. "What?"

"I just remembered!" Blinking, she turned to look at Don and her voice fell to a whisper. "He was at the restaurant the night we were at Jose's."

TWENTY-NINE

Don leaned forward and stared at Kate. "Tell us about it."

"His name is Barry Witt. He owns a real estate investment firm in Denver. I applied for a position there when I was close to my graduation from Boise State. I flew in for an interview, got the job, and moved right after I graduated." She sighed. "At first I didn't have much to do with him because I was in training. However, I learned a lot and worked hard. After a few months, he took more of an interest in me." She made a face. "He really started to come on to me sexually. I kept resisting, but it became a more and more difficult situation, so I looked for another job. As luck would have it, when he was out of the country I found my current job and gave my notice. I was gone before he got back. The first time I've seen him since was the night at Jose's."

"What happened there?"

"He was drinking at the bar when we came in. His back was mostly to me so he didn't see me, but I saw enough of his face so that I recognized him." Kate studied her hands. "I pretended I didn't see him and hoped he didn't see me." She paused and looked up. "But he did. You know how when you don't want to acknowledge someone, and your eyes meet for a split second and then you look away?"

"Yup."

"Well, that's what happened. It was a little bit later in the evening." She sighed. "It's kind of odd. That happened at work a few times and he actually called me in his office to talk to me about it."

"What'd he say?"

"He said I worked for him and he deserved respect. He said, 'You're my employee. Mine. You need to show me a certain regard. When you see me, you address me.'" Kate wrinkled her nose. "I mean, it was nothing. But he got really bent out of shape over that."

Luke let out a low whistle. "That's a problem."

Kate's forehead creased. "Yeah, creeped me out."

"It sounds like he thought of you as his. As a possession. Something he could control." Luke crossed his legs. "They've done studies on men who kill women. They think they own them. When the lady leaves, they go off the deep end and try to get her back. But when they can't, the process turns from recovery to elimination."

"Ugh," Don grunted. "That's right." His eyes lingered on Kate as he thought. "Did he ever try to contact you after you left?"

"A couple times, but I never took the call."

Don stared at his coffee cup and chewed on his lip. "Okay. So, Barry sees you, you ignore him again like you did several times in the past." He tapped his finger against his cup as he thought. "Maybe while he was at Jose's, Barry somehow got a copy of the list from Treavor. Or maybe some extra copies were left on the tables by a few ladies from your group. Barry picked one up." Don looked up. "Treavor might know something. I'll go down to the station and talk to Treavor and do some research on Mr. Barry Witt. Give me the name of his company."

"It's Witt Real Estate and Investments. His folks loaned him the money to start it and he began in commercial real estate. Later he became more involved in residential and I think he also expanded into other financial vehicles." Kate closed her eyes for a minute. "I can't believe I didn't tell you this before. I just didn't remember seeing him until now. Besides, it was just a fraction of a second. I got so caught up with the whole thing about Treavor and the devil worshippers and I guess I just forgot about it."

"Happens all the time. It meant nothing to you." Don paused. "But maybe it meant everything to him." Don turned to Luke and put a hand on his shoulder. "I've got the case. You have more than enough to worry about. If there is any change with Lucy, let me know." Don turned and sprinted out the door.

Kate watched him leave and turned to Luke. "I apologize again about the medal. Please forgive me."

"Yeah." Luke ran a hand over his head. "It's fine."

Kate gathered her belongings. "Do you know where the chapel is by any chance?"

"Chapel?"

Kate nodded. "Yes, I think all hospitals have one. No worries, I'll find it." She touched Luke's arm. "Take care."

The chapel was easy to find. Kate spent some time praying for Lucy and the Malone family. When she exited, she found Luke standing outside. Once again, she put a hand on his arm. "You okay?"

"God didn't help me with my brother. Why would he help me with my daughter?"

"Luke, what happened with your brother?"

Luke leaned against a wall. "The short story is my dad left us, my mom earned the money to support us, and my brother hung out with the wrong crowd. One night I heard him on the phone with someone and I could tell something bad was going down. I followed him and it was a drug deal. He pulled a wad of money out of his pocket to exchange for drugs. But instead of the drugs, the guy pulled out a knife and stabbed Jay like he was nothing. I ran after his attacker and we fought, but he got away." Luke's eyes welled up. "Jay died in my arms."

"That's just awful. I'm so sorry."

"I prayed as hard as I could but Jay didn't make it. Where was God then, huh Kate? Where was God then?" Luke leaned forward and closed his eyes.

"Luke, God didn't kill Jay, the drug dealer killed Jay." Kate paused. "God gave us free will. We can choose how we want to live. He gave us an example to follow and we either do it or not." She searched Luke's eyes. "But Luke, make no mistake, God loves you."

Luke rubbed the top of his head and took several deep breaths. Then he cleared his throat. "You still have that medal?"

She pulled it out of her pocket and handed it over to him.

"And when you ask this guy to pray for you, you get miracles?"

A corner of Kate's mouth turned up. "It certainly hasn't happened every time, but it has happened."

"Huh." Luke rubbed his lips together, considering. "I'll do anything to help Lucy. Okay, let's put him to work."

Down at the station, Don made slow progress. The office of Witt Real Estate and Investments was closed but Barry Witt still lived in Denver. Don wanted to know what Treavor remembered from that night in the bar. The problem was that last Don heard, Treavor wouldn't talk without his lawyer present. Don sat at his desk and stared at his computer screen. He was going to have to jump through some hoops and jumping through hoops always took time. In the meantime, the killer was still out there. Don's stomach churned.

THIRTY

Don went to talk to Treavor who was still being held at the station. Treavor stood leaning against the back wall of the jail cell, arms folded.

"Treavor, I have new knowledge in the case involving the women that are being killed. I just want to ask you a couple of questions."

Treavor shook his head. "Not without my lawyer."

Don tried again. "This will in no way implicate you in this case. I just need you to verify a small detail for me."

Treavor shook his head again. "Nothing doin'. Not without my lawyer."

Don's shoulders drooped. He was stuck.

A few miles away, the killer prepped to leave for Brazil. He stopped both the mail and the paper for the duration of his trip. The doors were locked, the lights were off, and the heat was set to low. He had his passport, so it was time to go. As he put his luggage in the trunk, he saw the axe. *Too bad that can't come to Brazil, too.* He took the axe out of his trunk and looked for a place to hide it.

More than once, he left the axe in a closet, got in his car, then got back out and moved it again. He stood in his living room looking at the collection of the medieval weapons. He tried putting it up amongst them, but he'd been polishing it so much the shiny blade stood out. He took it back down and looked at himself in the blade, mesmerized. All of a sudden he blinked and looked at his watch. Cursing, he ran back out to the garage and put the axe back in the trunk of the car. After all, the airport police didn't search car trunks! Then he backed out of his driveway and headed to Denver International Airport.

At the police station, Don called Treavor's lawyer several times but couldn't get any further than voicemail. He paced in front of his whiteboard and then leaned against a wall as he studied it.

Without warning, the sound of gunshots broke out near the entrance of the room. Don dropped to the floor pulling his gun out of its holster, and saw a man wearing the same red hood as the devil worshippers shoot in a frenzy, then turn and run out the door amidst a barrage of return fire. The prisoners in the jail cells cheered. Some of Don's colleagues were down and bleeding. Don checked to make sure that they were being attended to and yelled, "I'm going after him," as he barreled out the door.

The street was crowded with shoppers and citizens who were unaware of the danger they were in. Searching, Don spotted the man darting through the crowd and Don chased him, arms pumping and feet pounding as fast as he could go.

The shooter spotted Don and turned to fire. People near him screamed.

Don heard shots hit a van behind him. He turned to look. Van damaged. People okay. Don sprinted towards a doorway. "Get down!" Don shouted as he ducked into the doorframe and checked to see where the shooter was. He was running again. Don sped after him and closed the gap.

The shooter ran across the street through traffic and Don jumped behind a truck and crossed without losing any ground. The shooter turned to shoot again but Don reacted. Bellowing, "Get down!" to the pedestrians, Don fired a clear shot at the gunman and the bullet knocked the assailant to the ground. Running to him, Don worked to stem the bleeding before the ambulance arrived. He really wanted to have a conversation with this guy.

After watching paramedics load the shooter into the ambulance, Don clutched the wallet he'd confiscated and jogged back to the station to check the damage. As he neared, he saw the blazing lights of two ambulances out on the street and the injured were being loaded into them. Zach Daskalis stood near the ambulances and Don jogged over to him. "Zach how is everyone doing?" Don held his breath.

Zach beamed. "Everyone survived. The guy's a lousy shot."

Don let the air out of his lungs and leaned over, holding himself up with his hands on his thighs. "That's a big relief!"

"Did you catch him?"

"Yeah, I chased him and wound up shooting him." Don straightened up. "He's not in great shape. Not sure if he'll make it. I'm going to run over to the hospital where he is to get an interview."

"Good idea." Zach patted Don on the back. "Hey, thanks for nabbing him."

"My pleasure."

Don ran into the station and looked through the wallet for the shooter's ID. The driver's license showed one Avery Sanutchi, a twenty-year-old. He lived near Treavor. Don printed out Avery's crime sheet and stuffed it in a pocket.

Arriving at the hospital, Don identified himself and discovered Avery was in surgery. Don handed out his card and let the nurses know he wanted to talk to the patient as soon as possible. He headed back to the station.

Sitting at his desk in the homicide unit, he perused the wallet, speaking out loud in a low voice to no one in particular.

"Avery Sanutchi, what made you start worshipping the devil? You're twenty-years-old. Don't you have better things to do? And why would you walk into a police station and start shooting up my colleagues?" Don pulled Avery's record out of his pocket and reviewed it. Then, eyes intent on the computer screen, he searched further into Avery's record along with the records of anyone mentioned in the file.

The next thing he knew, his phone was ringing. "Detective Layden? I'm calling to let you know the patient is out of surgery and is coming out of the anesthesia."

"Be right there."

As soon as Don walked into Avery's room, an ominous feeling came over him. He found himself looking around almost as though he was investigating a crime in progress. By instinct, he put a hand on his gun, fighting the urge to pull it out of its holster. He laughed at himself and shook it off. He rubbed his hands together. *Why was it so cold in here?*

Avery's eyes flew open and he looked around jerking his head from side to side. "No! No!" he shouted.

Don grabbed his arm and spoke to him. "Avery, it's okay. You're in the hospital. Your name is Avery, right?"

Avery looked at Don, his eyes filled with terror. "Yes, I'm Avery, but don't let them know! Don't tell them! They're out to get me!"

Don put one hand on each of Avery's shoulders and clasped them. "Avery, I'm a detective with the Denver Police. No one here is going to hurt you."

"Yes! Yes, they are! They're right there!" Avery pointed over Don's shoulder. Don spun around but saw nothing. He turned back to Avery, who was having some sort of a seizure. Avery shook wildly as he lay on the bed, and his head jerked at random from side to side. It was time to get some help in here.

A tiny, elderly, gray-haired nurse responded to Don's calls. As she walked in, she stopped for a moment and gazed at Avery as he convulsed.

"He's having a seizure, is there something you can do?" Don looked at the nurse. Amidst the turmoil, Don noticed the nurse's nametag said 'Mary'.

Mary's steady gaze calmed Don. "The only thing you can do is wait for it to pass and hold the patient so he doesn't fall." She pointed to the handcuffs on Avery's wrists that were attached to the bedrails. "This patient is already restricted so he is as secure as we can make him."

"I see." Don paused and rubbed his arms several times. "Why is it so cold in here? It can't be healthy for a patient to be in a room this cold."

Mary checked the thermostat. "It's set at 72 degrees." She walked over to the heating unit and held her hand over the vent. "It's churning out hot air." She turned around and looked at Don with a wise gaze in her clear, blue eyes. "If I had to take a guess, I'd say this isn't the first time our patient has been in trouble."

Don remembered some of what was on Avery's sheet, the bombardment at the station, and the eerie ritual in front of the statue of Lucifer. "You'd be right." Don regarded the nurse. "What made you say that?"

"I've seen this happen before." She checked his vitals and read the screens on the machines that were connected to Avery.

Don opened his mouth with more questions when one of the machines screeched. A second later, several hospital personnel ran in and surrounded the patient with a variety of medical devices.

Don stood against the wall, trying to comprehend the whole situation. What had Avery so frightened? Why was he seeing things?

As the medical team worked, they exchanged clipped bits of information with each other. After a time, they backed up. One of them looked at his watch and gave the time of death. Then, one by one, everyone cleared out and before long the only two remaining were Don and Mary.

"What the hell just happened?" Don demanded. His palms were sweating as he stood looking down at Avery's body.

Mary tilted her head. "I have my own little theory about the cold and the seizures. I don't think he was having a medical seizure." She paused. "I think he was being chased." She glanced at Avery's body. "Or at least he thought he was being chased."

Don spun around and faced the nurse. "What are you talking about? We were right here. He wasn't being chased! What kind of drugs did you give him? Was he allergic?"

A small smile played about the venerable woman's lips. "Detective, if all of this happened because he was allergic to drugs then why is the room so cold?"

Don stood there, blinking.

"I think either he thought he was being chased by demons or…" her eyes pierced Don, "…maybe he really was." She walked over to the body and pointed to his hair and his face. "I was here when he came in. When the surgeons started working on him, they were working on a twenty-year-old man. Now look at him. Doesn't he look older than that to you?"

Don frowned and looked at Avery's face. "He was shot, he went through surgery…I've seen people's appearance change while they're sick. I don't think that's anything new."

Mary considered Don's response for a few moments and then finally nodded her head. "Okay, you have a point." She shrugged and pulled the sheet up over Avery. "Go ahead and think what you want, it's a free country. But that still doesn't explain why the room is so cold."

She smiled before she continued. "I guess we'll never know, will we?" She stepped towards Don and took something out of her pocket and handed it to him. He held it in his open palm. It was a rosary. "I've carried this with me and used it faithfully ever since the first time that I encountered this 'condition' so many years ago." She closed Don's hand around the beads. "Now I'm giving it to you. Use it, young man." She patted his hand and walked out of the room.

Don felt the blood drain from his head. He steadied himself against the wall as he gazed after the retreating nurse.

THIRTY-ONE

After Don tied things up at the hospital, he stepped outside to his vehicle. *What just happened?*

He sat in the car and stared at the rosary in his hand, then let it slide through his fingers into a cup holder in the console, watching the brown beads take on the shape of their round container as they slowly descended from his hand. He pinched himself. *Yes, that hurt. I'm awake.*

Don clapped his hands together a couple of times and warmed them with his breath. The cold night jolted the fogginess of his brain. He fumbled for his phone and called Zach.

"Daskalis."

"Hi Zach, it's Don Layden."

"Hi Don, what did you find out?"

Don scratched his head. "He didn't really wake up. He had hallucinations and a seizure. Then he died."

"Hallucinations? Was he on drugs? Maybe that's why he shot up the station."

Don raised his eyebrows as he thought about the events he'd witnessed. "They had to know if he was on anything before they anesthetized him. Said those came up negative. But I asked for a thorough autopsy to be done after his family was contacted. We'll see what comes of that. I also checked his shoe size. It's no match for the murders Luke and I are working on. Anyway, I wanted to let you know that

I'll be filing my report from home tonight. But first I have to stop by and drop off my gun while the shooting of the suspect is investigated."

Zach laughed. "I think the investigation will take about five minutes. The guy came in and shot at a lot of police officers. He signed his own death warrant." He paused. "Thanks for the capture and making sure he's not on the streets anymore."

Don ended the call and drove to the station to turn in his gun. Belinda stopped him as he was leaving. "What in the world were you thinking? A gun fight in the middle of downtown Denver?"

"He came in here and shot a bunch of police officers and I chased him. He fired first."

Belinda folded her arms and lifted her chin. "Guess what? Your little shooting spree hit a van that was carrying a valuable painting to the art museum. The van and the painting were damaged. That costs us money."

"Those were his shots, not mine."

"We'll see about that, won't we?"

Don felt his face redden and his heart pounded so hard he thought it might pop out of his chest. "Yes, we will," he said through clenched teeth. Spinning around, he stalked out.

When he got back in his car, he let it run for a minute as he stared at the rosary Mary gave him. He picked it up and talked to it. "You gotta help me out here. Anything you can do to help me solve this case would be appreciated. I do not want another woman to meet her death at the hands of this lunatic." He put the rosary back and continued "I don't think I can take walking into a scene like that again." The car moved along at a slow speed as thoughts about the case swirled in Don's mind.

A couple of blocks to his right, the bright red Marriott Hotel sign appeared in his peripheral vision and he found himself turning into the hotel's parking garage. He sat in his car and stared at the steering wheel without really seeing it for a few minutes. Then he walked into the bar.

Upstairs in her room, Kate flipped through channels. She shut off the television and glanced around. "I've got to get out of this room," she muttered to herself. She threw on her exercise clothes and walked through the lobby to get to the gym. When she passed by the bar, she did a double-take after spotting Don. He was at a table all by himself. She stood and watched him drain the brown liquid in his glass and signal for another. She wandered over to his table.

"Detective Don Layden, welcome to the beautiful Marriott City Centre." Kate gave him a puzzled smile. "What brings you here?"

Don waved his hand around in a gesture to include the room. "I remembered seeing this bar when we moved you in. I liked the jazz I heard." He shrugged. "I think I'm here because I just didn't want to go home to all of the quiet there. Wanted to be around people."

Kate's smile disappeared as she slid into a seat across from him. "What's wrong?"

Don swirled the ice around in his glass and listened to the music the cubes made as they clinked against the walls of their container. "Don't know if you're going to believe me if I tell you."

Kate settled herself and patted Don's hand. "Try me, Detective."

Taking his time, Don explained his last few hours from the shootings at the station to Avery's strange death. "Maybe I'm just weirded out by the whole scene from the shooting at the station, but man, I have a serious case of the creeps right now."

Kate sat back, eyes wide. "Wow!" She leaned forward and rested her chin in her hand. "He must have fed the evil wolf."

"Don't speak in riddles," Don sighed. "I'm tired. You're supposed to be on my side, remember? What are you talking about? The last time I looked there weren't a lot of wolves wandering around in downtown Denver."

"Of course I'm on your side." Kate tilted her head and grinned at him. "I'm remembering a Cherokee Indian legend I heard Father Tim tell at church one time. It's the story of an Indian Chief who walks in the woods with his two small grandsons as he explains human behavior to them. He says there are two wolves fighting inside of everyone. One is evil and mean and hates. The other is humble and kind and shows patience and forgiveness. As his grandsons listen to him, their eyes grow wide. 'Grandfather, Grandfather! Tell us! Which wolf wins?' Their grandfather stops walking and looks deep into their eyes and answers, 'It's the one you feed.'"

Don sat back in his chair, folded his arms, and became quiet. The faintest hint of a smile played about the corners of his mouth as he gazed at the ceiling. After a few moments he considered Kate. "That makes a lot of sense."

Kate shrugged. "A lot of what Father Tim says makes sense."

"Sounds like he's good at his job." Don yawned. "Anyway, right now this case is in the hands of the medical professionals, Detective Daskalis, and his partner. Avery's episode is their issue. I have a killer of my own to catch." Don leaned forward as he retrieved his pen and small notebook out of his suit pocket. "I tried talking to Treavor about the list, but he won't open his mouth without his lawyer. I want to learn more about Barry Witt. Tell me everything you know. The more I know about him the better. How long did you work for him?"

"I made it a year. Luckily for me, he traveled a lot so I didn't have to endure his advances on a daily basis. I wanted to have a somewhat solid level of experience on my resume for my first job."

"I see. What details can you tell me about his investments? How did he get clients?"

Kate pursed her lips for a minute. "I think his dad was in real estate, so he started out in that arena. He traveled all over the state, and then he started traveling all over the country to find investment opportunities. I think he also networked at cocktail parties and at art shows and art performances too."

"Performances?"

"Yeah, like the opera or the ballet. He would go to the endowment dinners and things like that. He rubbed shoulders with some real wealth that way. He always wanted me to come with him, but I never did."

"Do you have any idea why he closed his office?"

"My guess would be the real estate bust during the Great Recession caused a problem for him that he couldn't recover from." Kate drummed her fingernails on the table. Then she sat up. "I know someone who might know more. Her name is Rosalyn Walker. She is an heiress who had been close to his family for years. She seemed about as close as Barry ever got to having a real mother. His own mother was just a social climber. The few times she came to the office, all she could talk about was what kind of car she drove or what ritzy event she attended." Kate shook her head as if to dislodge some disturbing memories. "Barry's parents traveled quite a bit and didn't really pay that much attention to him. I think Rosalyn Walker had him over for dinner now and then and showed him some kindness. Barry talked about her all of the time."

"How would I get in touch with her?"

"She's hard to reach because she has a few layers of people you have to go through to get to her." Kate raised her eyebrows. "But I know she is a big supporter of the Colorado Ballet, and as I recall she usually goes to opening night." Kate held up a finger. "Hang on a minute." She hustled out to the lobby and came back with a brochure from the Denver Performing Arts Complex nearby. "We're in luck. The opening performance for their Christmas show is Monday. They always do a dinner for their major contributors beforehand. Maybe I could get us in. I know someone I went to school with at BSU who works for the Colorado Ballet in their Finance Department."

"All right." He paused. "But I want to make something clear. You're going as my *date*." Don put quotation marks in the air with his fingers. "You will not pull anything like you did the other night. Do you hear me? You're not a trained law enforcement officer. Period."

Kate folded her hands together and bowed her head. "Of course. I promise to be good." She looked at Don through her eyelashes. "I was cleared in the investigation of the devil worship scene shooting."

"I know," Don frowned. "But no need for a next time. Got it?"

Kate smiled and held up three fingers. "Scout's honor."

Don got up and threw a couple of twenties on the table. "Okay, let me know if you can get us into the dinner. Thanks." Then he strode out the door into the cold night air. Due to the three drinks, he called Lyft to get home. Keep life simple.

On another continent, the turbulence surrounding the jet as it approached the airport in Brasilia, Brazil, was disconcerting. Rain pelted the windows as they landed on the wet runway. The killer knew it was a city of about two million people in the central plains of the country. He also knew December was the wettest month of the year. *What was I thinking when I decided to come here?* His hands were folded tightly in his lap, knuckles white.

Several bumps later, the jet stopped on the runway amidst a torrential downpour. The killer stared out the window, his face as gloomy as the weather.

A couple of hours later, he made it through customs and stood in front of the airport out in the rain in the hopes of nabbing a cab. The newspaper that he held as an umbrella wasn't helping much. After what seemed like an hour, he got into a taxi and sat while it inched forward in the bumper-to-bumper traffic. The wiper blades beat back and forth against the windshield in rhythm, struggling to clear the torrents of water streaming in rivers down the glass. The killer stared out the window, his elbow propped on the armrest and his chin in his hand. He could see only foggy glimpses of the city through the windshield on the slow ride to his hotel.

It took forever until he was in his room. He stripped off his wet clothes and huddled under the covers, falling asleep.

When he awoke, his head felt as foggy as the weather. He grabbed the clock and then stumbled to the window. *How to get anything done on a Sunday afternoon? Why didn't I think about the time change?*

Smacking the window, he plopped down into a chair. The room service menu was right next to him. He knew enough Portuguese to order a bottle of Scotch.

In Denver, Don was in a convenience store near his condo buying some cereal and milk when his phone rang. He didn't look at the screen when he answered, "Layden here." When he recognized the caller's voice, he put his products down on a nearby shelf and leaned against a wall, grinning. "Ryan! How are you, bro'? It's great to hear your voice!" He nodded his head as he listened to his brother. "I'd love to have you and your family come and stay with me for a ski vacation. My home is your home. Hopefully I can get some time off to ski with you. And yes, March is good. Always a great time to ski." He listened.

"Oh, the job's a little tough right now. I'm on a brutal case and my boss keeps dictating that I go out and search a bunch of dead-end clues. It was a good way to start the case, but Luke and I just couldn't interview a gajillion people in two days. Now the case has moved beyond that. But she just won't let up that we haven't finished those interviews. In spite of her, I'm still working on any other leads I run into, of course."

Don sighed, "My boss has the department running too thin. But I'm making progress. It's just excruciatingly slow." Don paused. "Yeah, can't wait to see you. Hey, sorry for unloading on you. I'm just frustrated." Don smiled. "Yeah, love you, too. Give Gretchen and the kids a hug for me." Still smiling, Don looked at the phone for a few seconds before he put it in his pocket and headed for the checkout.

In another aisle of the store, Sarah Snow stood stock still, holding a bright orange container of laundry soap. Frozen in place, she watched the door open and close when Don exited. She ran her tongue over her lips as she pondered what she had just heard.

Time zones away from Denver, a clap of thunder startled the killer out of his sleep. *Ugh.* A moan escaped his lips when he grabbed the clock and read that it was ten in the morning. Glancing over at the bottle of scotch, he saw it was now three-quarters gone. He held his head in his hands for a while and then stumbled into the shower. *Whew. Feeling a little better.* Searching the clothes he'd packed, he picked out one of his best Armani suits. *They need to see who they are dealing with!*

Walking over to the window, he saw that the rain was still coming down in sheets. He steadied himself with coffee and pastries and took another cab ride, this time to the address listed on his certificates. It was time to make his next move.

After getting out of the cab, he tried to open the door to the investment offices and it wouldn't budge. It was locked. *What?* Peering through the windows, he saw the offices inside were completely empty. *What's going on?* He walked over to the business next door, and a pretty girl with dyed blonde hair looked up from her work. "English?" *She wasn't going to be bright enough to know English, he just knew it.*

She smiled and shook her head.

The killer grunted and pointed to the business name on one of his certificates. "Where?" He searched his brain for the word in Portuguese. "Onde?"

She shook her head again and shrugged her shoulders.

"How long? Como longo?"

She held up a calendar and pointed to last Thursday.

"Obrigado." The killer walked back to the closed business and beat the glass until his fists couldn't take it anymore. Head hanging, he stood in the rain and tried to flag down a cab. Traffic cruised by him as though he wasn't there, and several cars splashed filthy muck all over his Armani suit. *Perfect! Can this get any worse?*

A cab stopped. *Finally!* "Policia," he directed. After another interminable cab ride, he arrived at the downtown Brasilia police station, which looked like it was understaffed judging by the number of people that needed help. Asking for direction, he ended up in a line that wound by grimy walls and through a battered doorway. *This is not acceptable.* Jostling and shoving amidst shouted curses, he made his way to the front desk. He pounded on the desk and pointed to his certificates. "Money gone! Theft! Roubo!"

The thick-necked, gray-haired Brazilian sergeant narrowed his eyes. "Back in line," he shouted in English. "Get back in line, American!"

The killer slammed the certificates on the desk. "No! Theft! Help now!"

Two large policemen got up from their desks where they were taking reports, came over and folded their arms. "Back in line," growled the sergeant. "Back in line or we throw you in jail!"

The killer looked from one officer to the other and trudged back to the end of the line. About two hours later, he was finally at the front of the line. "English?"

"Yes, some English."

Pointing to the address and the phone number on his certificates, Barry explained the scam and summarized his problem. "I want my money. I invested thousands and thousands of dollars, but now I cannot get in touch with this business. I came all the way down here from the United States to talk to them and their offices are closed. They took off with my money!"

"Fill out the form and put it in that box."

The killer's face turned red. "What? I've been in line for hours! I expect some action!"

"You get the same action as everyone else. Fill out a report and we will call you."

"When?"

"As soon as we get to it." A shrug. "Shouldn't be too long."

The killer raised his arms and opened his mouth to yell, but once again the two officers came over and showed him to a table where he could complete the form.

One more endless cab ride brought him back to his hotel. After taking a lengthy hot shower, a big, juicy steak was right up his alley. He dug into his meal, angrily slicing the meat and smacking his lips as he chewed and thought about his day. As he cut the last of his food, his steak knife gleamed when it caught the illumination from the lamp. The killer stopped chewing and studied it, turning it from side to side and watching the light reflect off the blade. Thirty minutes later, he put the room service tray outside in the hall.

No one would notice a missing knife.

THIRTY-TWO

In Denver, Don was in a counselor's office at the high school Barry went to. A yearbook lay open to Barry's senior picture.

The counselor leaned back in his chair. "I got here after Barry graduated but there are a couple of teachers still here who might remember him. Wait a few minutes while I make some calls."

Two elderly teachers came down to look at Barry's photo, but they had no recollection of the student. Then an old shop teacher shuffled into the office and studied the yearbook.

"Yup. Barry Witt. I remember him." The old man pointed at Barry's picture. "He was a lost, lonely young man. Didn't have any friends, really, far as I could tell. I felt sorry for him." The teacher regarded Don. "He had good skills in my class. Did good work. I encouraged him. He often dropped by my classroom after school to ask questions." The instructor put his hands in his pockets. "I could tell he was figuring out excuses to just spend time with me. One day I noticed a sketch of a sword on his notebook and that gave me the idea to start a knife sculpting unit in my shop class."

"What? You taught high school kids how to make knives?"

"It was before Columbine. I don't teach that anymore."

"Good."

"Anyway, Barry really excelled at it. He made some beautiful knives in class. As a matter of fact, he made one for me. I still have it."

Don stood up. "I appreciate the information. Thank you for your help."

The old man stood there, shifting his weight from one foot to the other. "I hope Barry's okay. I try to help the lost ones. He was bullied back then. We know more now. We would've intervened. High school can be hard on the less popular kids."

"I can tell you one thing for sure: we could use a lot more teachers like you." Don shook his hand.

He got back in his car and leaned his head against the headrest to think. Belinda would want him work on the files. But he wanted to keep digging into Barry Witt. He gave Rebecca a call. Maybe she could do some research for him. Then he went to work on the files.

A few hours later, Don replaced a hated file into the hated box and slammed the trunk of the Crown Vic. After filling out his part of the paperwork to get the investigation into Avery's death closed and working on the files as he knew Belinda would ask about, he was tired. He looked at his watch and his face relaxed. The last game of the season was coming up. In spite of their recent losses, the Eagles still owned the best record. If they won this one, they would win the league championship. He got back into the car and wondered how he'd lead his team to victory without Luke. A smile crept on his face and he made a call.

"Hi Kate, this is Don Layden." All of a sudden, his palms were sweaty and he wiped each one of them on his pants, fumbling with the phone as he switched hands to do so. "Lucy's the same, but I do have an update on the case. However, right now I need a favor. With Luke out, I was hoping you wouldn't mind covering for him on the coaching front. It would really help us out and I can fill you in on what I learned about the case after the game." Don held the phone away from his ear as Kate's excitement spilled out of it and into the car. "I'll take that as a yes. I'll be there in a few minutes."

On the way to pick up Kate, Don found himself surprised at how much he was looking forward to seeing her. When he pulled up, he saw Kate waiting outside in front of the hotel wearing a big grin and a bright orange BSU jacket.

She jumped in the car and squealed, "Are you excited? Your team is playing for the championship!"

Don nodded. "Yes, as a matter of fact, I am."

Kate's smile broke for a moment. "How did you get your car? Did you call Lyft? I would have given you a ride."

"I just grabbed a Lyft here in the morning and then drove my SUV home and switched to the Crown Vic. I drank three scotches fairly quickly last night. Driving would have been a bad decision."

"Yeah, but I could have given you a ride."

"No big deal. I just took care of it." He held up his hand as if to signal the case was closed.

Kate shrugged. "Okay." Then she rubbed her hands together in anticipation. "So, fill me in on what I need to know to help the Eagles win this championship!"

Don threw back his head and laughed. Then he handed her a team roster and started in on the details. "So, there you have it," he summarized. "Now you know about a little about our offense and a fair amount about our defense. I need you to coach the defense."

He glanced over at Kate. She had her hands clasped together and was staring at them.

"Kate? You praying or somethin'?"

"What?" Kate blinked and looked at her hands. "Oh." She giggled. "No, I was thinking about different defenses I could run in different situations." Her forehead creased. "I hope I don't mess up!"

Don reached over and squeezed her shoulder. "You won't mess up. I have faith in you."

"Thanks." She clasped her hands together again. "Maybe praying is a good idea."

Don chuckled as he parked the car.

The game started and it was a defensive battle. No scores. Then right before half time, a Lions running back broke free for a touchdown.

The Eagles' defensive players trudged off the field, heads hanging. Don took a few steps toward them but stopped. Kate was already there to greet them and called to them to gather around her. She clapped her hands together. "That's okay, men, that's okay! It's one score! Not a problem! Let's talk about what happened so it doesn't happen again, sound like a plan?" Sad faces looked at her and nodded. She got down on her knees as she talked with each player so that she could look at them in the eyes.

By the time she was finished, the boys were pounding each other on their shoulder pads. "Yeah! Let's go get 'em!"

Don's heart softened and he found it hard to tear his sight away from the scene. A player tugged on his sleeve.

"Coach, what's the plan for the next half?"

He blinked and grabbed his clipboard as he focused on the offense. The corners of his mouth were upturned as he talked to his players.

The second half started and once again defense ruled. The Lions' running back that scored the touchdown got the ball, but the Eagles' defense closed in and tackled him right away.

Kate jumped up and down, screaming. "That's it! That's it! Way to do it! Great stop, men, great stop!"

Don grinned and ran over to her. "That was beautiful."

"Thanks." Kate's eyes shone.

As the fourth quarter wound down, the Eagles' quarterback dropped back and threw a beautiful pass to his receiver, tying the score. The Eagles punted the ball to the Lions, but their player fumbled. An Eagles' player recovered and scored! They won the game! The team fell all over each other in one giant, screaming mass of wiggling arms and legs.

Kate hopped around the boys and, as they peeled off of one another, she pounded them on their shoulder pads. The players pounded her shoulders in response.

Don's lips twitched as he watched. Then he ran over. "Hey guys, don't forget she's not wearing any shoulder pads."

Kate waved a hand. "I'm loving every minute! Don't worry about it!"

The referee called Don and the team over for the trophy presentation. Don beamed from ear to ear as he held it over his head. "Gentlemen! You are the champions!" The celebration continued for some time before Don finally called for everyone to go out for pizza.

Hours later, after the final Eagle player left, Don walked back to the table where Kate was and sat down to admire the trophy.

"Good job, Coach." Kate grinned at him.

"Good job yourself." Don held up his fist, and she laughed and bumped it with her own.

She sighed and rested her chin in her hand as she smiled at him. "I have to tell you, you do a wonderful job with those boys. It's really something to watch. They learn a lot from you; how to overcome making mistakes and to celebrate the right things." She paused in thought. "I've read that humans become what they celebrate. If they celebrate victories in gang violence, then they become violent. If they celebrate love, learning, and triumph over tough times, then that's the behavior they follow. They love, they learn, and they over-come problems." She swallowed the lump that formed in her throat. "Good for you, Don Layden."

"Thanks." He shrugged. "I have fun with it." Don then pulled his notebook out of a pocket. "Let me tell you about a meeting I had earlier at Barry's high school."

When he finished, Kate looked down at the table. "Wow. I had no idea. That's just terrible. And then I ignore him at Jose's. I feel awful."

"Maybe you can schedule a speaker to come and talk to your Bible study group about bullying when this is all over. Help someone in the future. But right now, I want to go over this with Luke. I'll drop you off at the hotel and head over to the hospital." He held up the trophy. "Besides, I have to show him this."

The next morning Don whistled louder than Belle as he made his morning coffee. In response, Belle chirped and whistled. "Today's going to be a good day, right Belle?" She chirped right on cue. Don laughed and sat down to read the paper, but he kept checking his watch. It seemed like forever until the time showed it was eight o'clock. He made yet another call to Treavor's lawyer.

He got an associate on the phone and listened to her reply. Don jumped up and yelled, "Are you serious?" Belle fluttered off his shoulder. "I can't believe I can't reach him again today! I can't ever reach him! When will he be in?"

"He's simply not here."

Don grunted in disgust. "Isn't there anyone else who can be present? I just want to ask Treavor a couple of questions!" Don sighed as he listened to the reply. "Yes, I know. And I want you to know that I have to be the first person he calls when he gets back into town."

Don hung up and plopped down. He put his elbows on the table and held his head in his hands as he stared at the table. In his peripheral vision, a movement caught his attention. He watched as Belle tottered over to him, climbed on his sock, and then made her way up his pants leg. As Don leaned back to observe her, his face relaxed. He held his finger out to her and she climbed on. Don held her up to his face and stared at her for a few minutes.

"Let's go visit Uelle, shall we Belle? Your wings were just clipped so you won't fly away and get into trouble. I think Uelle would like you there too. I haven't visited her as often since Lucy got hurt. I need to go."

In less than an hour he was at the cemetery. He watched Belle climb on the tombstone. Then he ran his hand through his hair and sighed. "Oh honey, this case is driving me crazy. I want it to be over. I live with the fear someone else is going to get hurt. I finally have a person of interest but tying him to the murders is slow. I just don't want anyone else to lose someone they love..." He looked at the tombstone. "...to feel this pain." He dropped his head and opened his hand, exposing the rosary Mary had given him. He stared at it for a long time.

It was early and the city of Denver was waking up. Anyone who was outside wore a big, warm coat. Sarah Snow sat in a coffee shop near the police station, wearing glasses and a green wool hat that hid her hair. She pretended to read a newspaper. There was no cameraman with her today.

Before long, two uniformed policemen walked in, one tall and burley and one shorter and paunchy. They sat down to order breakfast. Sarah listened as a heavyset waitress with curly gray hair and bright red lipstick bantered back and forth with them. They knew her name and she knew what they wanted before they asked for it. Sarah waited until the waitress left, then walked by their table.

"Hi gentlemen, how are two of Denver's finest doing today?" She beamed her best smile at them, focusing on the one who was not wearing a wedding ring.

He smiled back at her. "We're good. We're keeping Denver safe, as usual."

Sarah's smile faded just a bit. "What about the hatchet man? Any luck with him?"

The police officer became sober. "Can't talk about that one."

"Oh. At any rate, I am certain that you have every man on it. A case like that must take a lot of man-hours. Of course you don't want anyone else to get hurt."

The two men exchanged looks. One of them opened his mouth to answer when a call came over the radio. "Nine-twenty-one to sixteenth and Larimer. Investigate a 2-1-1."

Both men got up to answer the call. The one who had been talking to Sarah rubbed his eyes. "You've got to be kidding me! We've been on the run for ten hours. I'm hungry!"

Sarah moved to block their path. "Surely there is someone else who can take the call besides you. You were just getting a meal."

The married officer grunted. "Yeah, right." He frowned at Sarah and shook his head while his partner cancelled their order.

Sarah snatched a couple of wrapped muffins out of a basket on the counter and handed them to the men. "Here, take these. My treat."

Thanking her, they grabbed the muffins and dashed out of the door. Sarah watched the police car roar down the street, sirens wailing and lights pulsating. Her eyes narrowed. Spinning around, she went back to her booth. When the waitress came by to refill her coffee, Sarah pounced.

"Hi." Sarah made a point to look at the waitress's nametag, even though her name was already in Sarah's memory from listening to her earlier conversation with the officers. "Hi, Libby. Please put two muffins on my check. I just gave those two poor police officers muffins as they rushed out the door."

She shook her head in dismay. "I think it's terrible that they couldn't even eat breakfast after ten hours of work! That's almost as much of a crime as the things they have to give people tickets for, don't you think?"

Libby's eyes widened and she reached over to touch Sarah's arm. "Oh dearie, you are so right! Those poor men work their tails off!" She motioned to the door. "You saw what just happened? Dearie, I am here to tell you that happens all the time. As a matter of fact, it happens almost every day!" Libby clucked her disapproval.

Sarah's eyebrows shot up. "Really?"

"This place is a favorite stop for the cops. I've worked here for thirty years, and I swear on my mother's grave, it has gotten worse and worse for them the past couple of years."

Sarah frowned. "That's a shame." She patted Libby's hand. "Wow! Thirty years! I'll bet you know a lot!"

"Oh, yes I do, dearie." Libby rattled on and on as Sarah sat and nodded, offering an occasional murmur of sympathy and encouragement.

THIRTY-THREE

Downtown at the police station, Don surfed the Internet, researching old articles on real estate during the financial meltdown that kicked off in 2008, looking for any news on Barry Witt. There were hundreds of articles on businesses that failed during that period. Finally, he found two sentences in the financial section of *The Denver Post* that were significant to his query. The reported relocation of the offices of Witt Investments appeared and the address given was Barry's home address. Don sat back and folded his arms. *How did Barry make an income? Was he able to keep working out of his home?* He tapped a finger on his chin as he thought. With a sigh, he called Treavor's lawyer again and found himself speaking to the answering service. "Hi, it's Don Layden calling again. Has he called in to check his messages?"

"No, Detective Layden."

"Thanks." Don tried not to growl.

"Okay, let's try Barry's substitute mother yet again," Don muttered to himself. He dialed Rosalyn Walker's number and left another message.

Before he even put his phone back down, Rebecca called. "Hi, Don. I found something in the legal data about a suit Barry filed. He was developing a real estate app, but he claimed someone by the name of Patty Johnson stole his idea."

"Did he win?"

"No, not enough evidence to prove it."

"Can you get her contact information for me?"

"She retired and moved away but I'll see what I can find."

"Shoot. What was the app?"

"Just something folks looking for a home could put on their phones to alert them when a property came available within parameters that they set."

Don's jaw dropped. "I have that app. Needed it when I was looking for my condo."

"Yeah, I have it too. It's a good one. I'll bet a lot of people have it."

"Okay, thanks Rebecca. Let me know if you find anything else."

"Absolutely."

Don hung up the phone and leaned back in his chair. *Wow. If Barry's app got stolen, he'd be really pissed off. And I wouldn't blame him.* Returning to the Internet, Don searched for information tied to Barry Witt, Witt Investments, and even Barry Witt's father.

A voice behind him pierced the air. "What do you think you are doing, Don Layden?"

Don startled, then took his time as he turned around. "I am following up on a good lead, Belinda."

"And where did you get this lead?"

Don paused. "From the files."

Her eyes lit up in triumph. "Amazing! Isn't it crazy what a little leg work can do? If Gail and Wanda were still with us I'd bet they'd agree with me." She spun around and marched into her office, slamming the door behind her.

Don's chin dropped to his chest and a feeling of claustrophobia overcame him. He turned off his computer and walked outside. The air was crisp. The city smelled like ski season. He turned and gazed at the snow-covered mountains. Shaking himself, he pulled out the pocket-sized notebook he kept in his jacket and fingered through it. He stopped at a page containing Barry Witt's home address and stared at it. Spinning around, he headed for the Crown Vic and took off.

When he got off the exit leading to Barry's house, he spotted a convenience store that also sold tee shirts, sweatshirts, and some sweaters. On impulse, he pulled into the parking lot and rushed into the store, deciding on a navy blue Denver Bronco sweatshirt which would make it easy to blend in anywhere. After Don took off his jacket and pulled the sweatshirt over his head, he proceeded on his way. When he came upon Barry's house he slowed but continued down the street.

Barry's house was dark. Maybe he wasn't home. Maybe he was sleeping in late. Maybe he was in his office and his office was in the back. Don stopped on a side street and parked. He turned off the ignition and sat there a minute. "Don't do anything stupid, Layden," he muttered to himself. "You're just here to get a feel for this guy's territory. Don't do anything that will get any evidence thrown out." He took a deep breath, put on a Vail baseball cap and started walking towards Barry's house. He tried not to stare at it as he approached it, focusing on the home and on appearing nonchalant at the same time.

The next thing he knew, he heard a growl behind him and he spun around to face a Doberman pinscher's fangs about twenty feet away. Backing up, he held out his hands. "Go home, dog, go home. I'm not hurting anyone, just go home." Don kept his voice down. The last thing he wanted to do was attract attention. The Doberman moved forward step by step, head down and teeth bared. "Come on, you have a collar. Where's your owner for crying out loud? Just go home. Get some breakfast." Don found himself backed up against a fence. The dog continued to advance. "What is wrong with you, you mutt?" He turned and scaled the fence as fast as he could, but the dog sprang at him and grabbed his pants leg pulling him down. Don kept a tight grip on the top of the fence, shaking his leg trying to dislodge the dog. His sleeve caught on a nail as he tried to climb over and he struggled, tearing it. His pants leg finally tore, and the snarling dog dropped away as Don scrambled over the fence, but the top of the fence was unfinished and he ran his leg over a couple of nails drawing blood.

He dropped to the other side as the Doberman threw his body against the fence, barking and growling. Don leaned over with his hands on his thighs, breathing hard and watched as blood flowed down his leg. "So much for getting the lay of the land." He grabbed a handkerchief out of his pocket and applied it to the wound. "More stitches. This wonderful case is getting me all kinds of new scars." When the dog finally grew tired of his attack and took off, Don made his way back to the Crown Vic and drove to the hospital.

Kate was on her way home from an early morning of skiing at Breckenridge when her phone rang. She checked the caller ID and saw that it was Vicki Zurn, who was working with her on the toy drive. She put it on speaker. "Hi Vicki, what's up?"

"Hi Kate. I'm not calling you at a bad time, am I?"

"Nope, this is a perfect time. I'm just heading down the hill from a very pleasant morning of skiing."

"Sounds nice, I hope you took a few turns for me. Hey listen, I was thinking we could go through some of the toys before Gail's service tonight. We only have a couple of days before we have to get everything over to Father Bill at Regis University. I know I'm not going to feel up to it after the funeral."

Kate sighed. "You read my mind. That's why I only skied a few runs. I just hadn't gotten around to calling you yet. I'll meet you there at three."

"Okay, sounds good. See you then."

Kate's face darkened as she pondered the funeral of another friend. She arrived at St. James a couple of minutes early and opened the door to the meeting room they used as the drop-off for the toy drive. She stepped back and scratched her chin.

"Wow." Kate spun around at the sound of Vicki's voice behind her.

Vicki looked at her friend. "It's a good thing we came early."

"You walked in at just the right time." Kate put a hand to her forehead. "I was about ready to pass out."

Vicki wagged a finger near Kate's face. "No passing out allowed. No time for that." The tall, lanky woman ran a hand through her short, cocoa brown hair. "Let's divide the toys by age group first and then by gender."

Kate pulled a letter out of her coat pocket and waved it in front of her friend's face. "How'd you guess? That's exactly how Father Bill wants it. How about if I take the left section of the room and you take the right? I brought some Post-it notes to mark the age groups on the walls to help us stay organized."

Vicki agreed and both women set to work, chatting as they sorted. After about ninety minutes, Kate stretched her arms over her head and looked at the room. Although it was still full, the toys were now organized in bins and ready to go. Kate surveyed the scene and gave a thumbs up. "Miss Vicki, you do good work."

"We make a good team. I think all we have left to do is to load the stuff into the van and take it over to Regis and Father Bill."

"I've already cleared using the church van with Father Tim, so that's a go."

"Sounds good." Vicki glanced out of the window and then froze. "Whoa."

Kate followed Vicki's gaze. Outside, there were already hundreds of people streaming into the church. She blinked. "Whoa is right. Why are so many people here?"

"I don't know, but I think we'd better go grab a seat while we have a chance." The two women closed the room and made their way into the church.

Sarah Snow stood outside wearing her cobalt blue coat and some high fashion black boots. The soft wind ruffled her blond curls. She approached a husband and wife as they headed into the church with their hands entwined.

Walking up to them, Sarah introduced herself. "Would you mind taking a couple of minutes for an interview?"

The woman took a step back and shook her head. "No! We are here to pay tribute to our friend." Her voice started shaking. "This is not a circus event! Show some respect!" She turned away and her husband glared at Sarah as he put his arm around his wife's shoulders and led her into the church.

Sarah glanced at the cameraman. "Okay, that choice didn't work out. Let's try again."

Her colleague took the camera off his shoulder and scratched his head. "I don't know about this, Sarah. We might be crossing a line."

Sarah waved a finger at him. "Nonsense. Look at all of these people, Mike. This is clearly a news event. And it appears as though we have the exclusive coverage." Her eyes widened. "I love it when that happens!"

The cameraman grumbled to himself as she approached another couple. This time the response was positive and, after she smoothed her hair, Sarah signaled to the cameraman to start recording.

"We are here covering the memorial service for Gail Gonzalez, the elementary school teacher who met her death at the hands of Denver's still at large serial killer," reported Sarah while she gripped the microphone with both hands. "Three Catholic Denver women, all members of St. James Catholic Church, are now dead. We are here talking to some of the worshippers to hear their thoughts."

She stood aside and acknowledged the couple standing near her. "How did you know the deceased?"

A small, dark-haired woman stood with her gloved hands clutched to the front of her gray wool coat, attempting to tighten it around herself as a protection from the chill. Her husband stood close to her, his hand supporting her lower back as she answered, "We didn't know Ms. Gonzalez. We are here because the killer is murdering religious women. We want to stand up and show our support for the victim's family members. We also want to show support for religion." Her eyes bored into Sarah's. "If we lose God, we lose humanity."

Sarah leaned forward. "So, you think these are hate crimes?"

The woman nodded and wiped her eyes.

Sarah tilted her head in empathy towards the woman before addressing the next question to her husband. "And how do you expect the Denver Police Department to be handling this?"

"I have no doubt that every member of the department is working hard on this case. I'm a hundred percent certain that they will find the killer before another woman has her life taken."

Sarah pursed her mouth and brought the microphone back to her lips. "What if I told you I have a source who confirms that the Denver Police Department is spread so thin that they only have two men on the case?"

The man straightened up and his eyes darkened. "Is that true?"

"According to my source, only two detectives are covering this case and one of them has an extremely ill daughter in the hospital at this very moment."

The man clenched his fist at his side. "That's an absolute outrage! Women are losing their lives to a psychotic killer and only two men are working the case?"

Sarah turned back to the camera. "You can see for yourself. The citizens of Denver are infuriated over the lack of manpower on this case. While innocent religious women are being systematically murdered in their own homes, the people in charge at the Denver Police Department have reduced the staff to next to nothing, causing a strain on the overworked force. One of my sources tells me that the police think this crime might be the one that finally exposes this weakness to the public." Sarah peered into the camera. "I hope it doesn't take another murder to get additional staff on the case."

The reporter turned and thanked the couple and watched as they stalked towards the church entrance, waving their arms in frustration. They stopped other churchgoers, and soon there was angry undercurrent rumbling through the crowd.

Sarah turned back to the cameraman and patted him on the shoulder. "I do believe we just made the national news."

Inside it was standing room only. Father Tim glanced outside and he could see more people walking towards the church. He stood near the front, turned on his mic, smiled at the growing crowd and encouraged them to move up and fill in empty seats. Before long, the service began.

This time a tall, slender brunette walked up to the lectern to speak after the readings. "Hi, my name is Marilyn. Gail was a good friend of mine and I'd like to tell you about her." After about ten minutes of funny anecdotes, she paused and gazed out at the many attendees. "Gail kept a saying by a businessman named Stephen M. Wolf on her desk. It gives a good description of how she lived her life." Marilyn picked up a frame and took a deep breath.

"Each of us can look back upon someone who made a great difference in our lives,

Someone whose wisdom and simple acts of caring made an impression upon us.

In all likelihood it was someone who sought no recognition for their deed

Other than the joy of knowing that, by their hand, another's life had been made better."

Marilyn raised her eyes. "That was Gail."

While the hundreds of mourners contemplated her words as she walked back to her seat, the church was completely silent.

THIRTY-FOUR

Kate felt unsettled during the dinner that followed the funeral. After the scene Sarah Snow stirred up, the peace usually found there was diminished. Saying her goodbyes early, Kate left. Putting the key in the ignition, she stared out the windshield. Facing an empty hotel room was not doing it for her. Pounding the steering wheel with her fist she yelled, "Murderer! You're such a monster!" She thought for a minute. "And I'm a coward for letting you banish me to a hotel room. That's it. No more." She went to the Marriott to collect her things and then moved back into her condo. She sat and contemplated her walls for a few minutes and then got back in her car and drove to the hospital to see Lucy.

When Kate walked in, Sabrina and Luke were both standing next to Lucy. Sabrina's face was wet. "Are you two okay?"

Luke glanced at his wife and then back at Kate. "We're just tired."

"What do the doctors say?"

"Same thing."

Kate hugged both of them and stepped back. "I wish I could wave my magic wand and make Lucy better. But the best I can do is to pray for you."

"I know." Sabrina blew her nose and looked at Luke. "I'm going for a walk to get a little fresh air. I need a break from these medical fumes."

Luke kissed his wife, watched her walk out the door. He turned to Kate. "We're having a bad day."

They both gazed at Lucy and after a few moments Luke cleared his throat. "So, I have a question for you."

Kate raised her eyebrows with curiosity.

"How do you pray?" He shook a finger at her. "Tell me without one of your long lectures."

Kate smiled at Luke. "You just have a conversation with God."

Luke snorted. "How do you have a conversation with someone who doesn't talk back?"

Kate laughed. "He does talk back, but he whispers. You don't listen with your ears, you listen with your heart."

Luke's eyebrows drew together. "How?"

"Try telling him one thing you thought you did well today and one thing that you could have done better. Then you ask for his help on the things that you could have done better."

Luke considered. "Sounds easy enough."

"It is. And while you're at it, you could thank him for your beautiful family." Kate poked him in the chest. "See? It's easy."

The corners of Luke's mouth turned up a bit.

"Just nurture your relationship with God. Think about a plant. To get it started and keep it going, you have to water it. If you stop watering it and ignore it, it will die. Your relationship with God is the same. Just keep watering it. It works."

"Hmmm." Luke turned back to gaze at his daughter. Kate watched him out of the corner of her eye as he folded his hands and looked down.

After getting stitches, Don was on his way home when he decided to swing by The Children's Hospital. He stood at the door to Lucy's room for a second. Luke and Sabrina sat near Lucy's bed, staring at her and holding hands. Kate stood on the other side of the bed with her back to the door.

"Hi," Don said as he entered. He nodded to the others and walked over to Lucy. "Hi Lucy, it's Uncle Don. I didn't want to go home without coming to visit you." He gently stroked her cheek and held her hand as he murmured to her. Then he walked over to his partner, squeezed his shoulder, and handed him a laptop. "I brought one from the department like you asked."

Luke rubbed his head. "Hey, Cheeto. Thanks." He leaned his head from side to side, stretching his neck. "I feel like I'm in some kind of a trance or something." He gazed at the computer, blinking.

"Come on pal, can I buy you a cup of coffee? Do you want to talk about the case at all? You don't have to." Don shrugged. "Whatever you want to do is fine with me."

Slowly, Luke nodded. "Yeah, I'll drink some coffee and talk about the case." He turned towards Sabrina and rubbed her shoulder. "Okay with you?"

The corners of her mouth moved up ever so slightly as she leaned her head on his hand. "Sure. Maybe Kate should go too?"

Luke leaned over to give his wife a kiss and followed Don and Kate out of the room.

In the cafeteria, Kate, Don, and Luke sat around a table, each holding a cup of steaming hot coffee in white Styrofoam cups.

Don brought them up to speed. "So, he basically had no parents, got bullied in high school, and he invented a popular app but someone stole the idea. He sued her and lost. Then the Great Recession hit and his business eventually failed. And after all of that, he was sitting at a bar having a drink and was once again ignored by a former employee who he felt he owned when she worked for him," Don summarized. "It's like everything built up."

"Plus, now he's all over the news," Luke noted. "For the first time in his life he's actually getting some attention."

"Yup," Don agreed. "The other thing is that he's really into blades. He's definitely got my attention. However, I just can't make a connection to the case."

Luke patted his partner on the back. "Cheeto, when we get stuck, what do we always do?" He stood up and pantomimed digging a hole. "We keep digging man, we keep digging." He pointed at Don. "Sounds to me like you need to keep digging for more information on Barry Witt."

"I've found out about as much info online as there is." Don sat back and folded his arms. "I've been trying to track down this Rosalyn Walker. I guess she was the only one who paid any attention to him while he was growing up. But I haven't been able to get through. That woman has a fortress around her."

Eyes wide, Kate leaned forward. "I almost spaced. Don, after you and I spoke at the Marriott the other night I left a message for my BSU friend about getting tickets for Monday evening. She called me back this morning. She can leave me two tickets at will call if I still want them. Do you still happen to have that brochure I gave you by any chance?"

Don looked at his phone. "Yeah, I took a picture of it." He frowned as he scrolled. "Huh. Turns out they're high-lighting a chef from Paris. He's the brother of one of their new dancers. He'll be the one cooking the dinner."

Luke frowned. "Ballet is where they dance around the stage on their toes. What does dinner have to do with it?"

"It's a fundraiser. All of the rich folks that help keep the Colorado Ballet afloat will be there. It'll be perfect! Good opportunity to find Rosalyn and maybe even Barry." She patted her phone. "I'll call my friend and make sure about the tickets."

Luke leaned toward Kate so that his face was very close to hers. He pressed his lips in a straight line as he stared at her for a minute. "Calm down Miss *I-want-to-catch-a-bad-guy-but-am-completely-clueless.*" Luke leaned back and folded his arms. "What's the goal?"

Kate twirled her hair around a finger. "To find information on Barry Witt."

"How are you going to do that?"

"We're going to ask questions."

"What questions are you gonna ask? Who are you gonna ask? How will you approach them? What if you do see Barry there? Do you know enough about the law to keep from making a mistake that could get him off down the road? How are you going to be believable as a couple at the ballet?"

Kate blinked. "Well…"

"Yeah, that's what I thought."

Kate studied at her hands then smacked Luke lightly on the shoulder. "You make me so mad sometimes."

"You need to remember that you don't have a corner on the intersection of 'I'm Always Right' and 'I Know All.' You need to remember you have some things to learn." Luke's words were a little too clipped.

Kate folded her hands in her lap. "Okay, I hear you," she whispered. "I just really want to get this guy."

"Catching a murderer has to be approached carefully." Don squinted. "When you're putting your budgets together, what do you do?"

"I look at our history, our trends, the marketplace, the projections for the upcoming year, and then I map everything out on spreadsheets and…"

"Exactly," Don interrupted. "You take a methodical approach to get to the right outcome. We have to do the same thing here." He gazed at Kate for a few seconds. "Only here, the stakes are a lot higher if you make a mistake." He took a sip of coffee. "Let's put our heads together. Come up with a plan."

An hour later they all got up to leave. As Kate buttoned her coat she said, "I'm heading home for a good night's sleep so I can be ready."

Don looked at his phone. "It's pretty sad that you are calling the Marriott *home*."

Once again, Kate examined her hands. "Actually, I moved back into my condo."

Don nearly dropped his phone. "What?" He started waving his arms. "You kidding me? What are you thinking?" He put his phone in his pocket and grabbed her by the shoulders. "Why would you do that?"

Kate raised her chin along with her voice. "Because I'm not a coward, he is. I'm not going to let him make me live in a hotel room."

Don dropped his hands to his sides and clenched his fists. "Kate this guy wants to kill you. Don't you see that? Your dead friends set an example anybody with any brains wouldn't want to follow."

"I'm tougher than they were. He's not going to get me. I have a gun and I can defend myself. I'll see you at my place tomorrow night." With that, she marched out the door.

"How can such a bright woman be such an idiot?" Don spun around and glared at Luke.

"I dunno, Cheeto." Luke shook his head and pointed at the coffee. "Looks like you better invest in some more. I have a feeling I know where you're going to be spending the night. You have a blanket in the Crown Vic?"

THIRTY-FIVE

Belinda reached for her remote and turned off the TV. She felt the anger boiling inside of her after watching Sarah Snow on the early morning news. *Sarah Snot would be a better name for her. And where the hell did she get that information?* She reached for her phone and dialed.

"Don Layden, what the hell have you told Sarah Snow?" She paused. "All right, if you haven't spoken to her since Gail's scene then how does she know how many men I've assigned to the case? How does she know the number of interviews you were supposed to have? How does she have all of this information?" She listened again. "Sounds like she's too good at snooping and she's made this case even worse now. So, solve it and make sure you get that in the news!"

Across town, the mayor's PR manager leaned back in his recliner after watching Sarah Snow's news clip. Sipping his coffee, he stared at the TV screen without listening and then picked up his phone.

At Denver International Airport, the killer's flight touched down and taxied to the gate. As soon as the tires hit the tarmac, he had the phone to his ear. "Yes David, I think our investments in Brazil are set, but we are going to want to keep those funds there for a while so they have time to grow. Let's diversify by putting additional funds into some other investments." He listened. "Yes, just like you studied in school. We should branch out to other churches. Can you look into that for me?" A smile. "Great. Thanks."

As he walked to his car, he noticed the last traces of the night sky chased away by the sun as it rose up over the mountains and etched pink in the clouds. He got to his car and started it up, rubbing his hands together for warmth as he watched people carrying gifts wrapped in bright red, green, and gold Christmas paper.

He growled under his breath and glanced at his phone. Touching the stuffed dog in his pocket he said "Buddy, taking a picture of that list was smart, wasn't it?" Scrolling through his contact list, he stopped when he came to Kate's name and address. He pulled out of the parking lot.

As the dawn aged, the city came alive and its symphony of sounds strummed as buses braked, garbage trucks groaned, and cars cruised by. Still in the Crown Vic, Don watched the sky and his mind drifted to thoughts of Uelle. He shook himself and noticed a security guard walk into the lobby of Kate's building. He got out of the car and stretched. "Man, that was one long, cold night."

A jogger glanced over his shoulder as he ran by Don.

Don touched his head in a little salute to the retreating jogger. "You spend winter nights in a car waiting for a murderer to show up and you'll talk to yourself too, pal," he muttered to himself.

Don hastened to catch up with the security guard. "Hey, can I speak with you for a minute?" Don showed the guard his badge, and a picture of Barry Witt on his phone. After their conversation, Don handed the guard his card and took off.

As the killer drove into the city from the airport, he listened to some classical music while a spooky smile played on his lips. Buddy was on the front seat. "So, Kate thinks she can just ignore me like she used to when she was mine at work. Well guess what, Buddy? Something tells me she's not going to ignore me today." As the anger coursed through his veins, he stepped on the accelerator.

Before he knew what was happening, his car spun out of control on the icy streets. Crunch! The sound of metal hitting metal caused his stomach to flip. He gasped but couldn't catch a breath because his face was covered. "Are you kidding me?" He escaped from the safety device and pounded the dashboard. "I was two blocks away!"

He heard a man knock on his window. He opened the door and the man asked, "You okay?"

Barry nodded.

The man pointed to his crunched Ford. "You have insurance? I just called the cops. I think we should get a police report."

Barry closed his eyes in frustration.

Soon after he arrived for the work day at City Hall, the mayor's PR manager, Ethan Hamilton, strode into a conference room and placed a pen and a legal pad on a beautiful walnut table. He flicked a piece of lint off his charcoal gray suit, straightened his navy blue tie, and smoothed his ash-blonde hair. Then he walked out to greet the visitor in the reception area and introduce himself.

As Sarah Snow stood up to shake his hand, he bent down. At six foot two, he towered over her, but wanted her to feel comfortable. He hoped to get through this thing without using any strong-arm tactics.

Ethan led Sarah into the elegant conference room and motioned to a chair for her to sit. "Would you like any water or a soda?" She shook her head. Ethan sat down and folded his hands on the legal pad. "I saw your story on the manpower issue at the police department this morning. It was very interesting."

"Thank you." Sarah smiled her practiced smile and waited.

"How did you get that information, may I ask?"

Sarah raised her eyebrows slightly. "I'm sorry sir, but I cannot reveal my sources."

"I see." Ethan picked up the black pen and tapped it on the yellow legal pad. "So according to *your sources*, the entire police department is undermanned and overworked?"

"It's not the entire department yet, but that seems to be the trend. It started under the watch of Belinda Mann in the Homicide Department. She's received several awards and much recognition for reducing the staffing and maintaining crime levels. Because of that her staffing model is spreading to other departments." Sarah tapped a pink manicured nail on the table for a moment. "It sounds to me as though Belinda Mann was just lucky before now. Now she has a case that is a real problem and she doesn't have the manpower to solve it." Sarah leaned forward. "Mr. Hamilton, the treatment of the officers is an embarrassment. As I worked on this, I saw men that didn't even have time to take a thirty-minute break on a ten-hour shift. I'm appalled that our police force is treated like dogs."

"That's a little harsh, don't you think?"

"I call it the way I see it."

Ethan clicked his pen and held it over the paper. "Is there any information you can give me so I can make contact with some of the people you spoke with on this?"

"No." Sarah tossed her head and stood up. "Will that be all?"

Blinking, Ethan hastened to his feet. "Uh… yes, I suppose so." He straightened his tie. "Let me show you out."

Sarah waved a hand. "Don't bother, I can find my way." She marched out of the room, her blonde curls bouncing against her flashy pink suit.

◅◈ ◈ ◈▻

Don hung up his jump rope and wiped off the sweat after his morning workout. He glanced at his watch. "It's time to pay Treavor's lawyer a personal visit," Don muttered to himself. "Sounds to me like someone is just putting me off. If I can't get to him through the phone maybe I can break his door down or something, eh?" Don grabbed a shower and then headed out.

As he neared his destination, he noticed the buildings were weathered and in need of a coat of paint. He parked and walked into an office, moving slowly as he observed the dirty, worn carpet and rickety furniture. A heavy woman wearing bright red lipstick that clashed with her neon green dress looked up without saying a word.

"I'm here to see Jeff Mitchell."

"He's not in."

Don showed her his badge. "I just want to ask one of his clients a couple of minor questions about a case. I've called and left a number of messages. When will he be in?"

"Not for another couple of days."

Don felt his blood rise. "I'll just have a seat. Maybe he'll surprise us and drop in."

She smacked her lips and snorted, "Suit yourself." She turned her back to him and continued looking at various postings on Facebook.

Don squirmed on the hard chair, trying to get comfortable. After a few minutes, he leaned his head back against the wall and closed his eyes.

A squeak caused him to start. The receptionist got up from her chair and walked down the hall towards the ladies' room. Don jumped up and hustled through the rest of the office space, exploring. He swung open a door and found a room containing boxes with files and papers scattered everywhere. He opened the next door and found a run-down desk with shelves of legal books behind it. There was a calendar on the desk. Don studied it and found two weeks scratched out with the words "Mom - Florida" written across the dates. With a groan, Don spun around and strode to his car.

Chewing his lip, he sat in the driver's seat. "I can't catch a break!" He reached for the murder book that sat in the passenger seat. He thumbed through the pages until he found the name of the woman who might have stolen Barry's app. Scrolling through his contact list, he found Rebecca's name and made the call.

Early evening found Don standing at Kate's door smoothing his tuxedo and adjusting his red bow tie. He straightened his shoulders and rapped on the door. A Christmas wreath hung on the door with bright red bows and golden bells that jingled merrily in response.

Kate opened the door. She wore a shimmering strapless red gown and her dark hair was swept up in a French roll at the back of her head. "Hi Don, come on in." She touched his shoulder. "You look great."

"Hi." Don cleared his throat. "So do you."

He wiped his suddenly damp palms on his pants before he pointed to her neck. "First time I've seen you without the necklace."

"It didn't look right with this dress." Kate shrugged.

She walked over to a table and pointed to her gun. "See? I didn't have to use it once today."

Don took in a deep breath and walked over and unloaded it. "If we are going to make it to the ballet we'll have to talk about this later." He glared at her.

"Suit yourself."

Don helped her on with her long black wool coat and they headed out.

Don used the valet to park his SUV, then stood in front of Kate before they went in. "You ready?"

"You bet, Detective Layden."

He put his hand on her back and guided her into the room.

As Don took care of her coat, Kate looked around at the room filled with patrons of the arts all wearing their best attire. Women were dressed in gowns of all colors. Their faces were decorated with lots of makeup and sparkles of jewelry hung on their ears and around their necks. The men looked dashing in their tuxedos and expensive suits. A few patrons were casual, but they were in the minority. Probably due to the affluence of tonight's crowd. Kate walked over to a window that looked down upon the beautiful entrance to the Denver Center for the Performing Arts and sucked in her breath. Two story statues of dancers graced the acres in front of the glass building that was a piece of art in and of itself. The lighting on the statues was positioned to inspire. It succeeded.

Don walked up behind her. "Pretty isn't it?"

She spun around and closed her eyes for a second. "It's absolutely fabulous."

"Seen our friend yet?" Don asked as he surveyed the room.

Kate shook her head and studied the crowd for a few minutes. "No, but I see Mr. and Mrs. O'Donnell, Alicia's parents."

They walked over, greeted the elderly couple, and Kate gave each of them a quick hug.

"Interesting." Elizabeth O'Donnell looked from Don to Kate. "I didn't know you were a couple."

Kate touched the older woman's arm. "We met due to the case."

Elizabeth cast her eyes down to the floor and Elliott stepped towards Don. "What's this I'm hearing that there isn't enough manpower to work the case? Is that true? And why are you here when he hasn't been caught?"

Don paused for a beat. "I don't make the manpower decisions. But I'll do what it takes to catch this guy. Know that." He scratched his head for a second as a memory flashed in his brain. "Can't go into why I'm here, but I have a question for you. Is one of the firms that you are investing with named Witt Real Estate and Investments?"

"Why yes, it is. Why do you ask?"

"I remember the name from an envelope on your desk when Luke and I interviewed you. How did you find the company? Do you like the service?"

"It's all right. I invested a sum of money a couple of years ago and I keep getting statements showing good growth." Elliott raised his eyebrows. "I met the owner here at one of these functions as a matter of fact." Elliott's eyes narrowed. "What does any of this have to do with Alicia?"

"Mr. O'Donnell, I can't say right now. You'll have to trust me on this."

Elliott studied Don's eyes and took note of the dark circles under them and the bloodshot color due to a lack of sleep. "I believe there are others here who have investments with that firm. Let me introduce you."

Elliott led Don to a group of four gray-haired men in tuxedos sipping on what smelled like scotch. Don observed a group of four women near them who he assumed were their wives. Elliott introduced Don as the lead detective for the murder investigation of his daughter and her friends. Don found himself wincing. So much for being incognito.

"Detective Layden asked me about Witt Real Estate and Investments. My statements show good results. I thought I remembered someone in your illustrious group investing with him as well, am I right?"

"I did." Don turned to face a man of about five feet ten and about 180 pounds. Don guessed him to be about fifty, at least fifteen years younger than the rest of them. He was athletic-looking and had the goggle tan of someone who'd been skiing recently. The man reached out his hand to shake Don's. "I'm Cameron Ingalls. I met Barry here right at the time I was looking to invest after selling some real estate. I knew of his name from the real estate market and knew that he had achieved success there."

"How are your investments doing?"

"To be honest, about two weeks ago I thought about filing a complaint. I wanted to withdraw some funds to give my daughter a down payment on her house, and I couldn't get in touch with Barry or anyone else in his firm. Then he finally called me back and sent a check. He said he's been out of town or something. Bottom line - I have the money I wanted."

Don found himself jotting down information in the little notebook he thought to put in his tux. "So, you feel at ease about the rest of your funds?"

Cameron studied Don for a moment. "You can check them?"

"If you file a complaint, we can look into it," Don answered. "If I get enough evidence of possible improprieties, I can get something going."

"Good to know."

Elliott and Don moved towards the bar where a blonde man named Clark told Don a similar story. "Yes, Detective, I really was concerned with my funds being in Witt Real Estate and Investments for a while, but I was able to get the money out that I wanted."

A man standing nearby turned to them when he overheard the words 'Witt Real Estate and Investments.' Grinning broadly, he said, "Small world! Do you invest with Barry Witt? I just met him at church and I was very impressed with him. As a matter of fact, I believe our church's funds are with him now as well."

"What church do you go to?" Don asked.

"New United Community Church."

Across town, the light from the computer screen illuminated Barry's eyes. Cigarette smoked swirled around his head as he studied various growth projections.

He jumped when his cell phone rang.

"Hi, David." As he listened to David's news, a smile crept onto his face. He reached for a paper and pen. "Give me the address of that church again. I'd love to give a presentation to their finance committee next week. I was just looking at some fine investment options. This time we'll go domestic to diversify our assets. Great work and keep it coming."

He leaned back and stared at the address. Then he reached for the list in the leather folder.

THIRTY-SIX

The waiters had finished clearing the plates from dinner at the Denver Center for Performing Arts when a bell chimed and startled Don. He jumped and looked around left to right, turning around to get a full view of the room. Coming in through the doorway were several petite women wearing glimmering tutus, toe shoes, and pink tights. Delicate crowns on their heads sparkled along with their heavily made-up eyes as they appeared to float into the room. Some muscular male dancers wearing colorful costumes came in behind them. "Wow." Don glanced at Kate. "I've never seen anything like this."

"They're beautiful, aren't they?" Elizabeth murmured as she observed the dancers moving among the crowd. "Human beings who turned themselves into art."

The dancers filtered throughout the guests and some applause started. Then the chef swept into the room and waved to the crowd. Taking his white chef's hat off his head revealing jet black hair that matched his eyes, he bowed.

Some cheers broke out and he trotted over to one of the dancers and gave her a hug. "Welcome, everyone," he said in his charming French accent. "I hope you enjoyed the dinner. As you may know, I am opening my second restaurant in your great country this week. My sister asked me to stop here in Denver and give you wonderful patrons of the Colorado Ballet a preview of my cuisine." He hugged his sister again. "I was delighted to do so and am thrilled to know you all want to support this beautiful ballet company and the wonderful talent here."

Checkbooks and credit cards came out of pocketbooks and wallets. A line formed at an out-of-the-way table that was decked out with red and green satin ribbons and glistening golden ornaments. A small, tasteful sign indicated that this was where to make contributions. There were even computer stations set up so that online donations could be made right then and there. In addition, a smattering of signs that indicated how to donate using your phone.

Don leaned over to Kate. "Barry might be a really screwed up person, but he knew what he was doing by focusing on this group. Definitely some money in this room." He pulled out his notebook and looked at his notes. "Several of the guys I spoke with tried to pull out some funds but couldn't get in touch with Barry to get their money. Then, right about the same time, they all got calls from Barry. Got their investments back." He tapped the notebook with his index finger a few times. "You know, it almost sounds like a Ponzi scheme. Right about the time Barry got a lot of funds from a church in town, the clients from this group got the cash they wanted."

He reached for his phone. "I'm going to give Luke a call with the information I got tonight. See what he can find out." Don paused. "Oh, and please see if you can locate that Rosalyn woman. I haven't been able to get in touch with her. Have you seen her?"

"No, but I'll look for her while you call Luke." Kate searched the room but didn't see any sign of Barry's friend.

Soon the lights dimmed and got bright, the signal that it was time to get inside the theatre because the performance was about to begin. Kate's back tingled when Don put his hand on it to guide her to their seats. She gulped some air as they sat down.

Don leaned towards her. "You okay?"

She nodded and smiled at him. "I'm just excited to see this. My mom took me to see *The Nutcracker* in Chicago when I was a little girl. I'll never forget it. It was magical!"

"Nice." Don settled into his seat, stifling a yawn. Spending the night in the Crown Vic was catching up to him.

The lights darkened, and the music glided up from the orchestra pit and soared to the balcony as the curtain disappeared amongst the rafters to reveal the artists as they danced their story.

Soon, the performance was over. Don signaled for his car as he and Kate stood outside in the winter mountain air. He watched the crowd exit, heavy winter coats buttoned up and their breath creating steam as they raved about what they had just seen.

Kate huddled in her coat with her hands in her pockets as Don jumped up and down to stay warm. He was relieved when the valet drove up. "The seat heaters will kick in before you know it," Don said as he turned them up.

"I can't believe you didn't wear a coat." Kate stared at Don. "Are you crazy?"

"If I am, that's good because it's keeping me awake."

"Yeah, I noticed you were nodding off now and then. You probably aren't a big ballet fan. I understand. Most men aren't."

Don's face softened. "Actually, my wife Uelle and I caught a performance once or twice a year. We never went to *The Nutcracker* though." He turned to face Kate. "The reason I'm so beat is because I sat in the Crown Vic and watched your condo all night." Kate's eyes widened and her jaw dropped but no words came out of her mouth.

Don's phone interrupted the silence. Luke was on the other end. "So, based upon when the sale of his real estate transactions took place, it's likely that he sold most of his real estate holdings at a loss."

Don paused. "Any history of mental illness? Intelligent people can cover that up until they get under a lot of stress. Then they break. Can you check that out?" Don listened. "Yeah, still no probable cause. But we're getting closer. However, I have to get some sleep tonight. It's all I can do to sit in the car in this traffic jam. Let's touch bases in the morning."

As Don put his phone down Kate gasped. "I just can't believe Barry would do this. I mean he was definitely a creepy guy, but murder?"

Don tapped the steering wheel. "This is the first time since I've started working on the case that I feel like things are beginning to come together." Don paused. "A week or two after you see him at Jose's is close to the time his financial life was crumbling. It's also near the time Alicia was killed. Too early to draw any conclusions yet, but it's something to think about."

The traffic crawled forward and Kate noticed Don yawn again. "I'm sorry you felt like you needed to watch my place all night. That's just crazy. I'm fine, really."

Don took in a deep breath, let it out again, and closed his eyes for a second. In measured tones he said "Kate, quit being so incredibly stubborn. Use that brain of yours. This guy is unstable." Don ticked off the issues on his fingers. "One, the guy's business falls apart so he has to let all of his associates go and close his office. Two, he has to sell some nice real estate investments at a loss. Three, his name is on a list of foreclosure notices, which means that he has other bills that are past due too. Four, right around this time, he sees the beautiful employee that he lusted after and who rejected him come into a restaurant and ignore him. That's rejection. Again." Don paused. "And from what we know, he never really received any recognition for anything. He was bullied in high school, and even his own parents ignored him! Now he's all over the news. He's got a taste for murder. He wants to do it again. Next time it could be you."

Kate blinked. Voice trembling, she said, "Do you think the murders are my fault?"

Don looked at the ceiling of his car and stifled a groan. "No, Kate, I think this guy is nuts. He was ready to blow. You were just in the wrong place at the wrong time." He turned toward her and his voice rose. "But let's make sure that doesn't happen again. Because the next time you're in the wrong place at the wrong time, your blood and your brains could be splattered all over your beloved photos of Boise State University."

Kate sat back and stared at the lines of bright red tail-lights as they snaked forward. Short of breath, she had to wipe her forehead from the sweat that formed there. "I was on my laptop earlier so I took a look at the hotel's forecast before I left. We picked up some room nights. The hotel is sold out tonight."

"That's fine. You can stay at my place. I can't spend the night outside of your condo again, and I'm convinced the graveyard security guard couldn't catch a murderer if the guy walked right up to him and confessed." He let go of the steering wheel and briefly held up his hands. "No strings attached. I have a guest room and some clothes you can wear. You'll be safe and I'll get some sleep. Win, win."

They arrived at Don's condo and Don helped Kate with her coat. Kate caught her breath as Belle chirped. "You have a bird?"

"Yes, I do," Don laughed. "Do you want to meet her?"

They walked towards the chirping and Kate's eyes lit up when she saw Belle. "Oh! She is so beautiful! What's her name?"

"Her name is Belle." Don reached into the cage and waited for the bird to step onto his finger before he withdrew his hand and brought her up to Kate.

"Hi, Belle," Kate cooed. "What a perfect name for such a pretty birdie. Yes, you are, you're a pretty birdie aren't you?"

Belle looked at Kate curiously, tilting her head this way and that.

"I think she's checking me out!" Kate gasped.

"Cockatiels are almost like dogs," Don said with a grin. "They show affection, they listen when you talk to them, and they want to be with you." He stroked Belle's soft, yellow feathers and brought Belle around so that he could look into her eyes. "I miss you when I'm away so much, Belle. It's good to be home so that I get to see you." Belle stretched her wings and Don grinned. "See that? That's the same thing as a dog wagging its tail."

Kate let out a little squeal. "Do you want to hold her?" Don asked.

Kate's long silver earrings waved back and forth as she nodded her head, and Don showed her how to extend her index finger and put it up next to Belle. Without hesitation, Belle stepped on Kate's finger. Kate sucked in her breath and glanced at Don with delight before returning her gaze to the bird. After a few moments, Don laughed.

"It's okay to breathe while you're holding her. She wouldn't like it if you passed out, you know?"

Kate exhaled without making a sound and then stroked the little bird's soft feathers. "You're about the size of a robin, aren't you? I'm pleased to meet you. I've never held a little birdie before."

After a few moments, Belle looked at Don and flew over to him. She almost didn't make it. Kate raised her eyebrows as Don moved so that Belle landed on his finger. "I get her wings clipped every two months or so. I like to hang out on the deck with her. Don't want her to fly away. She could get lost." He stroked Belle again. "I would miss you, Belle." His voice became almost a whisper.

Kate's heart softened as she watched them. "I can definitely see why you are so careful with her. She's absolutely precious." Kate glanced around Don's condo. "This is a really nice place." Kate's eyes fell upon the pictures that were on the mantel above the fireplace and she moved towards them. She spotted Uelle's picture and picked it up. "This is Uelle, isn't it? She was really beautiful. Sabrina told me about her."

Don gazed at the photo as he had countless times. "She was perfect," he said in a low voice. They stood without moving for a few moments.

Not sure what to say, Kate offered the photo to Don. "Do you want to hold it?"

"No, that's okay. I hold it all the time. You can put it back."

Kate placed it back on the mantel and found another photo to take down. In the picture, Don stood next to a young man who held a football while Don gave him some sort of a document. "Is this one of your players?"

"Yes. That is Martin Martinez." One corner of Don's mouth went up in a half-smile. "He graduated from high school and earned the first annual Uelle Layden Memorial Scholarship for our recreational football league. He's going to college now and his books are free." Don paused. "I hand one out every year. I found a small way to let Uelle live on."

Kate patted Don's arm. "That's wonderful." Kate pointed to heaven. "I'm sure she loves it."

"I hope so."

Kate found Don's family ski photo to bring down and grinned. "What a neat picture! You were such a cute kid! Is this your family?"

"Yes."

"Where was this taken? Did your dad teach you how to ski?"

"It's Michigan. I grew up there. There was a ski slope not too far from our house. Yeah, he taught all of us. My mom could ski a little bit when I was learning and then we all just always went whenever he could take us. Great family time together." Don considered the picture for a moment. "My dad was a great man. My mom was pretty cool too."

Kate replaced the photo and noticed an intricately carved box next to it. She traced her fingertips along the carvings. "This is nice."

"Yes, that's where I keep my dad's badge."

"Oh," Kate breathed as she took it down and opened it. She took the badge out and held it. "Is this why you chose this profession?"

"I really want to live up to his memory."

Kate noticed something else as she started to put the badge back. "There are letters in here. Are they old letters from your dad?"

Don raised an eyebrow. "You ever thought about being a journalist? You ask a lot of questions." He waved off her look of dismay. "That's okay. Just kidding." He motioned to the letters. "My father was shot in the line of duty. Those are from the man who killed him. When I was in college, I found out where he was incarcerated. Decided to write him and find out why he killed my father. When I started writing, I just couldn't stop. Lots of pain and anguish ended up in that letter. He wrote me back begging for forgiveness. I was surprised." Don glanced at the floor for a moment. "He shared a lot of pain and anguish with me as well. Then he said that he found Jesus while he was in prison. A lot of inmates do that. Anyway, he taught that to others. I could tell he was sincere. I forgave him and we've been writing each other ever since." Don shrugged. "I keep some of the letters in with my dad's badge. Not sure why."

Kate replaced the box with care and turned towards Don. Her eyes were glistening as she placed her hand on his arm. "Don Layden, you have a beautiful heart. There is no doubt in my mind that your father is insanely proud of you."

"Thanks. Now let's get you fixed up with some clothes. I need sleep."

He showed her the guest room and then went into his room and stepped into his closet. With great care, he pulled down a pink box and grabbed a dirty T-shirt out of his hamper to wipe off the slight film of dust that had gathered on the lid. In the box was a woman's shirt that was just Kate's size. Closing his eyes, he rubbed it on his cheek and held it to his nose to smell it. After a few moments he kissed it, put it back, and returned the box to its resting place. Then he went through some hangers and brought Kate some of his own clothes. "These will be big on you, but I brought a belt to hold up the sweat pants." Don shrugged. "They're clean."

Kate thanked him and Don closed the door behind him as he left her room and walked back into his own.

A few hours later, the sound of the alarm rang in Barry's room and he turned to shut it off. Throwing the blankets aside, he got up and dressed in the same clothes he wore when he went to Alicia's. He placed the axe in a chair at his kitchen table and stared at it as he ate his muffin and drank some coffee. The knife he brought back from Brazil sat next to him, gleaming. Retrieving his black trench coat out of his closet, he placed the axe and the knife in a pouch he designed. *Perfect. That will work. Time to head over to Kate's condo.*

Picking up the stuffed dog, Barry held it so he could look right into its eyes. "Kate looked away when she saw me, didn't she? Tried to pretend I wasn't there. For crying out loud, she worked for me for a year! She was my employee. Mine. What makes her think that she can treat me like that?" He stuffed the dog into a front pocket. "Well she'll learn the hard way, won't she?"

After a short drive, he walked into the modern lobby of Kate's building. He looked over at the guard's station and smiled. The guard was asleep, head down on a fleece coat he'd bundled up as a pillow.

Barry wiped some sweat off his forehead and controlled his breathing. He held his arms close to his body, certain that he looked normal as he searched for a doorway to the courtyard, pressing on all the doors leading out there as he walked by them. *Bingo.* The door farthest from the guard opened.

He slipped outside and turned around to get oriented. He found Kate's side of the building, her floor and what had to be her unit. *Time to climb up the fire escape. So cool!* When he got to the sliding glass door on her balcony, he peered inside. Boise State was everywhere. A smile broke out on his face and his heart pounded against his chest. The curtains to the bedroom were closed, so he got some tools out of his pocket and worked on the lock to the kitchen. Before long, he slid the door back and crept into her condo.

He got the axe out and licked his lips as he made his way to her bedroom. He peered into her room and saw the bed wasn't slept in. The axe dropped to his side and he stood and stared at the bed. *Where the hell was she?*

He leaned against the doorway and looked around the room. A jewelry box was open, a satin hanger sat on the bed, and what looked like a bag of panty hose stuck out of a drawer that wasn't completely closed. *She went out on some hot date and wasn't home yet!*

Then he noticed a flyer next to the jewelry box. Vail. Picking it up, he studied it and noticed an ad for early ski season discounts at a ski shop he knew of. The ad was circled. He placed the flyer back where he found it.

His shoulders drooped as he trudged back to his car. Turning on the radio, he sat there staring at the dashboard while the engine ran so that the car would stay warm. He couldn't believe she wasn't there.

The radio blared *"And it's a beautiful day to enjoy some of that famous Colorado skiing listeners! Vail is still selling those early season discount passes! Come on up and take some turns at the world class Vail Ski Resort!"*

Barry turned his head and gazed at the radio. "Vail. Maybe she got home from her date and went up to Vail this morning, Buddy. I remember she talked about skiing there sometimes. Maybe she went to that ski shop." He checked his watch. "I bet we could get there right as it opens." He put the car in drive and headed up the interstate toward Vail.

THIRTY-SEVEN

Downtown in Denver, Don's phone interrupted his deep sleep. He groaned and rolled over to glance at the caller ID. It was Luke.

"Got some more information for you, Cheeto. Barry Witt was in Brazil. Looks like he invested some money there. The money trail after that is sketchy. I've got a call into the authorities down there to find out more. There's the time difference and the language barrier, but I'm working through that." Luke sighed. "We keep running up against these horrible hurdles."

"Yeah, I know. I haven't been able to get in touch with the app lady either." Don paused. "How's Lucy?"

Luke glanced over at his daughter. "She's the same," he said in a monotone.

Don fell back on his pillow. "Give her a kiss from her Uncle Don for me," he responded in a low voice.

As Don put down his phone, he saw the message that there was a voice mail.

"Hi, Detective Layden, this is Teresa Williams. I worked with Gail Gonzalez. I left for New York the same day Gail was…the same day Gail…" Her voice trailed off and she cleared her throat. "I think you were trying to get in touch with me. Please give me a call when you get this."

Don dialed and introduced himself. "When can you meet? I'd like to make it as soon as possible. I can come to the school or anywhere that's easy for you."

"Actually, I have a dentist appointment early this morning. There's a little coffee shop next to his office. How about if we meet there at seven? Would that be enough time?"

"Sounds good," Don said as he wrote down the address. He jumped out of bed, grabbed a shower, made some coffee, and wrote a note to Kate. He said goodbye to Belle and took off to meet Teresa.

About thirty minutes later, Kate stirred as the aromatic scent of coffee drifted into her room. Eyes still closed, a smile came to her lips. "Why is he up so early?" she murmured to herself.

She threw back the covers and sat up, stretching her arms over her head. She glanced over at her red gown, laid over the back of a chair, and her pantyhose and shoes on the floor next to it. Then she stood up and looked down at the huge Denver Broncos sweatshirt she had on. It was like a dress on her. And she'd pulled the sweatpants practically up to her chest. Thank goodness for the belt!

She sat on the ottoman and put on some socks Don had given her to wear as slippers. Running her fingers through her hair, she wandered into Don's kitchen. "Don?" She looked around and saw a coffee cup, a spoon, and a couple of muffins wrapped in plastic wrap. A note, a key, and some money were next to the little spread.

KATE – A COLLEAGUE OF GAIL'S CALLED AND I WENT TO INTERVIEW HER TO SEE IF IT WILL GIVE ME A LEAD. I PUT THE GRAY TOWEL OUT FOR YOU IN THE BATHROOM. IF YOU GO BACK TO YOUR PLACE

TO GET SOME CLOTHES, THAT'S OKAY, BUT HAVE THE GUARD COME UP TO YOUR ROOM WITH YOU. <u>THEN LEAVE YOUR PLACE.</u> YOU ARE WELCOME TO COME BACK HERE. I LEFT A KEY FOR YOU AND SOME MONEY FOR A CAB IF YOU NEED IT. WHATEVER YOU DO, <u>BE CAREFUL</u>. THIS GUY IS UNSTABLE. DON

Sipping coffee, Kate leaned against the counter and read the note again. Then she turned and headed for the shower.

Miles west of Denver, Barry sat on a bench that was near the door of the ski shop but situated amongst a few trees. He watched as an associate unlocked the door. No one was waiting to get in. He sat there until he had to stamp his feet to keep them warm. "Buddy, I think we got skunked. Let's go have some breakfast."

He walked over to one of the many spectacular hotels in Vail, and a uniformed bellman grasped a brass handle opening a beautifully carved oak door. "Is the Quaking Aspen restaurant still here?" Barry asked.

The bellman nodded and made a sweeping motion with his hand. "Right over there, sir."

"Yes, I remember where it is from my childhood. My parents used to bring me here frequently. Thanks." Barry walked in and was seated. He looked around and took in the luxurious linens, the rich curtains, the polished china, and the sparkling sterling silver. *Hasn't changed.*

His food soon arrived, and as he ate, the sound of a little boy's voice got his attention. A family of three sat near him. Barry looked at them without turning his head as he put some strawberry jelly on his toast. *Easy $5K just in ski clothing sitting right next to me.*

"Lookie at the Christmas tree over there, Mommy. It has Santa ornaments on it! I want to go look!" The little boy's face shown with excitement as he gazed at the tree.

"No, honey. You can see it from here. I'm sure they don't want little boys running around in here. You don't see anyone else running around do you?" The mother was decked out in the latest ski attire, including a fur-lined hood on the back of her jacket. Her emerald earrings glistened in the light and she pulled a compact mirror out of a pocket to check her make-up.

"I promise I won't run. I'll just walk. I'll be careful. I just want to see the Santas."

Still admiring herself in the mirror the woman shook her head. The boy's head fell as he looked down at the white linen tablecloth.

The father signaled for some coffee. Every hair on his head was neatly in place thanks to whatever hair product he used. He also was dressed in this year's top-of-the-line ski apparel. "Hey, Stewart, how about some hot chocolate?" Head down, his son nodded.

They ordered and the father patted the little boy on the back. "Ready for your ski lesson today?"

The boy raised his head and looked up at his dad. "Can I ski with you a little bit today, Daddy?"

"Oh, no honey, we're skiing with the Gleasons," the mother answered. "We already paid for an all-day lesson for you."

The boy turned to his mother. "But I want to be with you and Daddy. You said we would get to be together after you got back from your trip."

The mother put a hand on her son's arm. "Why, we are together right now, dear." She patted his arm, pulled her hand away, and addressed her husband. "Did you book the babysitter for tonight? Remember, we were going to meet Jim and Sheila for dinner." She didn't notice her son's head go back down or see him rubbing the tears out of his eyes.

Barry pushed the rest of his breakfast away and signaled for the check. Throwing some cash on the table, he hastened out of the hotel into the crisp air outside. He pulled out a cigarette and watched as the smoke curled up in the air against the backdrop of the snow-covered mountains.

The bellman finished helping some guests and spotted Barry. "Did you enjoy your breakfast? Was everything as you remembered it from your childhood?"

Barry looked at the bellman. "Yes. Everything was exactly the way I remember it from my childhood." The bellman smiled and turned to attend to a couple as they exited. Barry walked to his car and headed down I-70 back to Denver.

At the hospital, Luke sat by Lucy's bed staring at the computer screen. "Come on! Pull up the info for me. Why does it take so long for you to search?" He sat back and glanced at his daughter.

He put the laptop on a nearby table, clearing away some items to make room, including the little guardian angel Kate brought. Luke picked it up and put it in Lucy's hand as he leaned close to her. Stroking her forehead, he murmured to her, "Good morning, sweetheart. How is my baby girl today?" He kissed her head and smiled. "I want you to know that Christmas is coming pretty soon. You have to wake up so you can tell Santa what you want for Christmas. We have to write Santa a letter so he will know what to bring you. Why don't you wake up today so that we can do that?"

Sabrina walked in and stopped to watch for a second. Then she walked over to the other side of the bed and held Lucy's hand. "Yes, Lucy, and you have to help us put the ornaments on the tree. I'll make some cookies and hot chocolate and Daddy will put up the tree and we'll decorate it. Maybe we can go shopping and buy a new ornament this year. You can pick it out."

They were both silent for a few moments and then Sabrina covered her eyes as tears rolled down her cheeks. Luke walked over to his wife and hugged her, rocking her. Sabrina buried her head in Luke's chest and started moaning. "I want to go shopping with my Lucy. I want to take pictures while she is on Santa's lap. I want to make sugar cookies with her and decorate them and go around and take them to the neighbors." She took a ragged breath. "What if she never wakes up?" Sabrina sobbed.

Luke reached over to get a box of tissues by Lucy's bed and froze. He stared at Lucy's hand. What just happened? Did he just see that? Lucy's fingers moved! He stood stock still as he watched her fingers curl around the little angel. Heart in his throat, he leaned over his daughter. "Wake up, Lucy," he whispered. "It's time to wake up."

Lucy opened one eye and then the other. "Hi, Daddy." Sabrina squealed. Lucy looked at her mother. "Hi, Mommy." Lucy frowned. "Mommy why is your face all wet?"

Luke handed Sabrina the tissues and Sabrina laughed, "Sweetheart, you were asleep for a long time. I missed you! And now I'm so glad that you're awake that my eyes just started watering again. I'm so happy I think my heart is going to just come busting right out of my chest!"

Luke leaned over to give Lucy a hug and so did Sabrina. Lucy brought up the angel to show them. "This is from Uncle Don's friend, isn't it?"

"Yes, honey," Sabrina gasped. "How do you know?"

"I could hear you sometimes." Lucy looked around. "Am I in a hospital?" Her eyes fell upon the equipment surrounding her bed. "Oh look! Look at those machines! Aren't they awesome?" She threw back the covers so she could scramble out of bed and touch everything.

"Hold on, young lady, hold on," Luke chuckled as he put a slight pressure on her shoulders to keep her in place. "We need to get some doctors in here before you start terrorizing the place!" His face was wet too.

Sabrina pushed the nurse's button and when Esther came in she grinned from ear to ear and pumped her fist over her head. "Yeah, Lucy! You decided to join us!" She walked over and shook Lucy's hand. "Hi, I'm Esther. I'm one of your nurses. You've been asleep for a few days, missy. It's nice to finally meet you." She put her stethoscope in her ears to listen to Lucy's heart and examined Lucy's eyes. Then she called Lucy's doctor.

After a few minutes, several of the medical professionals that had been in and out during Lucy's ordeal stood around near Lucy's bed chatting with her and each other. Sabrina felt the tears welling up in her eyes once again. "I just want to thank each of you for all of your help!"

Esther spoke up. "It was a great team effort. You stayed with her so she could hear you, but Lucy did a lot of the work too. Her little brain worked hard to get better, right?" She patted Lucy.

Lucy raised her eyebrows. "I guess so. All I know is that right now I want to write a letter to Santa Claus." She looked at Luke. "Daddy, can we write a letter to Santa today?" A little cheer sprang out of the mouths of everyone in the room, and Luke grabbed a piece of paper and a pen. As he walked back over to his daughter, he pointed up to the ceiling and smiled.

Near the dentist's office, Don walked into a small coffee shop in a strip mall. A slender woman with short, brown hair wearing glasses and sensible clothing stood up. "Detective Layden?"

He nodded and extended his hand. "You must be Teresa Williams."

Don got some coffee for both of them and sat down, pulling out his notebook. "Tell me about the last time you saw Gail."

"She was tired. She hadn't slept well because of a weird incident with some guy at a Safeway near her house. She said she thought maybe he was following her around the store. Then he got way too close to her and tried to start a conversation with her when she was picking out some apples. And then after that he came right up to her in the parking lot. There was a distraction, and she jumped in her car quickly but he definitely scared her. I think she was afraid he was going to grab her and try to kidnap her or something. She even decided to switch grocery stores despite the fact that she really liked that Safeway because it was close enough to her house that she could walk there."

Don asked her a few more questions and then headed over to the Safeway. As he walked up to customer service, he glanced up at the ceiling and noticed the cameras. He waited in line and greeted the store's associate. "Hi, I'm Detective Layden. I need to speak to your manager." He flashed his badge and motioned towards the cameras. "I have to review some of your camera footage for a case that I'm working on." The manager wasn't there yet, so Don had to wait. He called Luke.

"Hey, Luke, found out anything else?"

Luke stepped away from the celebration. "No, Cheeto, I've been too busy talking to my daughter. We just wrote a letter to Santa Claus."

Don let out a whoop and jumped in the air. Several people glanced at him, but he ignored them and pressed the phone close to his ear as his partner described how Lucy woke up.

"Okay, that's been my morning," Luke concluded. "Now tell me about yours."

Don filled him in. "I'm at the Safeway right now. The manager should be here soon to let me look at the cameras." Don glanced up. "As a matter of fact, I believe he just arrived. Talk to you later." Don smiled. "And give Lucy a kiss for me."

Don and the manager reviewed the camera video and it wasn't long before they found the sequence with Barry in the produce section. "I can see why that bothered her," Don observed. "Can we back it up to see if he followed her in the store?" Sure enough, Barry was clearly stalking Gail. "How about the parking lot? Have cameras out there?"

"Yes, detective. Absolutely."

After Don finished watching that scene, he thanked the manager, got a copy of the video, and dashed back to the car. He gave Luke a quick call. "Who needs Treavor? I've got probable cause now." Luke agreed to put in motion a search warrant for Barry's house and an APB for his arrest.

Don made another call and listened to a voice mail greeting. He left a message. "Kate, I've got probable cause on Barry. He's our guy. Stay away from your condo and your usual haunts. Just call me as soon as you listen to this." Don paused. "Don't mess around, Kate. This guy is very disturbed and extremely dangerous." Don put down the phone and started the engine. "Come on, Kate Fitzgerald. Now is not the time to be stubborn."

THIRTY-EIGHT

Ignoring Don's advice to have the condo complex's guard accompany her to her unit, Kate rushed to change her clothes and get out. As she exited her condo, an elderly neighbor walked by with her little Pekingese and offered a greeting. "Hi, Kate. What are you doing today?"

"Hi, Elaine. I'm bringing a load of toys from church over to Regis. I'm in charge of the toy drive this year." Kate bent down to pat the small dog and its entire behind wagged in response.

Elaine smiled and pointed a finger at Kate. "A toy drive. Now that's what I call the Christmas spirit!"

At St. James, Kate shut the back doors on the church van and brushed her gloved hands together to get rid of the dust. She looked at Vicki and Father Tim. "I think that's it. Vicki and I can head on out to Regis University. Father Bill said he would meet us and open up the old chapel where they are going to store the toys."

Father Tim handed Kate the keys to the van. "Here you go. My thanks to both of you."

"You're welcome, Father," Vicki answered for both of them. She addressed Kate. "I'll follow you in my car. I promised to meet my mom as soon as we're done at Regis."

West of town, Barry headed down I-70 on his way into Denver. Buddy was in his spot on the passenger seat. "All right Buddy, we need to find that girl who used to work for me. She thinks that she can just ignore me the same way Mom and Dad always ignored me. We never liked that did we, Buddy? Maybe she's back in her condo now. Let's go surprise her, shall we?" He patted the pocket containing the knife from Brazil as he continued on to Denver.

Barry found a parking spot close to Kate's condo, turned off the car and folded his arms. He stayed like that for a few minutes, watching the pedestrian traffic on the street and waiting until it cleared somewhat. He opened the trunk and put the axe in the pouch in his coat, picked up the dog, and walked into the lobby. He kept his back to the security guard's desk as he studied the names of the occupants of the building.

It wasn't long before a couple swiped their key to step into the elevator. Barry followed and listened to them chatter to each other as the elevator climbed. He got out on Kate's floor and pounded hard on her door while keeping his finger over the peephole. No answer. He pounded again.

A neighbor's door opened and an elderly woman poked her head out. "May I help you with something?"

Keeping his head down, Barry turned. "Hi, I'm looking for Kate Fitzgerald." He held up the dog. "I brought her a little gift."

The woman smiled. "Oh, that is such a cute little doggie. How nice." Her smile faded a bit. "I'm so sorry but I'm afraid

Kate is over at Regis University right now helping to get their Christmas toy drive off the ground. Would you like me to give it to her for you or leave a message?"

Barry held up his index finger. "Ah. The toy drive. Of course. I'll just go find her over there. Thanks for your help."

Traveling to the north side of Denver, Kate found herself singing Christmas songs at the top of her lungs. As she made a left onto Regis Boulevard, her face broke into a smile. The statuesque brick buildings of the educational institution were nestled near tall, beautiful evergreens that were now draped with soft, white snow. It was such a picturesque scene she felt as though she had just jumped into a postcard. She pulled into a lane next to the soccer pitch and drove down to the Alumni Building. She checked her rearview mirror. Yup, Vicki was still right behind her. Just then her phone rang. It was Father Bill.

"Hi, Kate. I hope you aren't on your way to Regis yet. I have a conflict."

"What's up?"

"A parishioner is in the hospital and his family wants the last blessing – the last rites. I have to head over there right away."

"Oh, I'm so sorry for the family. Of course." Kate paused. "Are we still doing this toy thing today? The church van is loaded and Father Tim needs it tomorrow."

"Hmmm." A pause. "That's a tough one. I really need to stay with the family for a while. He's been sick for a long time and they knew this was coming, but that doesn't make it any less painful." A cough. "How about if we touch base in a few hours?"

"Sounds good. Tell the family I'll say a prayer for them."

"Will do."

Kate got out of her car to give Vicki the update and Vicki tilted her head. "Sounds like you'll just have to go Christmas shopping with my mom and me."

Kate grinned. "Fabulous! Let me give Father Tim a quick call so that he knows what's going on."

Barry pulled into a parking lot at Regis and looked around. *Pretty quiet.* "Okay Buddy, where is she? I guess we should just walk around and see what we can figure out. No students here due to the semester break. That's good." He got out of the car and put the dog in his pocket.

Before long he spied a van with lettering spelling out 'St. James Catholic Church' on the side. "She's here, Buddy," he whispered. Heart pounding, he got out of sight behind a building and waited.

And waited. After about twenty minutes he was stiff and his toes were cold. "What's going on, Buddy?" He walked back to his car and turned on the heat. "Let's call St. James and see what they know."

The phone rang twice. He listened to a recording and punched a key. "St. James Catholic Church. May I help you?"

"Yes, I was just wondering if I could still donate to the toy drive."

"No, the toys are over at Regis already."

"If I went over there, would someone be around so that I could drop them off there?"

"Actually, not right now. More like late afternoon or evening."

"I see. Could I call you later and get an update? It would help me out."

"Absolutely. The more toys the merrier Christmas for these kids."

Barry ended the call. *Looks like I have to wait.*

As she admired a skiing Santa Christmas ornament in a store, Kate placed a phone call. "Hi, Father Bill. Uh, not quite sure how to word this…"

"I understand. He passed away about thirty minutes ago. The family is tying things up and then they want to go out to dinner and they want me to join them." He paused. "I can refuse if you'd like me to."

"No, no. They need you right now. We ladies are thinking about going out to dinner downtown, so I'll give you a call when we are done."

"That works."

Kate placed another call. "Hi, Father Tim. Looks like I'll have the van back around ten or eleven. That's the latest update."

"That's fine. See you then."

As she put her phone back in her purse, she noticed the battery was low.

Barry killed time watching football in a sports bar near Regis. He placed a call to St. James and got the update. As he put the phone down, he breathed a sigh of relief. *Good. This will work after all. The idea of a night kill is more appealing anyway.*

Don was in his vest with his gun drawn. He, Belinda, and about ten other officers were ready to go into Barry's house, one way or another. A group went around back and Don pounded on the front door. "Open up! This is the police!" No answer. Kicking in the door, Don burst through followed by five others. Guns drawn, they rushed through the house, room by room. All clear.

Don walked through the kitchen and opened the door to the refrigerator. It was filled with perishable items. As he started towards the living room, he passed a block of knives. Using a handkerchief, he pulled one out. The blade was so polished, he could see himself. It was like a mirror. Spooky.

Don walked through the living room and stopped at the display of weapons above the fireplace. "This guy is into weapons." He glanced at an officer standing nearby.

"This guy is nuts," the officer responded.

They walked into Barry's office to find Belinda examining the corkboard. "Okay, we finally know who he is. How do you plan on catching him?"

"We know what kind of car he drives. Let's put an APB out for that. We'll put unmarked cars on all streets coming into this area. His refrigerator is full. It doesn't look as though he's planning to leave anytime soon."

Belinda studied Don. "Is the axe in the house?"

"I don't know." Don's blood ran cold. "Let's get everybody on that."

After dinner Kate made another call to Father Tim. "Okay, I'm on my way back to Regis. Father Bill just called to tell me he's there. We'll load up his storage area and I'll have the van back in two or three hours."

"See you then."

Kate followed Vicki to her car and noticed a slight stumble. "Hey, Vicki, I'll drive."

"I'm all right."

"Let's just be safe, shall we? I'm sure you're fine, but you know how many cops are out this time of year."

Vicki's mom piped up. "You and I did drink a lot of wine."

"Then it's settled." Kate slid behind the wheel and took off. After a couple of miles, she glanced over at her friend. Vicki was sound asleep.

Kate pulled up to Vicki's mom's house. "How about if I drop Vicki here? I'll lock her car at Regis and leave the keys on the front tire. Then you can give her a ride to her car tomorrow."

"That's a good plan. Vicki is lucky to have such a great friend." Five minutes later, Kate pulled into the Regis parking lot and went to find Father Bill.

Trembling with excitement, time slowed down for Barry as he watched Kate walk up to a door. A priest greeted her and gave her a battery-powered lantern. They went over to the van and started unloading the toys. "Buddy, I think we're finally going to get our chance." His heart glowed. "It was worth the wait, don't you think?" He smirked and sat there until the van was halfway unloaded and then got out of his car, making no noise as he shut the door and crept up to the chapel.

Kate and the priest came out the door, ready for the next load. Kate shivered and pointed up to the gargoyles. "Those things are spooky. I feel as though I'm being watched!"

Father Bill chuckled. "Sounds like you have an overly active imagination to me."

Kate forced her attention away from the gargoyles. "The toys from St. James are organized, but it doesn't look like the others are. We could do that tonight. It wouldn't take long."

"That'd be terrific. You saw how many toys are in there already and I have others dropping off more loads tomorrow, so that would make it much easier. I guess I should have done that sooner."

"Not a problem. We'll be done in no time."

Barry plastered himself against a wall and waited until they were back at the van. Then he slipped inside. There was a lantern on the floor and tables of toys of all kinds. Trucks, dolls, games, books. Images of children opening their presents with smiling parents by their side floated through his head. *Don't go there. Get those vile pictures out of your mind.*

He spied the oak doors leading to the chapel itself and went in. Positioning himself by the crack in the door, he peered out so that he could see what Kate and the priest were up to.

"Okay, we're getting closer to the finish line," Kate said as she placed an armload of toys on a table. She looked up at the priest with a frown and rubbed her shoulders. "Boy, the temperature in here dropped all of a sudden. I wonder what changed. It wasn't this cold five minutes ago."

The priest rubbed his hands together. "You're right. Let's move quickly and get this done."

At the hospital, Luke walked over to the computer to check for any updates about the case. On the screen was the police report from the accident Barry was in near Kate's condo. Realizing that it must have come up during the celebration of Lucy's recovery, Luke called Don. "I have bad news, Cheeto." Luke's voice was tight. "He has his sights set on Kate now. He got in a fender bender right outside her condo yesterday. His car has very little damage, but the car he hit has a big dent."

"Trouble." Don let out a breath. "I can't get a hold of her. She left me a message that she was Christmas shopping with some friends, but I've been calling her for about an hour and it keeps going to voicemail. I'm parking near her condo right now." Don hung up.

Luke stood there, holding his phone.

Sabrina glanced up at her husband and rubbed Lucy's shoulder. The others were gone but Esther was still in the room. "Mommy's going to go talk to Daddy for a minute sweetheart. I'll be right over there. And your best nurse is right here by you." Sabrina walked over to Luke and put a hand on her husband's arm. "What's up?"

"We know who the killer is and he's after Kate. Don can't reach her. He doesn't know where she is."

Sabrina bit her lip. She hustled over to the calendar that they'd hung on the wall. "I think today is the day Kate has to take the toys to Regis University. I remember that banner in the church and I heard her talking with her friends about it."

Luke grabbed Sabrina's shoulders. "Babe, you're a genius!"

Sabrina patted Luke on the chest. "One more thing. It's okay if you go help Don. Lucy's awake. She knows you've been here with her. But honey, it would be terrible if anything happened to Kate. Not only do I like her, but I think it would put Don over the edge."

Luke frowned. "What are you talking about?"

"Luke, Don is breaking down that wall he's been behind since Uelle passed. He actually laughs sometimes now. Heck, the man went dancing!" Sabrina grabbed her husband's arm. "I think he likes Kate. I don't know if he knows it yet, but I can see it." She poked her husband in the chest. "Now, you go out there and save that woman. Save her for her, but save her for us too." She took a step closer. "And be careful, honey. That man is a heartless killer. Lucy and I love you more than anything. You have to come home to us, you hear me?"

"I hear you. I'll come home." Luke kissed his wife and walked over to Lucy's bed.

"Are you going to go help Uncle Don get that bad guy you kept talking about Daddy?"

Luke smiled and nodded. "Girl, how do you read my mind? The two best women on the planet are both in my life and they're both geniuses." He kissed his daughter. "I love you baby girl. I'm so happy to see those big brown eyes wide open!" He pointed a finger at her. "And I'm also going to put ody. He let out a long breath and looked at the manager. "Okay, her condo is clean."

He walked around the kitchen and looked at the door. "Whoa. This lock is broken." He walked out onto the balcony and stared down into the courtyard spotting footprints in the snow. "That was a close one," he whispered. "He probably broke in late last night or early this morning. What do you want to bet she didn't even notice when she was here?" He looked back up at the manager. "We're going to have to get this placed dusted for fingerprints."

Don's phone rang. It was Luke. "Kate is supposed to be at Regis University for that toy drive she was doing," Luke said. "I called St. James and she is at Regis right now. They think she's in the Alumni building. Or a building near it. They aren't sure. I'm on my way. I'll meet you there."

"Luke, we have to hurry. He broke into her condo, but she wasn't here. He's stalking her. She's next."

THIRTY-NINE

Kate finished one table and stepped back to check their work. "I think that takes care of the dolls." She turned to the priest. "Can you believe how many different kinds there are? It's crazy!"

"All I care about is that these dolls become good friends for some little girls." Father Bill's eyes became wet and he blinked. "Okay, how about we do the books next?"

"My favorite. Wouldn't it feel good to be curled up in front of a fire reading a good book right now?"

"Mmmmm."

Kate moved to a pile of books at a far table and started leafing through them.

Barry's legs cramped as he viewed the two do-gooders. He rubbed the dog in his pocket. *How are we going to do this Buddy? I think we should take out the priest first.* He smiled to himself. *Kate will suffer as she watches him die.* He squinted. *It would be nice for Kate to go slowly.* He patted the knife from Brazil in his pocket. *Maybe slice her up a little bit first. Yeah, that's the ticket.* Yelling, he burst out from behind the oak door swinging his axe. Toys went flying. Father Bill hollered and grabbed a nearby hockey stick.

Barry laughed. "That thing is no match for this axe!"

Turning, Kate screamed at Barry as he rushed towards Father Bill. The priest scrambled around the tables of toys. Barry smashed through them with the axe, destroying everything in its path. Kate flung books at him. She found a baseball and hurled it at his head. "Barry, what are you doing? You have to stop this!" She spotted a baseball bat.

Father Bill dodged as Barry swung the axe through the air. The priest swiped a table to clear the toys and lifted it as a shield. The axe broke through. The priest threw the table at Barry, but Barry moved closer and struck his back. Blood poured out of the wound and the priest fell, hitting his head. He was still.

Barry turned to face Kate, growling.

Sirens blaring, Don guided the Crown Vic through Denver Christmas season traffic towards Regis University. He flashed his lights and pulled up to the bumper of a brown Toyota in the emergency lane. "Get out of my way!" he howled as he motioned at the driver to move. "The emergency lane is for emergency vehicles!"

Barry was too near the doorway for her to escape outside so she ran into the chapel with her bat. The chapel was as black as ink. Kate crept along the frigid stone walls without breathing. She hoped she could find that little door to get downstairs.

Barry burst in, snarling. "You aren't getting away from me this time!" He ran right into a pew and fell down but got back up, pummeling the pew with his axe. Blow after blow after blow he chanted, "I hate you! I hate all of you!" Another strike. "I hate my mother!" A thrash. "I hated the cheerleaders!" A strike. "Then, you quit!" A crash. "Then,

Patty stole my app!" A swing. "Then, the recession wiped me out!" A smash. "Then, I'm at dinner and you completely ignore me like I'm nothing! And on top of all that, some Brazilian thieves stole my money! That's it! I've had it! No more!" Barry beat the pew until it was pulverized.

Kate inched against the walls, sliding her hands along the stone. Then a smooth surface greeted her fingertips. She turned the door handle and slipped through the door. She stopped and gathered herself. Now she had to make it down the steps in the pitch black without falling or making a noise. She hoped the stairs wouldn't creak.

FORTY

Don approached Regis and silenced his sirens. As he careened around the driveway in front of the Alumni Building, he saw Barry's car and the church van with the doors open. Gun drawn, he hurtled out of his car towards the Alumni building and dashed around the dark structure, checking all the doors. Every one of them was locked. The windows were dark as well. He peered into them trying to spot movement. Nothing.

Kate sat on her butt and inched her way down each step. So far so good.

Barry found a lantern and roared through the chapel. "You can't get away from me this time, Kate!"

Don turned around to get a look at the buildings nearby and saw a glimmer of light coming through stained glass windows at an old church. He darted through the trees, towards the light.

Kate counted each step as she made her way down. She was on step seventeen. Three more maybe? The bat slipped out of her hand and clattered to the bottom. *Oh no!* Her hand flew to her mouth to stifle a scream. Moments later she heard Barry's heavy footsteps near the door.

Kate made it to the bottom and grabbed the bat. She ran her hands along the wall until she found one of the tiny rooms. Kate slipped into the room and spread her feet out, positioning herself to attack. She gripped the bat and took a deep breath.

Barry tromped down the stairs. "I heard you! Here I come!"

Kate found herself trembling at the sound of his voice. She opened her mouth to get more air.

Don listened at the entrance and pulled out a flashlight. He opened the door and was greeted with frigid air. He sucked in his breath. It reminded him of the cold in Avery's hospital room.

Laying on the floor in a pool of his own blood, the priest groaned. Don ran to him and called an ambulance. Ripping a dress from a doll, he used it to stem the priest's bleeding. "An ambulance is on the way."

"Don't worry about me. Help Kate. I'll bet she went downstairs." The priest pointed towards the little door.

"Here, let's see if you can reach well enough to stop the flow."

"I'm good. Go help Kate."

Don sprinted into the dark chapel.

Barry saw a closed door and ripped it open. There was nothing. *Where did she go?*

Kate heard Barry outside the tiny room. She held her breath and steadied herself.

Chest heaving for air, Barry held the lantern out. *Does she think she can hide against a wall?* Then he spotted another door, then another and another.

"Come out, come out, wherever you are!" he taunted. His voice rose along with his hysteria. He splintered each door with his axe.

Kate could hear him getting closer.

Don sprinted past the demolished pew.

Barry lunged at Kate's door and smashed it, then ripped it open with his axe swinging. Kate flattened her body against the wall, but he hit her leg and blood flowed. "You're done!" Lifting his axe, he held the axe over his head ready to bring it down. "Drop that bat and get down on the floor!"

Kate swung the bat at his feet and rolled.

Barry caught himself from falling and swore.

Don leapt down the stairs and saw Barry with the axe over his head and Kate crouching, ready to dodge the hit.

Don fired.

Kate watched Barry's face change before her eyes. Fury was replaced with shock. His jaw opened and he looked at her in disbelief. The axe fell out of his hands as he hit the floor.

Don kicked the axe out of his grasp and checked him; still breathing, but not a threat. He cuffed him then rushed to Kate.

"Boy, am I glad to see you!" Legs shaking, Kate stood up.

Don laughed and felt relief cascade over him like a waterfall when he heard her voice. Without thinking, he reached out and hugged her. After a few moments, he pulled back. "I'm glad to see you too," he whispered. He closed his eyes and soaked her in as he felt her soft hair against his cheek.

"Are you hurt?"

"Yeah, he hacked me in the leg."

Don helped Kate sit down, then sat back on his heels, and looked at her leg He took off his shirt and ripped it to make a tourniquet.

Kate's heart softened as she watched him. It felt really good to have him take care of her. She reached for his face, holding it between her hands. "Thank you for saving my life."

"I'm so glad I got here in time." He cleared his throat. "If anything happened to you I don't know what I would do," he whispered. He leaned forward, stroked her hair, and drank in her smell. His heart pounded. He gazed in her eyes and touched her soft lips with his own. Don held her as though he would never let her go.

Then the sounds of Luke banging down the stairs were heard. "Ow!" Luke wailed. "There's no way this room is meant to be for adults," he said, rubbing his head.

"Looks like Luke's gonna have a lump." Don grinned and then looked at Kate. "Here, let me help you to the ambulance."

"What about Father Bill? Barry sliced him, too."

"He's already on his way to the hospital," Luke responded. "I saw what Barry did to the toys and the pew and called for another. They should be here any minute." Luke looked at Barry. "Looks like he needs one, too." Luke made an additional call. "I'll stay down here with him until they get here." He looked around. "Man, it's cold in here."

A memory flashed in Don's mind. "Must be the evil wolf."

"Cheeto, you need a vacation."

FORTY-ONE

Hours later, Don found himself holding a vase of flowers and a couple of books while standing at the door of Kate's hospital room. She had an I.V., bandages around the sliced leg, and her face was the color of new fallen snow. Her eyes, however, were as bright as ever and he could see them flashing in anger as she watched the TV in her room carrying Sarah Snow and the news about the end of the search for the Denver serial killer.

Don stepped in. "Hi." He held up the vase. "I brought you some flowers." He held up the books. "I also found a couple of books I thought you might like." He grinned. "I didn't think being laid up in a hospital bed would suit you very well without something to do."

Kate laughed. "Oh Don, the flowers are beautiful! I love them! Thank you!" She held a finger to her lips in thought. "Where shall we put them so that I can see them easily?" She waved her hand at a nearby table. "I know, move this table a little bit down towards my feet and then I'll be able to see them every minute."

Don pulled a table over and placed the flowers the way Kate wanted them.

"Perfect!" Kate beamed. "Let me check out those books you brought, Detective." She scrutinized them and held up her thumb in approval just as a petite African American nurse came bustling into the room. Her dark hair was close cropped, and her big brown eyes twinkled.

She put her hands on her hips. "Rearranging the furniture already?"

Don apologized and she waved her hand. Smiling at Kate, she listened to her heart and took her blood pressure.

Don looked at her name tag. "Thank you for taking care of her, Haley."

"You're welcome."

"How long will Kate need to stay here?"

"Oh, at least two or three days. She needs to regain some strength after losing all of that blood." The nurse wrote a few things down on Kate's chart and marched out of the room.

Don moved over to Kate's bed and sat on the edge of it so that he could hold her hand. "You look pale." He gently smoothed her hair, and then squeezed her hand. "I'm so glad you're going to be all right, Kate." He shook his head. "When I got to Regis I didn't know where you were. I saw Barry's car and the van from St. James." He looked at the floor for a moment. "I knew Barry was after you. And then when I found the chapel and saw what he did to the pew…" His voice trailed off. "It seemed like it took forever to get to that room. And when I saw him ready to bury that axe into your head…" Don shivered. "I'm just so glad I got there when I did. One second later…"

Kate patted Don's hand. "He didn't win, Don, not this time. Thanks to you." She looked at her flowers and then back at Don. "I knew you'd find me. During the whole nightmare, there was some feeling I had in the back of my mind that you'd be there for me." She smiled at him. "I might be able to get used to it."

Don leaned close to Kate. He gazed into her eyes and stroked her lips with his thumb. He cradled her head with his hand and kissed her. Kate circled him with her arms and kissed him back for a long time. Then he leaned his forehead against hers and said in a low voice, "I'm thinking I could get used to this as well."

The television was still on at low volume. Sarah Snow's voice came into the room. "Barry Witt passed away in surgery a few minutes ago. We will provide updates as we learn more."

"Wow. That's such a shame," Kate observed. "I actually feel bad for all that happened to him."

"Yeah, it's sad. However, there are people who have really tough lives and manage not to commit murder. He didn't have to go down that road. His own choice."

"What hospital was he taken to? This one?"

"No, you and Father Bill were brought here. He was taken to Swedish Medical Center. My guess is Sarah camped out there to get the info. Paid off for her."

Later, after Don left, Haley came back to check on Kate. As she listened with her stethoscope, she moved Kate's necklace out of the way and raised her eyebrows when she noticed the necklace held an engagement ring. "Interesting necklace."

Her conversation with Sabrina about the necklace flashed through her mind and Kate chuckled. "Yeah, it is, isn't it?" She looked at Haley. "By the way, how is Father Bill doing? His name is Bill Crockett."

"He is a sweet man, isn't he?" Haley's eyes crinkled. "He's awake and he just finished giving me a dissertation on why he forgives the guy that did all of this." Haley shook her head.

"Either Father Bill has a big heart or he's crazy." She pointed out the door. "His room is right across the hall."

Kate sat up. "Is there any way I could visit him?"

"Let me think." Haley tapped her foot as she read Kate's chart. "I hate to tell you, but you're really hurt." She peered at Kate. "You lost a lot of blood. Don't you feel weak?"

"I refuse to answer on the grounds that it may incriminate me."

"Yeah, that's what I thought." Haley put down the chart and folded her arms. "We can't get you up right now, not even to get into a wheelchair. That's just the way just the way it is."

"Phooey."

"I can understand after having gone through what you did with Father Bill that you'd want to see him." Haley sighed. "That's good medicine too. How about if I give you his hospital room number so you can call him?"

Kate gave a thumbs up. "Yes, that'll work. But could you be in here while I call him? I have a surprise for him." She tapped her chin in thought. "Give me about thirty minutes or so. Would that be all right?"

"Looks like you've got something up your sleeve." Haley's eyes twinkled as she looked at her watch. "I'll be back in thirty minutes."

Kate made a couple of calls. Haley was back in no time with Father Bill's number.

Kate dialed. "I hope I didn't wake you," she said when the priest answered. "I know it's late. But I couldn't go to sleep until I knew how you were doing."

"No problem, I appreciate the call. I'm all right. How about you? I was worried about you, too."

"I'm okay, I guess. I have to admit I've felt better. I can't even get up to go to the bathroom. Normally I'm not fond of hospitals, but I'm glad I'm here right now."

"Yeah, me too."

"Have you heard how things are at Regis?"

"Barry destroyed most of the toys. We have a few deliveries coming tomorrow, but that won't be enough." His voice shook. "I don't know how we are going to be able to replace them in order to give those families a nice Christmas like we promised them."

Kate heard the tears in his voice. "That's another reason why I wanted to talk to you, Father. I think I can help with that. Hang on a minute." Kate took off her necklace and handed it to Haley. She put her hand over the mouthpiece. "Please go give that to Father Bill," she whispered, and then waited a few seconds.

"Did Haley give you the necklace?"

"Yes. What is it?"

"This is what we can use to get the funds to replace those toys. I've already called a couple of ladies and they will drop everything to shop for a couple of days to replenish the gifts. Can you reschedule the event for the families?"

Father Bill gasped. "Kate, I don't know how to thank you! You're the miracle I've been praying for."

Kate smiled and shook her head. "No, Father, it's just like Jesus always said. Love is the miracle."

FORTY-TWO

Early the next morning, Belinda's phone rang and she reached for it. Her caller ID indicated it was the police commissioner. She cleared her throat. "Hello Chief, what can I do for you?" She listened. "Yes, I'll be free then. I'll see you in my office at 5:30 tonight." She set her phone back down on her nightstand and stared at it.

Sitting in the Crown Vic at the cemetery, Don's stomach was in knots. He kept wiping the sweat from his palms on his pants. He took his time exiting the car and stepping over to Uelle's headstone. "Hi, honey." He shuffled his feet. "Uh, I have something I need to tell you." He scratched his cheek and moved over to rub the rose-colored marble for a minute. "I met someone. I...I met a woman during this last case. I've grown to like her. She's nice. She's an accountant and she really likes football. She knows a lot about it, too. She's intelligent and she's a very caring person." Don smiled. "She can be a little weird sometimes, but in a good way." He touched the marble again. "I think you would like her if you met her, Uelle." He inclined his head towards the headstone. "I think you would approve." He looked up to the sky. "I want you to know that she's not taking your place. No one could ever take your place." He stood there, looking at the sky. "Crazy, huh?" He kept looking at the sky, watching the clouds as they drifted east. Soon, he nodded. "Thanks honey. I love you." Then he got into the Crown Vic and drove to work. The clock seemed to crawl until he could leave to go visit Kate. Hours passed. He finally got up from his desk and rode the elevator down to his car.

A few minutes later, Police Commissioner Craig knocked on Belinda's door. Belinda straightened some papers on her desk, then got up to greet him. The assistant commissioner was with him as well.

Tall and imposing with dark hair and blue eyes, the commissioner came in and studied the framed articles for a few moments, then turned towards Belinda. He stroked his well-groomed beard for a minute. Then he motioned for everyone to take a seat.

On her guard, Belinda sat.

"I hear you closed the Kendrick case."

Belinda beamed. "Yes. We got our man. That brutal killer won't hurt anyone else."

"Three dead." He looked up at the ceiling and then back at Belinda. "Let me ask you something. How many detectives did you have on the case?"

"Along with my help, two experienced detectives brought him down." Small beads of sweat broke out along Belinda's forehead. "Of course, if they needed other help it was available."

"Of course." He paused. "Belinda, what's your mission?"

"Be efficient as possible in solving crimes."

"Sounds to me like you have the priorities mixed up. Your first goal is to keep the citizens of Denver safe by solving crimes. You have a fiduciary responsibility, but solving crimes is number one. Period."

"I thought my bonus was based on efficiency."

"Bonus?" The commissioner's eyebrows drew together. Then his jaw dropped. "You mean the $250 gift card at the end of the year?" He rubbed a hand over his face. "That's not a bonus. It's a gift card."

He shifted in his chair. "Belinda, we've looked into how your department is being run. Not only have you cut things too thin, but you treat your staff poorly. That is never acceptable, and we have signed forms in your file indicating you've been trained on that. Your priorities are not in line with mine or with the city of Denver. You're fired. Doug here will help you pack up your things and take them out to your car after you sign the paperwork." He got up and walked out the door.

Belinda's jaw dropped. She just sat there, blinking.

Later that evening, Don stood at Kate's bedside and pulled a phone charger out of a plastic sack. "I figured your phone needed this. Where is it so I can make sure it fits?" He tested it. "Perfect. Want me to plug it in for you?"

She gave him a thumbs up. As he plugged in the cord, a familiar voice came into the room from the television mounted on the wall. Kate turned up the volume.

Sarah Snow stood next to the mayor of Denver. He wore a conservative gray suit and a yellow tie. Sarah had on a smart looking red suit. She turned towards the mayor. "Mayor, what do you want the citizens of Denver to know about the staffing of the police force?"

"I want them to know that their safety and well-being is our priority. When I came into this office, the police department was too heavily staffed. But if my directive to take care of the people's tax dollars was taken too far, studies will show this and action will be taken to correct that. As a matter of fact, some steps have already been taken. I want our citizens to know that I would match our police force against that of any city in the world. We have outstanding people on our squads and we want to take care of them. We want them to be operating in an environment that fosters success. You have my heartfelt assurance that I will do what it takes to make that happen."

"Whoa!" Don looked at Kate. "I'm shocked!" He ran his hand over his hair and beamed. "I'm scheduled to have a meeting with a guy by the name of Ethan Hamilton. He's from the mayor's office." He raised his eyebrows. "Some of the guys have already been through it. They weren't supposed to talk about it, but they told me anyway. It's about staffing and how we're treated." He shook his head. "Huh. It'd be great if it got better. But that's almost too good to be true." He folded his arms. "I wonder how this will affect my boss…" His grin widened as possibilities swirled around in his head.

"I didn't know. Are you understaffed?"

Don nodded his head and pulled up a chair to tell her about it.

FORTY-THREE

The intoxicating scent of grilled steak greeted Don as he walked into the restaurant with Kate by his side. Don rubbed his hands together. "Yeah, baby! There's a smell I know and love!" He turned to Kate and grinned. "And this place is within walking distance of your condo. I have a feeling we're going to be on a first name basis with the folks who work here!"

"And they were nice enough to be open on Christmas Eve," Kate laughed. "I think that's a good omen."

"You crutched it over here pretty well," Don mentioned with a glance at her crutches.

"I don't let minor details keep me from a good dinner."

The hostess found their reservation and seated them at a deuce table near a window. Don looked around observing the leather chairs near the mahogany bar and the hundreds of bottles displayed behind the bartender. Their waiter appeared. "I'd say the size of the crowd is a good omen too. That means good food and good service."

Their waiter poured water out of a gleaming silver pitcher and lit a red candle on their table. "It's great food and great service." He gave a slight bow and smiled at Don and Kate. "My name is Jack and I will be your server this evening. What would you like to drink besides the water?"

After their wine was delivered, Don looked across at Kate. "You look great!"

Kate laughed. "I think that's the fifth time you've told me that tonight. I believe this emerald green dress is your favorite."

"No, the lady in the emerald green dress is my favorite," Don responded. "I can't believe how lucky I am to be with a beautiful, intelligent, and energetic woman!" He held up his glass. "Merry Christmas, Kate Fitzgerald. Having you in my life is the best gift I could ever imagine. You make me feel alive again."

Kate's eyes sparkled as she held up her glass to meet his. "I feel the same way. Not only do you make me feel alive, but I actually *am alive* thanks to you!" They clinked glasses and sipped. Kate tilted her head. "We have so much to be thankful for. It was good to spend some time with Luke and Sabrina and watch Lucy jump up and down every time she thought of Santa Claus."

"No kidding!" Don let out a deep breath. "That hospital scene was bad news. I'm so grateful to see her at home and back to normal."

Don enjoyed the rest of the meal, chatting animatedly and rarely taking his eyes off Kate. He didn't notice anyone else in the room and found himself wishing the night would last forever.

EPILOGUE

Later that evening, Kate's neighbor, Elaine, looked out the window of her condominium as she pulled on her mittens to take her pet outside. Snow drifted down out of the sky and the block was quiet. She saw Kate exit a restaurant down the street with an attractive man. They headed toward the condo building. Kate stopped to catch the snowflakes on her tongue and her male partner laughed and kissed her on the forehead. They crossed the road and walked into the building, Kate hobbling on crutches assisted by the very attentive man.

Elaine stooped to put the leash on her Pekingese. She exited her condo as the elevator bell dinged and announced its arrival. The doors opened and Kate and her date stopped at Kate's door. They chuckled as the man jiggled a bell on a wreath, causing it to play *Jingle Bells*. Kate's date sang along to the tune.

Giggling, Kate found her keys and they entered the condo. As Elaine passed by the door, she saw the couple in a passionate kiss. Without looking up, the man booted the door with his foot and the wreath jingled its merry song as the door closed.

BOOK CLUB QUESTIONS

1. Was the book hard to put down? If so, why?

2. Who was your favorite character in the book? Why?

3. Who was your least favorite character in the book? Why?

4. Were the characters well-developed? Did you feel as though you knew them?

5. If you could meet one of the characters right now, who would it be and what would you say?

6. What purpose did Kate's necklace serve?

7. Share a favorite quote from the book. Why did this speak to you?

8. What was the theme of the book?

9. Did you like the pace of the book? Why?

10. How did the characters change throughout the book? Did your opinion of them change?

11. How do you feel about the ending of the book?

12. Did the book change your outlook about anything? If so, how?

13. How would you summarize this book in a couple of sentences?

14. If this book became a movie, who would you want to see play the main characters?

ACKNOWLEDGMENTS

It takes a team.

You'd think writing is an individual sport. Like tennis, you don't have a team to help you succeed. You serve up an idea and wallop it over the net. You're confident that it will do well, because you practiced and practiced. You refined your stroke, working on it over and over.

At least, that's how I thought it worked.

But after lots of classes; lots of effort; and lots of pounding my head against the wall, I learned the truth. Writing is a team sport.

And I wound up with a great team. Stacy Dymalski was my story editor. She read through my manuscript over and over, making excellent suggestions and imparting much wisdom having to do with the craft of writing. Just like a pro tennis player, I had my own coach.

Michelle Rayner created a beautiful cover. She is astonishingly talented, and I feel incredibly fortunate that I found her.

Katie Mullaly did the publishing and my web site. She was patient above and beyond the call of duty as I put her on hold during budgets, forecasting, and all the projects that required lots of time while I was still employed as a controller. Then she was patient again as I researched marketing, found punctuation editors, and established connections in the writing community. I'm one of those people who has to learn before I leap, and Katie was kind enough to let me do that.

My husband provided constant support over the years, and my children have too. My instructors, my classmates, my writing groups, my church, my on-line friends, and my friends that I know in the flesh and blood have all bestowed their time and encouragement. I can't tell you how much I appreciate it.

I also appreciate my readers. You make writing fun. Hearing you tell me how much you enjoyed reading *Deadly Gratitude* absolutely makes my day. I'm thrilled to know the time you spent reading my book was enjoyable.

Last but not least, thanks to God for this beautiful life and all of the wonderful people in it. He helped me walk not once but twice. His work and words inspire me each and every day.

ABOUT THE AUTHOR

Lori Donnester started out life in Illinois and then traveled west to study ballet at the University of Utah. Deciding finance would be a better bet, she made the switch, but her creative genes encouraged her to study writing as well. It all worked out because today she is a newly retired financial controller, is writing full time, and recently won an award in a writing contest.

Lori remains steadfast in her conviction that her parents' prayers and positive thoughts helped her overcome a devastating bicycle accident from which doctors said she would never walk again. (Spoiler alert: She walks just fine today.) When her father passed, she decided to honor him with a story that both entertains and inspires, thus leading to her to write the suspense, crime novel, *Deadly Gratitude*.

In her spare time, Lori skis, hikes, and enjoys life with her husband in the beautiful mountains that surround her Salt Lake City home.

NOTE FROM THE AUTHOR

Thank you so much for buying and reading *Deadly Gratitude*. If you enjoyed the ride, please leave a review on Amazon for me. The number of reviews received by a book really helps it sell. Plus, I love writing and I love entertaining my readers. I know your time is precious to you, and if I gave you a few hours of fun, then it makes me happy! Reading or hearing someone say that they enjoyed it warms my heart the way a flickering fire warms a room. You can contact me or read more about writing and other good things on my website: *www.loridonnester.com.*

If you want to know how I got into the amazing world of composing cliffhangers, keep reading.

I wanted to write something positive, hopeful, and inspirational. So I wrote a story about murder.

It all started in 1995. I went on a bike ride. I believe I was looking at the sunset as I rode west on a residential street.

The next thing I remember is a feeling that I was in a hospital. But I couldn't wake up. I heard my husband near me. But I couldn't talk to him.

I was finally able to come to long enough to ask where I was. He told me I had a bike accident and was in the hospital.

I had a TBI, a traumatic brain injury. I learned I was paralyzed. I sunk back into blackness.

I was transferred to a rehabilitation hospital. I kept sinking in and out of consciousness. I couldn't remember my therapists. I couldn't remember what I'd done the day before. I couldn't solve simple problems.

Was I going to be stupid for the rest of my life?

As an accountant, I managed millions of dollars. I was used to solving problems. I was used to a high level of performance. This would not do.

Luckily, I had terrific health care and terrific support. And I had prayers.

I started biking three months after the accident, and I now snow ski, water ski, hike, jog, and lift weights. I'm active. I just recently retired after a successful career managing millions of dollars as a financial controller.

My recovery shocked my doctor. When he looked at my MRI, he said he thought I would never walk again. I looked at my MRI. It shows some big holes in my brain.

I give God the credit. And my parents. I figured He listened to their prayers and decided to give me a break.

And I will thank Him as long as I live.

Then in 2007, my parents came to Salt Lake City from Florida to visit. And my dad got sick. Very sick. He was admitted into a hospital here but did not recover. The morning after he passed a shooting star shot across the sky as I was jogging. He was sending me a greeting. His funeral was that December.

My dad was a great man. He was honest, loving, and hard working. He supported his wife and four children without question. I always felt safe. I always felt secure. I always knew he wouldn't ever let anything happen to me if he could possibly help it.

I wanted to honor my father…but how? Answer: write! Something I've always studied and done for fun.

I spent years learning the craft. I worked with a professional story editor which was the equivalent of having a private instructor. It was a blast!

I want my readers to be entertained as they are transported to that world that is in my book.

Be aware this is a work of fiction. Any similarities with real people or real events are merely coincidental.

Made in the USA
San Bernardino, CA
13 November 2018